Doodlebug

Calum E. Rogers

Doodlebug
Copyright 2025 Calum E. Rogers

All rights reserved. No portion of this book may be reproduced or transmitted by electronic or mechanical means, including photocopying, recording, or by an information and retrieval system without written permission from the author, except as permitted by law.

This is a work of fiction. Unless otherwise indicated, all names, characters, events and incidents in this book are either the product of the author's imagination or used in a fictitious manner. Any resemblance to actual persons, living or dead, is purely coincidental. Real locations and events may have inspired parts of the story

A message from Calum.

I found out recently that, while thought I knew what to do if I found wildlife entangled in fishing nets (or similar), I was completely wrong. Do not cut it free or untangle it. It needs specialist care by specialist people. Being the 'hero' will likely only further injure or kill the creature. At least €1 from each paperback sale goes straight to the Palma Aquarium Foundation.

https://palmaaquarium.com/en/fundation

For the quiet, patient people.

1.

The engine rattled and the brakes squealed in protest as they reluctantly complied with David's wishes. He killed the engine yet somehow, even after it had stopped running, its loose jangly accompaniment persisted. Eventually the car accomplished silence, and all was well with the world.
"That doesn't look right." said Sarah from the passenger's seat.
"Eh?" replied David.
"Their car is still on the driveway – they always park it in the garage if they are going away."
"Oh, yes, you're right they do. Hopefully everything is Ok. Maybe their flight has been cancelled."
"Oh, I hope not. What a pain."
"Weren't they supposed to go last night? There will be some sore heads if they have been up drinking instead."
"Come on. Let's go and have a look."

They both got out of the car and closed the doors, with David mis-judging the force needed, leaving the door latched but ajar. Sarah didn't. Her relationship with the car was one of contempt and mistrust. She slammed the door closed, partly to ensure effectiveness, but also as punishment for the vehicle being such a heap of crap.

As they strolled towards the front of the house Sarah admired the flowers that had recently come into bloom despite, or perhaps because of, the winter's cooler weather. David appeared to have been keeping on top of his jobs looking after the Köhler's Garden, but he hadn't visited for a couple of weeks and the weeds were beginning to assert themselves.

David grabbed the key from his pocket and inserted it into the lock.

"Hello?" he called, as he eased the front door open. He couldn't hear any voices but there was music coming from somewhere and followed the source through the living room and into the back garden.

It took a few moments for the reality of what he was seeing to settle, to become real. His initial disbelief, his hope that all of this was some kind of sick joke, was gradually replaced by his resignation that it was all, in fact, all too real. Lying there on the patio were Mr. and Mrs. Köhler - dead.

"Oh my god," said Sarah, "I can't believe what I'm looking at, what the hell is going on?"

There was a short pause while they both surveyed the scene.

"Have they just collapsed or are they dead?" asked David.

"Well, they look pretty dead."

They looked to have just collapsed, straight down, where they stood. It wasn't like they'd fallen asleep after drinking too much. Ingrid was lying on her back facing the sky, her tennis racket lying next to her. Gunther was almost completely face down. There was no sign of bleeding, only a small, red, circular mark on Ingrid's forehead.

David was having a hard time processing all of this, he only saw Mr. Köhler a couple of days ago. He was his normal jovial self, reminding David which way around he liked the car to face in the garage, where the tools were, and where the battery charger was. In fact, it was a repeat of the same conversation they had every time the Köhlers were returning to Germany. It was supposed to be an easy day today - a completely normal mothballing of a villa, followed by the gym in the afternoon.

"This is going to be grim, but I suppose someone will have to confirm there is no pulse." said David.

"Rather you than me, Dave." she said. From the look on her face, he could tell she was only just holding herself together.

Slightly unsteady on his feet, David gradually moved over to Gunther. He gradually got a hold under the shoulder. He found it quite repulsive – like most people, he'd never touched a dead body before. As he hefted the weight the body began to comply and began a slow uncooperative roll. Once David had turned Gunther enough, he could see his face. He looked grey and there were flies buzzing around him. He also had the circular red mark on his forehead. David took a deep breath and held it as he placed two fingers on his neck in an attempt to check for a pulse. He was cold. The shock made David pull his fingers away quickly. Having re-gained his composure he checked for a pulse again, but of course he found nothing.

"Goner," he said.

"Ok, I'm calling the police," Sarah said, "are you going to check Ingrid?"

"Do I have to?" he asked in a somewhat downbeat surrender. He took a deep breath and let out a sigh. David moved over to Ingrid, where he once again attempted to check for a pulse. Expecting the worst, he gently prodded her neck with his fist two fingers.

To his surprise she was still warm, and she had a pulse. It was faint but it was there.

"Oh my god she's alive." he exclaimed at Sarah. She had just got through to the authorities and gave him a thumbs up.

The first thing she asked them was if they spoke English. David and Sarah had lived Mallorca and, while they did speak quite a bit of Spanish, important moments called for clear communication. It took them a moment to find an English-speaking member of staff, but then Sarah carried on with the emergency services while David turned his attention back to Mrs Köhler.

She had a pulse but was she breathing? He knew he would have to get in close to hear her breathing. This was really creeping him out. He knelt down and reached over her with his left arm and supported his weight while lowering his right ear towards her mouth. It was very faint but listening carefully he could just about hear her breathing. Gentle in and out rhythmic breathing - just like she was asleep.

"She's breathing," he exclaimed at Sarah.

Sarah waved him off as she continued talking to the authorities. She was now speaking English to them and was explaining where they were.

David decided it was best not to move Ingrid in case he made her injuries worse.

"How does it go with that CPR stuff? ABC? Airway, breathing, circulation? Is that right?" he said talking to himself so as not to distract Sarah. It had been quite a while since he'd had any training, so he wasn't that confident that he was correct, but the fact that she had a pulse and was breathing, he thought, meant that the ABC was Ok.

Sarah was now finished on the phone, but she continued looking at it expectantly.

"They are going to send me a WhatsApp message," she said, "they want me to reply with a Google Maps location pin."

"Did you get on all right with them? Did they understand what you were saying?" he asked.

"Well, I think so, but you can never be sure."

With that, there was a ping from her phone. Sarah raised an eyebrow and nodded.

"That was quick." she said.

"Not bad," he replied.

She opened the message and, as expected, it was the Guardia Civil asking for a location.

Sarah opened Google Maps, shared their current location and pressed send.

"Done." she said.

"How long do you think it will take them to get here?" he asked.

"Well, I imagine they will have to finish their coffee, so who knows?" she said. "I think they'd like us to leave everything alone, not touch anything."

"Ok, let's back off a bit and have a think about what we have and have not touched. I'm going to turn the music off," said David.

"That's not exactly leaving everything alone, is it?" Sarah asked.

"Well, no it isn't. It just feels a bit weird leaving it to play like that."

A quick examination of the speaker revealed an on/off button. It was one of those portable Bluetooth speakers and was still plugged into its

USB charger. Ingrid's phone was plugged in next to it with 12 missed calls.

Everything seemed a little calmer without the music, David felt like he had more space to think. He looked around the garden. Nothing else seemed out of place. The table with the speaker also had two half-drunk glasses of white wine, along with the rest of the bottle. There was no condensation visible on the bottle or the glasses, indicating that they had been out of the fridge for some time. Both of the Köhlers were dressed slightly more formally than normal.

"It looks like they were getting ready to leave," he said.

"Oh yes," said Sarah "Ingrid always likes to dress up a little for travel."

"So. what do we do now?" he asked. "Do you think we should go and wait at the front of the house? Maybe go out to the van?"

"Well, I could do with some water. This whole episode has left me a bit shaken. But, if Ingrid is still alive then I don't want to leave her here alone like this."

"Right, Ok then," he said, "I'll head out to the van and grab a couple of bottles". He lifted his left arm and brought her in for a quick cuddle. After a few moments, she gently moved him off towards the front door. In situations like this she preferred to be busy, not standing still for too long. As he walked through the house, it became more obvious that they were correct about them being ready to leave. The suitcases were at the bottom of the stairs, everything was tidy and Ingrid had left her usual "thank you" note in the kitchen. He guessed they were just waiting for the taxi. All those missed calls would be the taxi driver. As he opened the front door he imagined that they must have been ringing the doorbell too.

"I wonder how long he hung around for?" David mumbled to himself.

Having opened the side door of the van, he grabbed a couple of water bottles then headed back to the garden and handed Sarah her bottle. She was staring off into space as she took several small sips, whilst seemingly on autopilot.

"How are you doing, babe?" he asked.

"Oh, you know, same shit - different day." came her standard, cocky response. "This whole thing is making my head spin. This can't be happening…. It's not real…it's like a dream."

"Unfortunately, honey -"

"So what do we do now," Sarah interrupted "just wait here for the rozzers to turn up?"

"I don't think there's anything else we can do. Just wait and keep an eye on the place." he said.

It took about 20 minutes before they finally heard a siren in the distance. It felt like their response should be quicker, but he knew everything happened at a more leisurely pace here. As the Guardia Civil officers were parking their Landcruiser, Sarah's phone rang. She wrestled it out of her pocket and pushed the answer button.

"Hola?" she said.

There was a brief burst of machine gun Spanish from the earpiece.

"Whoa, whoa, whoa, slow down. No hablo Español," said Sarah.

David left her to it and approached the Landcruiser. He raised my hand and waved. One officer exited the vehicle, while the other remained, talking on his radio.

"Hola, bon dia." said David.

"Hola, was it you that found the dead body?" he asked. According to his name badge, his name was Jimenez.

Credit where it's due: his English was very good - much better than David's Spanish would ever be.

"Yes," he said. " My girlfriend and I found them in the garden. One is dead, the other is still alive."

"Still alive?" he said. "Why didn't you tell me this?"

"I just did. Do you want me to show you?"

"No, no, you stay out here. I don't want you touching anything inside. What have you touched already?"

"Well, I opened the front door, after that I don't think I touched anything. I had to turn Gunther over – I needed to make sure …" David said.

"And your wife?", he asked.

"You will need to ask her."

Sarah had now finished her phone call and was heading over towards the front of the house, where David and Officer Jimenez were standing.

"That was the damned local police," she said, "they don't seem to be able to find the road, let alone the house. Useless."

This was pretty standard for the Spanish authorities to send two different branches of the police. It had never really been clear which branch was responsible for what duties, but the local police seem to be good at putting up signs and enforcing parking restrictions whereas the Guardia Civil seem to be more interested in "proper" crime.

"This chap wants to know what we touched inside the house," said David.

"I don't think I touched anything." Sarah responded, furrowing her eyebrows in thought. "Nope, you opened the front door and then I followed you. I don't think I touched anything."

"Ok," said Officer Jimenez, "later we will take your fingerprints and then hopefully eliminate you."

Officer Jimenez strode purposely towards the front door. Having made sure his gloves were secure he then pulled a torch out of the top pocket on his flak jacket. He clicked the torch on and slowly pushed the front door open and proceeded inside. They followed him towards the front door but thought better about going inside.

"Shall we give him some space?" David suggested.

"Maybe we should just wait out here until we are told otherwise." said Sarah. She sounded slightly monotone and was again staring off into space. David knew the signs: it was all getting too much - they both needed to get away from all this madness.

"Shall we stop at the bar on the way home?" he offered as a distraction.

"You're a mind reader," she said, "which one?"

"At this point, I'm happy with whichever is closest."

The idea of going to the bar seemed to spur her on a little. Nice cold beer was always a welcome punctuation mark on a difficult day.

They had been hanging around the front door for about 5 minutes, kicking their heels and looking at the floor, patiently waiting to be directed by the officer.

"Hola," came from behind them.

The sudden unexpected words gave them a start. It was the officer who had stayed in the car - Officer Marquez, apparently.

"He wants us all to go inside," said the officer.

Again, his English was quite good.

"Ok," David replied.

The front door was still open wide enough for them to walk inside without touching it. David went in first, followed by Sarah and then officer Marquez. David guessed that Marquez wanted them to go to the garden, so that's where he headed.

Nothing had changed. Ingrid and Gunther were still sprawled out in an unkempt manner. As he cast his eyes around the garden again, he could still see everything else looked normal.

"Have you touched anything here? asked Jimenez.

"No, of course not. I told you before, we haven't touched anything. Except for Gunther." The feeling of touching him came back.

"Everything looks very neat here, in the garden. You haven't cleaned anything up or taken anything away?" asked Jimenez.

"We have touched nothing," David repeated.

"Like we told you," said Sarah," we haven't touched or moved anything. This is how it was when we found them."

David felt like they were being accused of being involved in the crime.

"Ok," said Jimenez. "My colleague is going to take you back outside the front of the house. The other Guardia Civil cars will be arriving soon. One of those will give you a lift to the station."

David suddenly had a thought. It wouldn't just be more police arriving soon. There would be ambulances too. This would be a big story on the island.

"Shall I move the van?" he asked. "Get it out of the way so there's more space for your people?" What he was really thinking was *I don't want loads of people associating our company name with whatever it is that's going on here.*

"Sure, I don't see a problem," said Officer Jimenez. "Marquez, can you get their details first? Let's make sure they don't drive too far away."

Officer Marquez led them outside and took their details from their driving licences and identity cards. He then ran an identity check on the van and, surprise surprise, it came back as being registered to David.

Once he was satisfied that they were who they said they were, he indicated a side road about 100m away where he suggested the van could park. It only took a moment to move the van, but it had been just in time - the rest of the circus was arriving. Once he had strolled back to where Sarah and Officer Marquez were waiting, they were introduced to another officer who would be taking them to the police station in Inca, the nearest big town.

It took about 3 hours for the police at the station to sort out all of the paperwork, identities, fingerprints and anything else they could think of.

Eventually, they were allowed to go and to their surprise, they were offered a lift.

"Our regular isn't the closest anymore." David said to Sarah.

"I know, but I'd still like to go there if we can. Good people, friendly faces, cold beer. Just what we need." she replied.

The officer driving them grumbled a little bit, but agreed to take them to their chosen bar.

They were both completely spent by the time they walked into the bar. The barman had spotted them coming and already retrieved the appropriate beers from the ice-cold fridge.

"Siempre?" he asked.

This literally meant "always", though in this context it meant "the usual".

It was quite normal for there to be no English-speaking people in this bar, so it was the perfect place for them to discuss the day's activities without being interrupted or overheard. They grabbed the beers, which literally had ice on the outside of the bottles.

"Cold beer," said Sarah.

"You know it, it's always cold here."

They clinked their beer bottles together.

"Salut"

"Cheers"

They both took a long cold drag on their bottles.

"Christ, I needed that," said David.

"Me too, hits the spot."

He was already into his second pull on the bottle. These beers were going to go down a lot quicker than they usually do.

He was taking his third deep pull in quick succession when he realised the barman was hanging around and making himself available.

"Dos mas?" he asked as soon as David clocked him.

"Sí", he nodded.

Two more beers appeared in very short order. He also brought a small plate of olives and some chicken wings. These were their favourite tapas at this bar. He had loaded the plate up more than usual. They must have looked like they needed it.

"Graçies," said David.

The bar man nodded and rattled off some more Spanish that was way too quick for David to catch, but David gave him a thumbs-up and smiled anyway. The food and second beer were polished off in no time.

Beer and food had been their main focus since arriving at the bar. Sarah pulled a tissue out of the dispenser on the bar and, as she wiped the grease from her bright red fingernails, she regarded David and furrowed her brow.

"So, can anybody tell me what the hell is going on?"

"Sorry babe, I'm as lost as you are. What happened to them? What was it that killed him and nearly killed her? They both look like they have been shot in the forehead, but isn't there supposed to be more blood?"

"It looked like just one shot to the head for each of them. So what is that? Murder? Assassination?" she asked, desperate for answers. "They've clearly been killed, rather than just died, I think we can agree on that.

It wasn't a robbery, there were no signs of a struggle, and nothing had been taken. Well, not that I could see. Someone gets into the house, then pop pop and they're gone?"

David took another drink from his bottle and replied "It doesn't add up, we must be missing something."

"But what are we missing, Dave?"

"I wish I knew."

With that, Sarah's phone rang again. She would normally wrestle the phone from her pocket, in an effort to answer the call quickly. Clearly half defeated by the day, she pulled the phone from her pocket in a slow, resigned, half-beaten manner. She thought it would be the police, and was expecting more questions that didn't have answers.

"It's mum," she exclaimed with a happier expression now showing on her face.

"We don't really need to tell her about all of this, she will just worry," he said.

"Oh, I'd rather talk to her about anything else except today," she said.

She answered the call and was already saying hello to her mum before the phone was at her ear.

"Hi mum, how are you? What have you been up to?" she said.

She actually sounded cheery, which made David smile for a moment.

Sarah took the phone and her beer outside the front of the bar. David watched as she walked away. Platinum blond curls tied up in a red scarf, thick eyeliner and at least head and shoulders taller than any of the locals. He had a momentary flash-back to the day he'd first seen her in a rock 'n' roll bar in Inca. In a sea of darker complexions, she seemed to have a spotlight on her wherever she went.

The door thumped closed behind her bringing him back to the present. He made a conscious effort to slow up on his drinking. Without really thinking he retrieved his phone from his pocket and did as he usually would do while propping up the bar - he went on to social media to see what was happening.

Amongst all the regular cat and dog videos, he noticed one of the local groups had put up a post asking if anybody knew what was going on with the police up at the top end of Lloseta. Well, he knew… and he figured the news was going to break eventually. There were several responses to the original post, but it was clear that everybody was guessing. As usual with social media, lots of speculation, no real facts. He was actually quite relieved that nobody knew any of the specifics. Just at the moment, he was quite tired of having to think and talk about the whole thing.

2.

The next morning David woke up at about half an hour before sunrise, the morning sky already beginning its deep orange introduction to the day. Sarah hadn't had a good night's sleep, so he treated her to a bit of a lie-in. They'd had several beers but hadn't overdone it too much and had gotten a taxi home, but he didn't really recall what time.

David sat at the dining table, sipping his first cup of coffee. He flicked the TV on, just in case there was anything interesting on. Yesterday's events in Lloseta hadn't made the headlines - which wasn't really a big surprise. He checked his phone and there was nothing mentioned in any of his feeds either.

About an hour and another coffee later, Sarah emerged from upstairs.

"Morning," she said, did you sleep Ok?"

"Not really, and you were up for half the night as well."

"Yep, a bit of a crap night's sleep. Still, we can sleep when we're dead...." she trailed off.

"That *is* quite funny, but I think maybe it's a bit too soon," he said.

"Brain on autopilot. It's the sort of thing I normally come out with, but I guess it's not funny any more."

"Oh well, never mind, it's only me."

"Are we still going to the gym this morning?"

"Yep, of course. Exercise isn't going to do itself. Leave in about 45 minutes?" he suggested.

"Yep. What's for breakfast?"

"Scrambled egg on toast?"

"Sounds good to me."

Breakfast was ready in short order, and they ate while the TV played to itself in the background.

"So, what's the plan then?" she asked.

"Well, I figure we'll get a phone call from somebody at some point. Until then, I'd just like to enjoy my day, it's supposed to be wall-to-wall sunshine today and - aren't we meeting Miquel and Angela for lunch today?" he asked, the memory popping up from nowhere.

"We are. I'd forgotten about that. Do you want to go or should we give a miss?"

"I'm up for it if you are. Might be good to talk to some normal people."

"They're not normal! Actually yes, it would be quite good to just have fun free flowing conversation, in English, where I don't have to explain yesterday." she said.

Having loaded the plates into the dishwasher, they headed back upstairs to sort out what they'd be wearing for lunch. David always liked to wear a shirt - and to make sure it was one that hadn't been seen for a while.

He had noted that some people seem to wear the same shirt every time you see them and didn't want to fall into that trap. Sarah did her usual trick of asking for his opinion on various outfits, but he decided that retreat was the better part of valour and snuck off downstairs, leaving her to make her own choices.

They double-checked their gym bags and headed out of the door. The van was still parked at the Köhler's house, so they took the car. As soon as he started the engine, the stereo announced that it had paired with Sarah's phone.

"What are you putting on the stereo, DJ?"

"Rock. I might just hit play and see what comes out."

Some classic old-school track came on which they both recognised immediately. They couldn't resist singing along to the song.

The smiles and energy that the music brought lifted the mood and for a few minutes all was well with the world. Once that song was finished, Sarah turned the stereo down a little and gazed out of the passenger window, staring out into space. The low morning sun streaked the mountains with long, sharp shadows. Endless olive trees blurred past as they cruised through the foothills of the Tramuntana. Sarah's elbow rested on the car door as she wrapped her hair around her finger in an endless curl. He decided to leave her to her reverie and drove in silence for the rest of the journey.

They both went pretty hard down the gym. It was nice to be immersed in an environment that kept the brain busy enough not to think too much.

They pulled up at the restaurant, which was in one of the coastal towns north of Palma. It was a pleasure to see familiar faces. Having said hello to Miquel and Angela they settled into their places at the table, with David sitting opposite his good friend Miquel. He used to be quite senior in the police force but had been retired for a number of years. His work had taken him and his family all over Spain. Madrid, Valencia, Barcelona, you name the city - he'd been in charge there at some point. Maybe David could pump him for information.

"David, how's things?" he said in impeccable English.

"All good, thank you. How's things at your end?"

"Well," he said, "I'm good, but I'm a bit worried about what's going on in Lloseta."

That stopped David in his tracks. He hoped he was going to have more time where he didn't have to talk about this.

"Oh, you've heard." he relinquished, as he did a quick check of the room to see who was listening.

"I had a call from one of the senior people at the Guardia Civil - he had this idea that we knew each other and wanted to see if I can get any more information about yesterday. I told him I would help, of course I did, I don't think I had a choice. Anyway, I'm here as a friend if there's anything you want to talk about."

"How does he know that we're friends?" he asked.

"Well, to be honest, David, you two aren't exactly inconspicuous. I wouldn't read too much into it. I think a lot of people recognise you, even if they don't know who you are."

"Ok, I guess." he said. This conversation wasn't really what he needed to hear. Now David felt like he was being watched - was he a suspect?

"I don't know what to tell you," he said, keeping his voice deliberately hushed. "We went to close up a villa for the winter and the owners were dead in the back garden. I did get a feeling that the police thought we were more involved, but we aren't. We just turned up for work and walked into a crime scene. Sarah phoned the police straight away."

Miquel settled back into his chair. He had done as requested and David's answers seemed honest.

"So, then let's talk about something else. How's your house coming on?"

David was more than relieved at the change of direction.

"Oh, it's all happening, just slowly. There's still lots of work to do and I'm getting really bored with all the decorating," he replied.

Eventually, the conversation and the lunch began to follow a familiar routine, but David was kind of on edge the whole time. It was always a long leisurely lunch with these guys, with plenty of gossip, news and checking on each other's families. Three hours later everyone was fed and watered and needing their siesta. He had just finished paying up when his phone rang. He let out a sigh as he realised that it was all about to start again.

"Hello?" he said as he answered the phone. He could feel his stress levels rising.

"Hi, is that David? It's Torsten here. Torsten Köhler. You look after my parents' house."

"Oh, hello. I'm very sorry about everything that's been going on. What can I do for you, Torsten? How is your mother getting on?" He looked around for a quieter, more private place to have the conversation and decided to step outside. He could feel himself relaxing a little now that he knew it wasn't the police on the phone.

"Well, as you know she was in a very bad way when you found her. She hung on for a while, but she didn't make it through the night." He paused for a moment. "This whole thing is awful, I can't get my head around it. As I understand it, the police will probably be finished at the house later today. We need someone to go by and make sure everything is closed up and make sure it's secure. I figured this is what you normally do for my parents anyway, so you must still be the right man for the job." he said.

"Yes, of course, no problem. Are you going to be headed over here at some point? If there's anything I can do to help, please ask. A lift from the airport, a recommendation for a hotel or restaurant? I'm here if you need me."

"Thank you, David, I'll probably fly over in a few days. In the meantime, I think one of the officers will call you when they are done."

"Ok, no problem. I'll make sure the house is taken care of for you."

"Thank you, David, see you later."

"Ok, that's great Torsten, thank you."

He went back to the table where everyone was getting ready to leave. They said their goodbyes and agreed to meet again soon. As they headed towards the exit David told Sarah about the phone call.

"Torsten Köhler has just called, he's Gunther and Ingrid's son. Once the police have finished with the house, he'd like us to close the place up, do our normal winterisation. One of the officers will call when they are finished." he said.

Sarah wrinkled her nose; she was obviously not keen on revisiting the scene. "Ah, Ok. I hadn't planned on going back quite so soon."

"It'll be Ok. It won't be as grizzly this time. Torsten will be coming over in a few days. I said we would be here if he needed any help."

"Oh yeah, poor bloke. I guess I had forgotten that there might be a family involved here too," she said.

"Bloody awful all around. If we are just about done here, I might go and bring the car around?"

"Good idea, have we paid?"

"We have," he said over his shoulder as he turned to walk away.

By the time he had retrieved the car and driven around the front of the restaurant, Sarah was already waiting.

"The police have already phoned," she said as she opened the door, "they have finished and the house is now ours."

"The van is still there, well, assuming they haven't towed it as evidence. Are we going straight there or home first?" he asked.

"Yes, assuming they haven't towed it. Shall we get changed at home first? Get out of out posh clothes and into our overalls."

3.

It took about an hour to get back to their house, then another hour to change and get ready to head to the Köhlers' house. Neither of them was in a rush. Sarah didn't want to go back to the house at all, and David wasn't particularly looking forward to it either.

"You about ready?" he asked.

"I don't think I'll ever be ready…... come on, let's get it over with." she replied.

They lived on the opposite side of Lloseta to the Köhlers. They had gotten about halfway to the house when Sarah asked, "Are we parking out front, or in the side road again, near the van?"

It was a good question. They had no idea if we were expecting the press or other unwelcome onlookers.

"How about we drop off our gear, then I'll go and park around the side?" David suggested.

"I like it."

Five minutes later they were unloaded, parked and stood outside the front door.

"Oh my god," Sarah quivered. "It was one thing talking about coming back here, but now that we actually are here … I don't think I can go in."

David could see that she was visibly shaking.

"How about if I go in first and do a recce?" he suggested "Then I'll come back here to get you?"

Sarah nodded while looking down at her feet.

"Ok then, I'll be back in a minute...."

He grabbed the key from his pocket and inserted it into the lock.

"Hello?" he called, as he eased the front door open. He wasn't really expecting an answer, in fact he would have been worried if there was one.

The silence was very eerie, in perfect contrast to their last visit. Everything was perfectly still until the door hinge let out a comedy haunted-house-style squeak. It was probably his nerves getting the better of him, but David couldn't help himself - he had to copy the squeak and repeated the noise back to Sarah, who swore at him.

"Grow up, Dave."

"Oh, it's way too late for that..."

He had a quick look around the house and out into the back garden. Everything was empty and peaceful so he went back to get Sarah at the front door.

"All clear out the back," he said to Sarah.

"Thank goodness. No ghosts hiding in there?"

"Not that I can see. Shall we just get on with our jobs and get this over with?" he asked.

"Yes, you're right. The sooner we start, the sooner we can leave." Sarah was still clearly spooked out by being back in the house, so he sidled up to her and put his arm around her shoulder and gently pulled her in close.

"It'll be Ok, babe. We'll get this done, then we can go for a drink. Your choice of venue." he said quietly and kissed the top of her head. Usually, when he let her have the choice of venue, that meant they'd be going to a smarter bar, where people dress up a little and the drinks cost more.

"Oooh, you do know how to spoil the girl," she said, with a little more bounce in her voice.

"You know it."

"Is that little wine place in the market open today?"

"Oh honey, it's Thursday, they close at 2:30 today."

"Damn. Well, Bar Altura then."

David gave her an approving smile. More because they had agreed on a reward and because of the encouragement that it offered them, rather than the actual choice of venue.

With that he let her go, and they both got started on their usual jobs.

Sarah liked to start with emptying the bins and David liked to sort out the customer's car. He opened the garage door and reversed the BMW into the garage.

The owner preferred it to be facing nose out, so that's how David parked it, realising that it wouldn't make any difference this time, but that didn't mean he could let standards slip. Having parked the car he disconnected the battery, which in this case was in the boot. This meant that the car could be left standing for a longer period of time, without the battery going flat. As he closed the garage door, he had a sudden wave of sadness come over him.

Something about the act of closing the door had made him realise that this was the last time he would be doing this. He paused for a moment, leaning on the garage door. He closed his eyes and took a long, slow breath.

David opened his eyes and focused back on the task ahead. Back inside the house, he headed towards the back garden where his next job waited. He needed to make sure that all the water was switched off, and that the rear gate and door to the shed were secure. He headed out the back door without really thinking and was confronted with the patio where he'd last seen Gunther and Ingrid. He took a moment to compose himself and then carried on with the job at hand.

As he was checking the taps to make sure they were off he became aware of a buzzing sound. It sounded like a mobile phone vibrating, but surely the police would have taken them. He then carried on checking the gate was locked and the shed was secure.

A quick visual scan around the garden ensured there was no food or drink left outside. Everything was clear and ready to be left over the winter. As he headed back to the house, he could still hear that buzzing noise. It was coming from one of the windows near the back door. In Spain, most windows have slatted shutters covering them, which keeps the sunlight out while allowing air movement, and also for security. In this case, something appeared to be wedged between two of the slats. It looks like a big bee. David was very familiar with carpenter bees which he enjoyed seeing around the garden which are about 3 to 4 cm long. Mostly harmless but look like they could do some damage. This looked to be one of these carpenter bees.

He thought he'd see if he could free the insect from its captivity and decided his large pair of tweezers was needed, which he knew he had in his tool kit next to the front door. These were usually used for gripping cotton wool while cleaning difficult corners, or retrieving dropped items from difficult corners. He returned to the back garden with his oversized tweezers and squeezed the bee a little to get some grip. He then pulled gently to remove it from the shutter.

It buzzed again and made him jump. He lost his grip on the bee and dropped it. It made an audible "dink" as it hit the patio and continued buzzing. As a result, it danced around in a circle. Odd-looking bee. Anyway, it was no longer stuck so it would fly off when it was ready. HE decided to leave it to it's own devices and, as he was finished with the garden, he headed inside where Sarah had mostly finished in the kitchen.

"Strange-looking bee in the garden," he said.

"Oh cool, a new bit of wildlife I haven't seen before?" Sarah asked.

"Oh, definitely. We have not seen one of these. Very strange looking."

"Can you head upstairs and put the moisture traps out?"

Without central heating, the houses in were quite good at trapping moisture in the cold of winter. It got down to about zero degrees and houses that were not lived in could get big condensation problems. Mould would grow everywhere if you weren't careful. Moisture traps were available in just about any supermarket. It's basically a giant "Do Not Eat" bag in a plastic container of some sort. Each one would probably take about half a litre out of an average room over the winter.

Dave headed upstairs and placed one moisture trap in each of the five bedrooms. He also placed one in each wardrobe that contained clothes. Wardrobes without clothes he just left open to allow air to circulate. He then mothballed the bathroom.

He double-checked everywhere upstairs to make sure windows and shutters were closed and unlocked. He then headed back downstairs where Sarah was just finishing up and getting ready to head out of the front door.

"I think we're just about done," said Sarah "shall we have to see if your bee is still there?"

"Yeah, come and have a look at this," he said, already headed towards the back door, "maybe you'll recognise it, but I don't think I've seen one like this before."

The bee had probably moved a little, but it was still there.

"Wow, you're right, that is a strange-looking bug," Sarah exclaimed, "sort of half bug, half bee."

Sarah snapped a quick picture with her mobile phone.

"Shall we put it in a matchbox or something?" she asked, "we could take it back to ours and get a better look at it, before we let it go."

"I'll have a look in my tool bag, I must have something to put it in," he said.

Once he'd got to the tool bag he rummaged around and found an old tobacco tin which he used to keep spare nuts, bolts and screws in. He tipped the content out into the tool bag - and made a mental note to tidy that up later.

He reappeared in the back garden victoriously brandishing his tin.

"This should do the job," he said, waving the tin at Sarah.

"Perfect," she said.

He opened the tin and used the lid to flick the insect into the tin, then replaced the lid making sure it closed firmly. They headed inside and locked the back door. He put the tobacco tin into the tool bag and then, with one more quick idiot check, they were done.

They gathered their bags on the driveway and David headed off to get the van. Within minutes he was back and they loaded their gear into the van. Sarah double-checked that she had the keys for the car.

"It's quite sad to be leaving the place under these circumstances," said Sarah.

"I know, it's ridiculous, isn't it? I'm not sure we'll ever find out what actually happened."

"Probably not. What are we going to tell Torsten? Poor bloke must be going through hell at the moment."

"Cup of tea, is it?" David asked.

"Yeah, a nice cuppa will go down a treat."

David took the van and dropped the rubbish bags off at the local bin, while Sarah headed straight home in the car. Having unloaded the van and sorted out a few other chores, David went into the kitchen to make the tea. Once the kettle had boiled, he took his mug of tea into the workshop.

He sat at the workbench and took a sip from his mug.

"Right, let's have a look at this thing," he muttered to himself.

He prized the tin open and tipped the contents onto the bench. There it was, the same strange-looking bug as before. He grabbed a magnifying glass and examined the bug in more detail.

Sarah had been spot-on with her comment earlier. It kind of was a bee, but then it kind of was a bug. It didn't show any signs of movement or vibration, after everything it had been through it was probably dead.

Like all insects, it had a head and abdomen and a thorax. Overall, it was about 4 cm long. Its left wing appeared to be broken about halfway along the length. That explained all of the vibrating and going in circles, it was probably trying to fly. The thorax made up about half of the overall length, and the head looked really odd.

It was becoming obvious that David had no idea what he was looking at. This was the sort of thing you look up on the internet. He also had some buddies back in the UK that might be able to shed some light on its identity.

It was at this point that Sarah poked her head around the workshop door.

"I've done an internet search on the image I took of the bug. It's drawn a complete blank. Computer says no," said Sarah.

"I thought the internet knew everything." he mused.

"It does, well Everything except this."

"I've still got no idea what I'm looking at." he said "I'm going to get some more pictures and send them to my mate in the invertebrate house at London Zoo. If anybody can figure this thing out, it'll be him."

"I'll grab the big camera." said Sarah.

By "big camera" she meant the DSLR. Much better for high-resolution images than a phone.

He adjusted the position of the bug and the light so that he could get the clearest image possible. Once they had taken some pictures, he sent off a quick email to his mate.

He took another big slurp of tea and put the bug back into its tobacco tin and put the lid on.

It was starting to get late and somebody needed to start thinking about food, otherwise they were going to end up getting takeout pizza. He headed back to the house and regarded the contents of the fridge. It looked semi-promising; he should be able to throw something together.

4.

On Fridays, the alarm goes off at 8am unless there's something special planned. After they had sorted themselves out, they left the house at precisely 9, as planned. It was about a 30-minute drive to the gym and Sarah was DJ, as usual.

"Looks like all the idiot drivers are out early this week." David said as he only just managed to avoid another demented driver on the motorway.

"There must be something in the water." said Sarah.

During their overtake of the demented driver, they both peered in through the side window as they passed.

"It's just another old timer on his way to God's waiting room." said Sarah.

"Same crap driving, different day."

He had been hoping for a normal day and all this crap driving was standard issue Spanishness. So far it was all business as usual.

As they pulled up outside the gym, they were fortunate enough to find a car in the middle of vacating its parking space. With a couple of moments of patience, the spot was theirs.

"That's handy." said Sarah.

"We do occasionally get a win on this parking game."

Once they had gotten changed and into the cardio area they settled onto their usual cardio machines. Sarah on the treadmill and David on the stationary bicycle. As he peddled he took note of some of the usual faces around the gym. There were those that were there to actually work out, then there were those that were there to be looked at. He glanced around to find Sarah and caught her eye. They both did a little nod and a shrug as they jointly acknowledged the poseurs - business as usual at the gym. After their cardio session, Sarah went on to her class while David headed for the pool. A nice lazy 30-minute swim.

They usually met up in the café after their gym sessions, so David headed over there. He was drinking his coffee and surfing social media, when he bumped into an article by one of the local rags on the island. Of course, it was about the dead couple. It stopped him in his tracks for a moment. He guessed that he shouldn't be too surprised, the news of two dead Germans on the island was bound to make the media eventually.

"How was your workout?" Sarah asked as she sat down next to him.

"Quite good for a Friday." he replied, "Have you seen the article in the paper about our Germans?"

"Oh gosh, no I haven't. What does it say?"

"Almost nothing, really. Dead Germans, Lloseta. That's about it."

"Wow, they've really dug into that story."

"Oh, it's the normal top-quality journalism. They don't know anything, but they thought they'd write about it anyway. Do you want a drink, or shall we get going?"

"I could do with a lemonade or something, do you want another coffee?"

"I might have a coke with you." he said.

With that, Sarah got up and headed for the bar. While she was sorting our drinks out, he looked at some of the other local papers online to see if there were any other articles about the Köhlers. A few minutes later Sarah returned with the drinks.

"I can't find any other articles about the Köhlers." he said as Sarah placed their drinks on the table.

"So, we aren't famous then?" she asked. She had the usual Friday cheeky look in her eye, confirming that they were going to the wine bar later.

"Not famous, babe, not yet. Anyway, I don't think this is what I want to be famous for. How was your class, were your usual girls there?"

"Yeah, all the usual gang. Quite good fun really."

The trip over to Son Caliu was uneventful, apart from the usual traffic on the Palma ring road. They arrived at the normal car park and found a parking space straight away. In the off-season parking was easy, in the summer season it was almost impossible.

The English bars in Son Caliu and the surrounding areas are a heaven for Brits in Mallorca. As they walked in and found a table, he found himself relaxing more with every breath. The sound of English voices, the smell of English food, and the anticipation of a nice cup of tea.

They didn't even need to look at the menu - they had the same as they always have. Full English for him, jacket potato for Sarah. Two mugs of tea.

David was just finishing off his lunch - chasing the last couple of baked beans around the plate with his toast - when his phone pinged.

"Who's that?" asked Sarah.

"It's Paul from London Zoo," he replied. "He has had a look at the pictures of the bee. Apparently, he can't identify it. He can't find it in any of the reference books or online and it doesn't really look like a bee."

"I guess we knew all this already?"

"He'd like us to get some better pictures of the wings and legs. He has suggested using some special close-up lens for the camera, which we don't have."

Sarah thought for a moment then suddenly clicked her fingers and pointed at him.

"Maybe one of the photography groups on social media will have one that we could borrow, or rent?"

"I never would have thought of that myself, it's a good job you're here."

Within seconds, Sarah was on social media and looking for a macro lens to fit the camera.

David started writing an email to Paul saying they'd see what we could do about getting better pictures.

"There," said Sarah, "I've asked the question, now we wait to see if we get an answer."

"Fingers crossed," he said.

He slurped his tea and sent the email. His gaze drifted off to the music videos that they always have on the TV here. This was bliss. Good food, good tea, and now a few moments with his brain in power save mode. Sarah's phone pinged.

"We have a response." she said, "Rachel and Allen have a lens we can borrow."

"That's amazing," he said, "what was that 5 minutes? And their house is on the way home. Are they at home now?" he asked, knowing that she didn't have an answer.

"I'll find out."

David caught the server's eye and waved his bank card at her. She nodded in response. A couple of minutes later Sarah's phone pinged again, just as the waitress arrived. He blipped his card.

"They are home for the next couple of hours", said Sarah.

"Thank you," he said to the waitress, "perfect, as usual."

"You're very welcome," said the waitress "See you again soon."

"Are we ready to go?" he asked.

"I'm ready if you are?"

He nodded and they both got up to leave. They smiled and waved at the owners as they made their way back out onto the street and towards the car park.

"Bit of a result with that lens, isn't it?" he said, "amazing what you can get the internet to do these days."

"You're starting to sound like an old man," said Sarah.

"Starting to…?"

Binissalem is a small town about 5 minutes from Lloseta. The Keelers have a beautiful house here which they've owned for more than 10 years. David and Sarah have known them for about 3 years and first met them over a pint of Guinness in a bar somewhere in Inca.

"Afternoon Dave." said Rachel, popping her head out of the front door.

"Good afternoon, are we all keeping well?" he asked.

"Very good thank you. Allen is getting that lens out now. Come on in, he's expecting you."

He followed Rachel into the house and shut the door behind him, Sarah was staying in the car.

"Hello mate," said David "here's that macro lens. Have you got a new photography project?"

"Well sort of, I found this weird-looking bee in the garden which I can't identify. I have a friend at London Zoo who is trying to help me look into it, but he needs better pictures than the ones I took with my normal lens."

"Oh well, this ought to do the trick." he said, handing David the lens.

"Any particular advice about using it?" David asked.

"Not really, it's just a lens. You will probably need to put it on a tripod, otherwise you will never keep it still."

"Ok, sounds good."

The lens itself was comically long compared to a normal SLR lens. It had its own special case to protect it from knocks and bumps.

"I'll get this back to you tomorrow." David said, hefting the lens in his right hand.

"Oh don't worry about that Dave, we are visiting Rachel's family in Devon for a couple of weeks. Get it back to us after that."

Back at the house, Sarah decided she was making tea while David headed for the workshop. He removed the normal lens from the camera and fitted the macro. He took a couple of practice shots of various workshop objects before reaching for the tobacco tin.

He tipped the bug out onto a piece of paper. Not exactly a photo-quality background, but better than a dirty workbench. He aimed the camera at the bug and tried repositioning himself several times, but he couldn't hold the lens still. Just as Alan said, he was going to need the tripod. He headed back into the house to find it. It took a couple of minutes, but eventually, he found it lurking in the spare bedroom.

"Your tea is on the side." Sarah shouted up the stairs to him.

"Coming." he shouted back.

He picked up the cup of tea on his way back out of the house.

Back in the workshop he had a strange feeling that the bug was watching him. It was quite spooky. He also had a suspicion that it had moved while he was back in the house, but he couldn't be certain. They regarded each other for a moment, but then David decided that he was being silly, it was a bee and it was dead.

He mounted the camera on the tripod and aimed it at the bug. Instead of moving the camera to focus, or using the focus ring, he found instead that he got better results if he moved the paper on which the bug was sitting. He got several decent shots of the sides, front and rear of the bug. The front half of the head appeared to be missing - maybe it got knocked off in transit. He looked for it in the tobacco tin but it was empty.

He couldn't really get a good angle to photograph the top and underneath of the insect. He reached across the bench and picked up his large tweezers, grabbed the bug by its abdomen and lifted it up to a better angle to photograph the top.

Suddenly the wings started buzzing. It made him jump out of his skin. He dropped the bug and the tweezers, while simultaneously knocking over his tea which went everywhere. He jumped back suddenly to avoid getting hot tea all over his legs. Damned thing, why did it have to go and do that?

Maybe it had been watching him after all when he entered the workshop. It was clearly still alive, even after a whole day in the tin. There's nothing worse than a spiteful insect. They observed each other for another moment before he decided that he was being stupid. It's a bloody bee. If it wants to buzz, let it buzz. David grabbed some kitchen roll and used it to mop up the spilt tea.

He took a deep breath and resolved to man up. If it made him jump again, he would stamp on the damned thing.

Using the tweezers he gripped it more positively this time. Of course, this time he was ready for it to buzz and scare the crap out of him, so it sat there and did nothing.

Having photographed the top and wings he turned it over to photograph the underneath. He photographed the abdomen and the head eventually coming to photograph the thorax - the bit where all the legs join together. He had clicked off a few photographs when he noticed something strange. At the point where all the legs meet, he could see the head of a screw.

He put the bug down and grabbed the camera. He reviewed the pictures he had taken and zoomed in on the screw. The screw had a dot marked on it at the point closest to the head. The body of the insect had a dot on it in the same place and another dot at 90° anti-clockwise.

"Oh my god, it is actually a screw. On an insect." he said to the air around him.

He leant over to the toolbox and opened the drawer where he kept the screwdrivers. He offered it up to the screw on the bug and, gently but firmly, rotated the screw anti-clockwise 90 degrees. There was a quiet click. The bug fell into three pieces on the paper. Head, thorax and abdomen. The legs had straightened themselves and now aligned with each other neatly under the wings.

He literally sat with my mouth open for a few seconds.

"Ok," he said to the air around him, "this isn't normal."

So, what he was actually looking at was a drone of some sort, disguised as a bee

"Oh crap, I need to tell Sarah about this."

He scraped the three sections of the bug into the tobacco tin, sealed the lid on, then placed it on the bench and put a heavy tub of grease on top of the tin to make sure it couldn't escape.

He almost ran on the way back to the house. He must have burst into the kitchen a bit too suddenly and made Sarah jump.

"Whoa. Where's the fire?" Sarah asked as she steadied her nerves.

"Oh God, no fire but something weird has happened."

"Yeah, what's that?" asked Sarah.

"Oh, you have to come and look. You wouldn't believe me if I told you."

Back at the workshop, he tipped the bug out of the tin and back onto the paper.

"So, what am I actually looking at here?" asked Sarah.

"It's a drone made to look like a bee."

"Who would -"

"I don't know, honey, but it's scaring the crap out of me. Who would make such a thing and why? What's it for?"

As neither of them had any suggestion they just looked at each other for a moment.

"Right," said Sarah, "pack all this crap up. I need wine."

"Yes ma'am."

David put the sections of the drone back into the tin and put the lid on. He wedged it into the vice and applied gentle pressure.

That ain't going nowhere, he said to himself.

They always celebrated Fridays by dressing up little and heading to slightly more formal bar and he had promised her a night out. David emerged from the bedroom in a smart shirt. He was freshly shaven and his semi-mohawk hair was perfectly quaffed. Sarah had gone full-blown rockabilly chick. Her blonde explosion of curly hair was tied up in a bright red scarf which matched her lipstick. She wore a figure-hugging white vest top that showed off her curves and her tattooed arms. On her bottom half, she wore baggy dungarees, and her thick soled boots finished the look. She grabbed her favourite old biker jacket as she headed out of the door. It might not be the fashion, but it was her look ad she rocked it. David gave a wry smile - he knew she'd be turning heads tonight.

They dumped the car in town and were walking into the wine bar within 5 minutes.

"Ok," he said, "wine first then pictures after.'

"Yes, please," said Sarah "the usual."

David caught the owner's eye and he nodded. Maybe they come here too often - the owner knew telepathically what they wanted to drink. Their usual wine was served in short order and they exchanged pleasantries with the owner. Apparently, everything was fine, and it had been busy earlier but quiet now.

"Come on, show me these pictures." said Sarah.

David opened the folder on his phone and shared it with her. Almost instantly her phone pinged. From his side of the table, David couldn't see what she was looking at, but the expression on her face told him everything. She looked through the pictures for a few moments and then looked at him.

"What am I looking at on this part of the thorax?" she asked.

"Let's have a look." he replied.

She zoomed in on the front part of the abdomen where it would join onto the thorax. It took him a moment, but he had a good idea of what it could be.

"I think those are electrical contacts," he said, "maybe the rear part is a battery?"

"So, the thorax would be the motor, or something?" she suggested.

"Seems reasonable, that's where the wings are. What about the head? The front part is missing."

"Well, the head ought to be a camera or some other method of seeing or thinking or ... I don't know, I guess it doesn't have to be modelled on a real insect."

"Yes, but it does need to navigate somehow. I wonder what its actual purpose is?"

"I'm guessing we won't figure that out till we know what the head actually looks like." She was now zooming in on one of the pictures of the head. "The head isn't just missing, it's broken. It looks like it has broken off, or maybe it's exploded?"

"Exploded?" David asked, a bit louder than he had intended, causing him to look around to check that no one was listening.

"Well that's what it looks like to me, have a look."

She angled the phone around towards him.

"Yeah, I see what you mean."

He thought about it for a moment and had one of those light bulb moments. He suddenly realised that the bug had a smell - and I knew exactly what it was.

"The bug smells like a spent shotgun cartridge," he said, "smells like a dirty shotgun before you clean it."

"Did you not want to mention this before?" asked Sarah.

"Well, I guess I hadn't consciously noticed. Anyway, why is it going to have an explosive head?"

"Oh my god," Sarah exclaimed, "it's a weapon, and it's what killed the Köhlers."

There was a long moment where everything seemed to go quiet. They both sat staring at each other across the table.

"Yeah, it's a weapon. It's like a little flying shotgun or bomb. It lands on your head and then boom, you're dead." Sarah suggested, she felt like she was on a roll here. "And there must have been at least two of them. This bug only killed one of the Köhlers, there must have been another bug."

He was hoping there would be another explanation but, as weird as this all sounded, it was the only thing that had made any sense from this whole thing. Then another light went on.

"This is the bug that killed Gunther." he said "I didn't think anything of it at their house, but Ingrid had a tennis racket next to her. I reckon this bug killed Gunther, and she smacked it with the tennis racket. That's how it ended up wedged in the shutter. It must have been after that when the other bug came in and got her."

"So where's that one gone?" she asked.

"Well, that is a very good question. "Can they fly without their heads? I'm going to assume they can. This one was still buzzing away while wedged in the shutter, so I assume it was trying to fly away."

"Flying away to where?" asked Sarah.

"Back to whoever is controlling them." he replied.

Sarah cupped her forehead with her hand and closed her eyes. She let out a long sigh.

"They navigate by GPS. If it's able to fly home with no head and therefore no camera, then it has to navigate somehow."

"Oh crap," he said, "the bug in our workshop has GPS?"

"That means they know where it is." said Sarah.

"Not necessarily," he replied, "it's been in a metal tin the whole time. That would have blocked any signal.

"Not all of the time, " said Sarah "*most* of the time."

"Oh. It was out on the bench when I was looking for the tripod. Maybe 5 minutes?" he conceded.

How long does your fitness tracker take to get a GPS signal?" asked Sarah.

"Depends on what mood it's in, sometimes 15 seconds, sometimes 2 minutes." he reluctantly agreed.

"So they know where it is and, I'm going to assume, they know we live there too."

"So what does that mean?" he asked.

"I assume it means that we are expecting visitors."

They spent the next couple of hours using wine as a lubricant. The conversation flowed freely about conspiracy theories, spies, their imminent death and why the Köhlers would be targeted like this. There were too many unanswered questions for them to really make any sense of the situation. Eventually, they decided that the simplest solution would be the best.

"Shall we just pretend that we found a strange-looking insect in the garden and brought it home so we could look it up on the internet?" asked Sarah.

David thought about how that plan would fit into the overall picture for a moment.

"Yeah. I'll see if I can reassemble it without letting it get any signal out. Then put it back in the tobacco tin and leave it casually on the shelf or bench. Make it look like it was no big deal."

"Ooh, I like it." said Sarah. "We were interested in it but we couldn't find anything about it on the internet. We only took pictures with our phones, not with the SLR or the macro lens."

"We probably need to do something about hiding these high-resolution pictures, too." said David, "I'm not going to rush into anything because I've been drinking, but we could move them to a different cloud account, or someone else's cloud account. Not sure."

"I like the idea of not rushing. These people can probably hack into all of our accounts, so we need to be careful. If we are caught hiding things, then it will be obvious that we know more than we are claiming to." said Sarah.

When they eventually got home David had time to think about what their next move would be. First of all, they needed to deal with that bug. If people were going to come looking for it, it needed to look like it did when they found it so the sooner it was re-assembled and put away the better.

In the workshop, he tipped all of the tools out of his metal toolbox. This left him with a metal box big enough to work inside and reassemble the bug. Hopefully, this would act as a Faraday cage and stop any signals from getting out. To test his theory he put his mobile phone in the box. He opened Google Maps and waited to see if it could identify where the phone was - it couldn't. He counted this as a successful first test. He then went back into the house and asked Sarah to call his phone. It went straight through to voicemail. He just wanted one more successful test before trusting the box. He put his Garmin fitness tracker in the box and tried to get it to start measuring a run. After five minutes it hadn't got a GPS lock, so he took it out of the box and it locked onto a satellite in less than thirty seconds. He took this as proof that his system worked.

He tipped the parts of the bug into the toolbox and fitted them together. He was expecting it to vibrate but felt much braver about the situation after the wine. The parts fitted together very neatly, and he inserted the screw, turning it 90 degrees clockwise. It's clicked into place in a positive, satisfying manner. He had to admit the engineering was very good, whoever built this had done a nice job. The legs, which had been tucked under the wings, re-deployed themselves. As quickly as possible, he got it back into the tobacco tin and closed the lid. After a pause of approximately 5 seconds, the bug did one long vibrate, then fell silent again.

After a little bit of thought, he figured the best place to leave the tobacco tin would be in one of their plastic boxes that contain all the cleaning materials. He went out to the van and placed the tin between the toilet bleach and sponges. It seemed to him that the plan was working, so far.

All of the high-resolution close-up pictures were on the memory card in the camera. He turned the camera on and flicked through the pictures to confirm. They could now delete all of the pictures from online accounts knowing that the pictures were safe on the memory card. They just had to keep the memory card safe and after a couple of minutes weighing up the pros and cons of different hiding places, he decided to put the memory card in a sandwich bag and then hide it in the tool shed behind the leaf blower.

"Hey Sarah," he said, "we'll need to delete all those pictures we were looking at last night."

"I've already done the ones on my phone." she replied.

"Ok, just me then." He went on to his cloud account and deleted all the pictures. He then had a search around on his phone and made sure that he couldn't find any close-ups.

5.

They both kept waking up during the night with paranoia swimming in their minds. Maybe they were worrying too much, maybe not. time would tell. They must have eventually dropped off to sleep because the alarm woke them with a start at 8:00 am.

"Morning honey," he said, "we've got two houses to close down today, hopefully with no dead bodies."

"Still not funny." said Sarah.

"Did you get a crap night's sleep?" he asked.

"Yeah, don't know really - 3 hours maybe?"

"Well, let's get the work done. Then we can have a siesta."

"Looking forward to it already." she said.

After breakfast, they headed out in the van to the first house. They pulled up outside and both did synchronised sighs.

"Let's hope everything's normal in there." said Sarah.

"Couldn't agree more."

They grabbed their kit from the back of the van and headed towards the front door. David inserted the key into the lock and they both looked at each other with raised eyebrows.

"Here goes nothing," he said.

"Come on, open it." said Sarah.

He eased the door open and they headed inside.

Everything appeared to be normal. This couple had flown back to England yesterday for the Christmas period. David wasn't sure, but he thought Sarah had said they were going to be away for one month.

They proceeded to go around the house doing their normal shutdown procedure. They made sure all the bins were empty and the cupboards and doors open with humidity traps in the right places. He went around and double-checked that all the windows and doors were closed and locked and that there were no dead bodies in the garden. All clear.

These guys didn't have a garage, so the car lived on the driveway. As usual, he disconnected the battery to make sure it wouldn't go flat while they were away.

Within the hour they were finished and headed back to the van.

"That's a relief." said Sarah.

"You're damn right, I really didn't want to go out into the garden, but it wasn't so bad in the end. It's nice to get back into the usual routine after everything we have been going through." he said.

"Do you want to head straight over to the other property that we are doing today? It's a flat, isn't it?" asked Sarah.

"Yeah, it's a flat on the other side of town. Should be an easy one."

"Should be."

Fifteen minutes later they were at the flat and started their normal close down. Once again there were no surprises, and the job went smoothly.

After sorting out both of these properties they were free to enjoy the rest of the weekend. As planned, they went straight home and dozed in front of the TV.

Before they knew it the weekend was over and they were back to work on Monday. More cleaning and tidying of people's houses and gardens. Same thing on Tuesday.

Wednesday they only had work in the afternoon. They allowed themselves a brief lie-in and then planned to go out and do some grocery shopping. Sarah was in the front room trying to sort out their reusable shopping bags into some kind of order, when she shouted upstairs to David.

"There's a black van that's just pulled up outside."

David crept into the bedroom that overlooks the front of the house and sneakily peered out of the window. It was a black people carrier or minibus with dark windows. It sat stationary parked directly across the front of their property. He couldn't see the driver or any passengers.

"Who the hell is that?" he shouted downstairs.

"Dunno", Sarah shouted back.

He slowly moved back away from the window and then made his way downstairs to find Sarah. He sidled up behind her so he could see what she was seeing.

"Any sign of movement?" he asked quietly so as to not make her jump.

"Nothing, absolutely nothing. This is starting to give me the creeps. Are these the visitors we said we were expecting?" she asked.

"Well," he said, "if it is, we've already got our story straight. It's in one of the cleaning boxes and we haven't seen it since you took those photographs with your phone. We couldn't find anything on the internet and then we forgot about it until now."

"I guess we'll find out shortly if they are going to buy that story or not."

The side door of the van slid slowly open. A young man stepped out of the van and gently closed the door.

Compared to most people around here he was smartly dressed.

He turned around and looked directly at their house and made his way, slowly and deliberately, up to the front door.

"Oh, Christ, here we go." said Sarah.

"Right, I'll get the door. Wish me luck!"

David slowly walked towards the front door while taking a long deep breath. The doorbell rang and the sound seemed to hang in the air for ages. He glanced over at Sarah, their eyes met and they both shrugged their shoulders. He didn't want them to think that they'd been seen arriving, so he deliberately left it a while before answering the door. It felt like forever but, after about 10 seconds, he opened the door.

"Hello?" he asked as he regarded the young man.

"Hello David," he said, "it's nice to meet you, I've heard a lot about you."

He spoke in an even tone with an accent which, under the circumstances, David was finding difficult to place.

"Ok," he said, "how can I help you today?"

"Oh, of course. I'm Torsten, the eldest son of Gunther and Ingrid. We spoke on the telephone."

"Oh thank goodness for that." David realised he had been holding himself rigidly because he was suddenly aware of his muscles releasing the tension.

"Is everything all right?" Torsten asked.

"Oh yes," he replied, "it's just that it's all been such a terrible business. Would you like to come in?"

He opened the door further and backed away, giving Torsten more room to come inside the house.

"Hello, Torsten," said Sarah "it's a shame we aren't meeting in better circumstances."

Torsten nodded.

"If it's Ok, I'd like to take the keys so I can go and have a look around the house?" he asked.

"Yes, of course, no problem. But ... sorry to be difficult, Torsten, but I need to see some photo ID before giving out the keys."

"Of course, standard security."

"Well, yes. I wouldn't like to be the person who gave the keys to a stranger."

"I wouldn't like that either." he agreed, reaching into his pocket. He produced his wallet and extracted his driving licence. David compared the picture on the licence to the young man in front of him. As he regarded him, he changed from being some nondescript young man on the street into the son of Ingrid and Gunther. David didn't really need the ID, Torsten had his mother's eyes.

He gave the driver's licence back to him and then headed off to find the keys. He left Sarah chatting with Torsten. She was much better at small talk than David. What do you say to a lad in his situation?

"He's going to be staying at the hotel next to the fountain." said Sarah as he returned to the room.

"Oh yeah, it's quite nice there. I think I prefer that one to the one over the road." he replied.

Both Sarah and David knew that the one over the road can be a bit of a knocking-shop for local young people during the off-season.

"Torsten, if you need anything during your stay, you'll let us know." he said.

"Thank you, that's very kind." he said. "So, my taxi is waiting, I guess I should be going. Thank you for everything you've done."

"You're very welcome." David said, "Do keep in touch."

He was already turning towards the door as David opened it for him. As he walked out of the door, he thanked them again and headed towards his taxi.

"It's such a shame to see a young man have to go through all this." said Sarah.

"I know, poor bloke. He's far too young to have lost his parents, I can't imagine what he's going through."

They watched his taxi drive off down the street and then got back to their routine.

A couple of days later Sarah got a phone call from one of their regular customers in the next village over. The Fabers were heading home to Germany for a couple of months and needed their house mothballing and then watching over the winter. They hadn't spoken to them in almost 9 months and they were keen to show them around the house to make sure everything was done as they would like it.

They had arranged to meet at 3 that afternoon and they rolled up in the van at precisely 2:59.

As the Fabers were showing them around the house, the conversation naturally drifted towards their fellow countrymen Gunther and Ingrid.

"It's a terrible thing that happened over at their house, and you were the ones who found them, weren't you?" Mr Faber asked.

"Yes, we found them in the garden. It was a real shock. I've never seen anything like that before." David said.

"Well hopefully it's not the sort of thing you see every day." said Mr. Faber.

The two of them were now working their way around the back garden and swimming pool when Mrs Faber came over to see how we were getting on.

"Of course," she said, "you used to work with Gunther didn't you, at the Air Force base in Schleswig?"

"Yes I did, that was a long time ago now, darling. It's still supposed to be a secret, but I don't suppose it matters too much, we have both been retired for so long."

Now David's ears had pricked up - this guy used to work with Gunther? So, were these guys at risk as well?

Instinctively he had a quick look around the garden and the air above him looking for any flying insects. He couldn't see any but decided they should head back inside, just to be on the safe side.

"I think I've got everything under control out here." he said, as he corralled the Fabers towards the back door. "Perhaps we should head inside and you can tell me what you want me to do with your car?"

"Oh yes, I'm glad you reminded me, it's due for its ITV test and will need a service too. Are you Ok taking care of that?" asked Mr Faber.

"Yes, no problem, as long as I have access to all the paperwork." David replied, almost pushing them inside through the door.

"I knew you were going to say that, so I've left all of the paperwork in the glove box."

Having made their final arrangements, David put their house keys in his pocket as they said their goodbyes and headed out to the van.

David was almost bursting to tell Sarah what he had found out.

"Oh my God," he said as soon as they were back in the van, "did you know that Mr Faber and Gunther worked together years ago for the German military?"

"You're kidding me? Christ, I wonder if that means these guys are in danger too?"

"I don't know, but I wasn't taking any chances. When I found out we were in the garden and I had to get back inside as quickly as possible. Call me paranoid, but I felt very exposed out there."

"Did you see any bugs flying around?"

"No, but that doesn't mean they weren't there."

"Shouldn't we be telling somebody about all of this?" asked Sarah.

"Well maybe, but who are you going to tell? The police won't be interested, and to be honest, no one is going to believe us."

"Yeah, you're right, if I hadn't seen it with my own eyes, I wouldn't believe you either."

"Instead of telling someone, maybe we should have this documented somewhere." said Sarah.

"Well, yes, but I don't want to get caught with any incriminating evidence. At the moment our cover story is that we found a bee."

"We *think* that's our cover story; it hasn't actually worked yet."

"Yes, well, thankfully it hasn't needed to work yet."

Later that night they were watching TV in the living room. Dinner had been delicious and now they were chilling. The TV program was something about police and spies. David was half watching the TV and half surfing social media, but Sarah was paying closer attention.

"We need to do what these guys just did on the telly." she said.

"Oh?", he asked. Nope, he'd completely missed what she was talking about.

"These guys," she said, indicating the TV, "they have the same problem that we've got. They have files they want to keep safe and hidden.

"Right ... "

"They have just used a cyber café computer to upload pictures to a new cloud account that no one knows about."

"Oh, " he said, suddenly cottoning on to what she was saying. "Yes, that's something we could do."

6.

The next day they planned to get to the Fabers' house at about 11:00 and hopefully be out by 12:00. As they pulled up outside the house everything looked normal, and they both proceeded to get the gear out of the van. David grabbed the key from his pocket and inserted it into the lock.

"Hello?" he called, as he eased the front door open. They went in and started their jobs around the house. Within a few minutes, David was already upstairs sorting out bins etc. He was making good progress when Sarah called to him quietly from downstairs.

"Dave," she called in an exaggerated whisper. "Dave, can you hear me?"

"Yes dear," he called back as he headed back towards the top of the stairs, "what's up?"

"Ok, stay calm, but I think there's one of those bugs on the outside of the kitchen window."

"Shut up! Oh my god, I've got to come and see this."

David was downstairs in a flash. He crept into the kitchen and Sarah pointed towards the bottom left corner of the kitchen window. He couldn't quite make it out at first, there was a dark bush behind it which was camouflaging it. As he moved his head around the background became bright green grass and he could clearly see the suspicious bee on the window.

"Told you." she said.

"You're not wrong. God, this is giving me the willies."

"What's it doing? It's not trying to kill anybody. Maybe it's listening or watching."

"You think? Can they do that?"

"How the hell should I know, Dave? I don't think it's killed anybody, so it must be doing something else."

"Do we know it hasn't killed anybody?" he asked with growing unease.

"Well no, but I haven't seen any dead bodies."

"Have you looked for any dead bodies?"

"No Dave, That's your job."

Oh, for Christ's sake. Not what he wanted to hear, but somebody did need to check for dead bodies. He really didn't want to go outside with it, so he rushed back upstairs and peered tentatively out of the window overlooking the back garden. He got himself up close to the glass so he could see all of the garden including close to the house - no victims.

He breathed a sigh of relief and then headed back towards the top of the stairs.

"All clear in the back garden", he gently called down the stairs.

"Well, that's a bonus."

"Sarah." He loudly whispered down the stairs.

"What? " she called as she arrived at the bottom of the stairs.

"Is it here to spy on them or for us?" he asked.

The look on her face told him that she had not considered the latter as an option.

"I don't know."

David paused for a moment as he considered what he was about to say. This was either uncharacteristically stupid or uncharacteristically brave, and he didn't know which. From the look on Sarah's face, she didn't know either.

"We should catch it." he said.

"Um, we're going to do what?"

"Catch it. It's a whole example. None of it has blown up yet."

"Are we sure this is what we want to be doing?"

"No, not at all. But I think it's the right thing to do."

Sarah couldn't quite believe she was going to go along with this.

"Have you got anything to put it in?" she asked, meaning did he have a metal tin so that it can't connect to its GPS or to home base.

"I'm sure I'll find one somewhere. I have an idea about how to catch it too."

Sarah shook her head, clearly unable to believe what they were talking about.

"Ok, but so we're clear - this is all your fault."

He kind of nodded and shrugged his shoulders at the same time. Yes, this was always going to be his fault.

David knew he'd be able to sneak out of the back door, as long as he went slowly. He grabbed a hand towel from the downstairs toilet and wetted it under the tap to make it heavier. He knew that Mr Faber kept some spare fuses in an old air gun pellet tin in a kitchen drawer - which he located, emptied and pocketed.

He snuck out of the back door with slow deliberate movements. Within a minute or two he had been able to reduce the distance to his quarry to about three metres. Luckily, he was able to get a good angle of attack with his right arm, there was no way he would have made the throw with his left.

With a couple of preparatory deep breaths and a little sigh, he was ready to go. He breathed in, held it, stepped forward and chucked the towel at the bug. The shot was dead on, landing squarely covering the bug and then the towel fell to the ground. The bug went with it, ending up covered with the towel on the ground. David couldn't help himself and did a little fist-pump.

He hurried over to where the towel and hopefully the bug were on the ground. As he gathered up the wet towel, he could feel the bug buzzing inside. It was clearly trying to make a bid for freedom, and thus far was unsuccessful. He wrestled the pellet tin from his pocket and ripped the lid off. He covered the bug with the upturned pellet tin and then gradually pulled on the towel to remove it. After a few seconds of delicate manoeuvring, the towel was removed, and the bug was now under the pellet tin. A quick flick and the bug was in and the lid was on.

"Oh my God, you've done it!" said Sarah, not sure whether to be happy or annoyed.

He let out a big sigh. David had definitely caught the bug, but quite what he had started with the bug's owner he had no idea. David grabbed some aluminium foil from the kitchen and wrapped the pellet tin in the foil for extra GPS protection.

"I can't believe I've let you talk me into this," said Sarah. "just when we thought we had a reasonable get-out story, now you've gone and dug the hole deeper."

"I know, I know. But what could we do? Just let it fly away? We are never going to get another opportunity to look at one of these things up close. If we've done this right we can keep it for as long as we like, they'll never know that we've got it."

He figured that any kind of insect out in the open could be attacked by a cat or a gecko or a bird. Ok, so this attack had come from a wet towel, but they weren't going to know that, were they?

As soon as they were back at the van he pulled out a metal toolbox and shoved the pellet tin inside. There were now three separate layers of metal between it and the outside world. He thought that ought to be enough to stop any signal from getting out.

Once they were back at the house he moved the bee into the workshop, still wrapped and boxed. He knew it was very much alive and able to communicate but was less certain whether it was going to try to kill or photograph him or do something else that he couldn't imagine.

Then he remembered something they'd said earlier, maybe it could listen too. It would probably be best if they just kept away from the damn thing for a while. Having double checked that the wrapped tin was secure, he closed the toolbox, pushed it into a corner and closed the workshop door.

7.

For the next week or so they were quite busy working and socialising. David also had a period of renewed focus at the gym - these things happened from time to time but would likely soon pass.

One morning he was enjoying his post-workout coffee and social media session, having had a big workout at the gym. While he was engrossed in the contents of his phone a strange man sat opposite him at the table. For a moment he was completely confused. Even though he'd lived there for a while, he still got surprised by some of the local behaviour and customs, like their complete lack of the concept of personal space.

"Hello, David." he said with an English accent.

Now he was completely taken aback. Not only had this stranger invited himself to sit at his table but he knew him by name.

"Is there something I can help you with?" David demanded.

"Yes, David, I think we both know that there is. You have something that doesn't belong to you and I have been sent to retrieve it."

This confused him. For a short while he had allowed himself to forget about the dead Germans and the bug, so for a moment David really didn't understand what he was talking about. Maybe he'd borrowed something from a friend and forgot to take it back. Was this some kind of joke arranged by Rachel and Alan about him returning their camera lens?

"Would you like a little refresher?"

"Mate, I literally have no idea what you're talking about. Is this some kind of joke arranged by one of my so-called friends?"

"David. This is no joke, this is quite serious. You were working at the Köhler's house when you discovered them dead in the back garden. While you were there you would have removed various items to do with cleaning the house. The item I'm talking about would have stood out in your mind. I'm very surprised you have forgotten about it."

Holy crap, this was the moment they had been talking about, the moment that he had been rehearsing in his head and when it had been time, his moment to deliver his lines he'd completely fluffed it.

"Um…. Oh, wait. I get it. You want to look at that strange bee that I found in the garden."

"Strange bee, that's the one. I've been sent to retrieve it. You have it and you are going to give it to me."

"It's a bit dramatic, don't you think? It's just a bee." David said, finally hitting his stride, "why the hell are you so interested in an insect? In fact, now you've got me interested. What is it about this bug that's got you so wound up?" He hoped that he hadn't overdone it.

There was a bit of a pause while they looked at each other across the table. If David was honest, this guy didn't seem like the sort of bloke he should be testing.

"Look, David. I've got a job to do and I'm going to do it. I have no idea about the object, I've just been sent to get it back off of you." He leaned forward across the table shortening the distance between them and spoke in a quieter voice. "We can do this the easy way, or we can do this the hard way, David. At the end of the day, I just want to do my job and go home. At the moment you are preventing me from doing that."

"Ok, Ok. It's yours, take it away. Who knew that an unidentified insect could cause so much trouble? I don't have it with me, obviously. I think it's in the back of the van which is at my house."

"Great," he said, "time we were going then."

He nodded his head towards the exit and then continued regarding David from his side of the table.

"What, right now?"

"Yes David, chop chop."

At this point, David was crapping himself. He knew this was going to happen at some point because, of course, they hadn't found a bee, they'd found some weird man-made killing machine. His shoulders lowered and he let out a sigh as he gave up and decided to go along with his demands. He took one last sip from his coffee and put the cup down on the saucer and pushed it away from him.

David led him out of the gym and towards the car. He got in the passenger seat next to David and they drove in silence for the 20 minutes or so back to the house.

As they pulled up onto the driveway next to the van David decided to break the silence.

"Will it be alright if I explain this to Sarah, what do you want to scare the crap out of her as well?

"Cocky little shit, aren't you? Ok, I'll let you explain it to your missus. Then you'll get the bee for me. Anything stupid and I move onto plan B."

David headed over to the front door and let himself in. As he entered the house he called out to see if Sarah was around. It took him a moment to realise that her bag and phone were missing from their usual resting place, so she was probably out.

"I don't think she's here," said David.

"That saves us a job then, doesn't it? Now, where is it?"

"I told you it's in the van," he said, grabbing the van keys and heading back out to the driveway. He unlocked the van with the blipper and opened the rear doors. David made a show of rummaging around a couple of tool bags pretending to search for it for about 30 seconds. Eventually, he pulled the foil-wrapped tobacco tin from its hiding place.

"Here it is." he said, rattling the contents inside of the tin.

The man looked a bit perturbed that David would be rattling this precious object that he had been sent to retrieve. He extended his right hand towards David and beckoned. David gave up and placed the tin in the man's palm.

"Thank you." he said. "You're not to discuss this with anybody. You never had this object, you don't know what it is and I was never here."

"Ok, I understand - I think."

With that he turned and walked down the street towards, David assumed the train station. He watched for a moment as he disappeared around the corner then took a deep breath and let it back out again.

He sent Sarah a text message:

We have had a visitor.
He and it are gone now.
I'm going for a beer.

Ok babe, back in 10

She was back in less than 10. They went to the usual venue where they got to prop up the bar and nobody spoke English. Over a few beers, he explained to Sarah about a bloke and what had happened. Actually, now that it was gone, he felt a bit more relaxed. It was no longer their problem, and they were no longer dreading the arrival of its owners, assuming the other bug was still their little secret.

A few weeks later they also returned to the UK for Christmas. They'd been there for just over a week, but it was really good to catch up with family and friends and to be reminded of how good the curry was back home. The days flew by and in no time at all, they were back on the island and looking forward to the Spanish celebrations on New Years Eve

All thoughts of strange visitors and strange insects had disappeared out of David's mind. Even the one hiding in the workshop didn't seem important anymore. It was something he would get around to looking at some point, but he found the whole concept of it troublesome and could always find other jobs that needed attending to, rather than investigating the bug that lurked in the workshop.

Days turned into weeks, and they had gotten back in their normal routine. They were regularly going into the houses where they were responsible for checking for damp, mould and any other uninvited visitors. They were even starting to get emails and phone calls about people planning their return to the island in the next couple of months, once the cold season was over. Spring was on the way.

One bright but cold day they had been down to the gym and were preparing to get into a couple of chores around the house when the doorbell rang.

"I'll get it." shouted Sarah, already heading towards the door.

"Ok, babe." he continued soldering the wiring on one of his old guitars.

There was a pause for a moment. Sarah was chatting to someone at the door.

"Dave," she called, "someone here to see you."

"Coming dear."

He put his tools down and made a point of keeping them in order. David could be very good at misplacing tools when he wasn't paying attention. He walked over to the front door wondering who it could be. It obviously wasn't anyone they knew because Sarah would have said their name. He figured he'd find out shortly.

"Hello, David."

It was the man who sat opposite him at the gym and who'd come to retrieve the bug.

"Oh god. What do you want?"

He produced a small tin in his right hand, and gently shook it. It made a familiar noise, and straight away David knew what it was.

"You bringing it back?" David asked cheekily.

"I wish. I found this one sitting outside my living room window, it was watching me. There was another one near the front door, but that one flew away."

David had to take a moment to think about what was going on.

"So, are you now the hunted, rather than the hunter?" David asked.

"I was never the hunter, I was the courier. I was asked by the UK government to retrieve what they called a 'missing device'. I was never told what it was, or who it belongs to. I know this isn't just an insect. Yes, it does look a bit like a strange bee, but there's a lot more to it and I think you already know that. This is some kind of drone, some kind of weapon and I think you're just the chap to help me investigate it further."

David thought for a moment. He figured that this guy might have the inside information, skills and equipment to help him to investigate the bug more thoroughly. This could be a big step in finding out why the Köhlers had been killed in the first place. David stepped back slightly and opened the door a little wider.

"You'd better come in."

8.

The office around him was a drab, well used space. The few pieces of furniture the previous occupants had left behind were of the cheap brown laminate-on-chipboard variety. In places the plastic wood had peeled away from the sawdust and glue interior, threatening to pinch or embed itself in careless flesh.

He presumed the walls had, at one time, been painted white but were now nicotine brown with the occasional blemish of mildew for additional interest. The Venetian blinds showed the scars of decades of abuse; most of the slats were bent or folded with some missing completely. They had suffered their years of abuse relatively well and still functioned as designed, keeping the daylight and prying eyes out, though they too were covered in a sticky film of tar and poison. The window behind was similarly tiger-striped, with years of smoke and damp collaborating to form the vertical striations of cancer and condensation.

Klaus would have liked a better office to use as his temporary base of operations, but at the moment the budget didn't stretch that far. He sparked his lighter, producing an even triangle of golden-orange flame. He brought it closer to the cigarette that he had clamped between his lips. As was his habit, he held the tip of the shark-fin flame a couple of centimetres below the tip of his cigarette, gradually reducing the gap until the tobacco ignited under his gentle draw. He inhaled. He loved the feeling of the smoke reaching into the depths of his lungs - filling every corner with its calming caress. He held.

After a couple of puffs, his attention returned to the computer screen while the cigarette was relegated to its place between his right index and middle finger. The blue smoke curled into the air above him, rippling and tightly ruffling, before eventually dispersing into an even haze.

"Carl, have you got the hive setup in the other room?" asked Klaus.

"Yes, all the equipment is set up and I've got eight units on the docking station as you requested four video and four sound. I think we're just waiting for you to turn on the main computer and we should be ready to go." Carl replied.

"Excellent news. I've been in contact with our buyer and they are keen to see a demonstration. I thought we'd start by sending a few units out to

watch Gunther and Ingrid." said Klaus.

"That sounds like a good idea. We could send them a video of the units arriving and getting themselves into position. Then we can demonstrate the high-quality sound and video they are capable of capturing." said Carl.

Klaus leaned over towards the computer cabinet near the door. He was careful not to over-extend himself and put the chair under too much stress as it was of the same quality and vintage as the desk. It had some suspicious staining around what had once been chrome plated metal. He hoped the brown crust was due to spilled coffee or rust. He pushed the 'on' button and the various racked units whirred and chattered into life. Green lights blinked. As the main computer sorted itself out, he clicked on the icon that would launch the control software on his laptop.

There hadn't been any time or budget for aesthetics in the software. The result was a crude but effective user interface, with a screen that was crowded and chaotic. But all the necessary information was there. The display confirmed what Carl had told him: eight units, four video and four sound. That would need to change. The ultimate demonstration of the capabilities of article 79a involved killing. The video units would be useful as they could capture the action from various angles. But for the moment Klaus was going to keep Carl from seeing the killing. Partly, he supposed, this was because he still viewed Carl as the new boy. The last recruit to join the team and the youngest by a good margin. Klaus had taken him under his wing when he saw the young man struggling with new technology that was beyond him. He had trained him. Encouraged him.

Even at this late stage in the project, with all the bold moves and dreams, all the sacrifices and regrets, it was still Klaus and Carl after everyone else had left. It was a shame.

Their history together would complicate things in the end game.

Klaus turned the laptop towards Carl and swept his upturned palm towards the screen.

"There you are, Carl. You can launch them whenever you're ready." said Klaus.

"Oh, Ok. I thought this was usually your job?"

"It usually is. On this occasion and trying to sweeten you up, so you'll do me a little favour."

"Oh?" enquired Carl, pressing the enter button on the keyboard.

Klaus was already out of his chair and parting the blinds with his thumb and index finger. He peered through the stained glass, admiring his babies as they came to life. The eight individual units of article 79a began to stir. Their beating wings' low hum rapidly increasing in volume and pitch until all eight units became airborne. From his south facing vantage point they headed left, eastwards towards their target location. Each flying as an individual, not a swarm, so as to attract less attention.

Klaus allowed the blinds to reform their shape, to go back to their job of collecting cigarette slime.

"I'd like you to go down to the shop and buy me some more cigarettes." said Klaus, pulling a €10 note from his wallet.

"Ok, no problem. They are going to take 10 or 15 minutes to get to Lloseta, I'll be back in plenty of time to get them set up."

Carl took the €10 note from Klaus and headed towards the door, checking that he had his key. Even before Carl was out of the door, Klaus had turned the laptop back towards himself and issued a recall order on two of the sound units. He then picked up the transport case from next to his leg and placed it on his desk.

He popped the lid open and removed a smaller transparent plastic container. These each contained two more bees, but this time of a more sinister design. These weren't for watching. Taking the container with him, he walked around into Carl's office next door, then open the door onto the balcony.

The empty base unit stood in front of him. Externally it resembled a computer printer or scanner, but made of material designed for longevity, not aesthetics - rugged plastic protecting its precious cargo. He removed the two units from the plastic container and carefully positioned them onto two of the available ports. After a few moments of impatient toe-tapping the recalled sound units returned and docked themselves into available slots. Klaus removed them and placed them in his clear plastic container.

Ensuring the balcony door was closed and locked, he hurried back to his office and the laptop. He hurriedly accessed images of the intended victims, Gunther and Ingrid Köhler, which he copied and pasted into the mission file. Location was similarly copied. They were then instructed to identify their targets and wait. He hit the enter key and heard the mission begin. Two murder bees off on their mission to start what would be the beginning of the end of article 79a.

Decades of careful research and development. Trying and failing, technologically and financially. All the hard work eventually being rewarded with small successes, followed by larger ones. It seemed like it had taken half of his career, but eventually his dream had come to fruition. Autonomous multi-function units that could function individually or part of a team. Hiding and travelling in plain sight. The perfect surveillance tool. The perfect weapon.

9.

After a degree of fiddling and fine tuning. Carl was happy with the video and sound feed he was getting on his laptop. He had positioned the various units around the Köhlers' property so as to get a good overview of the activity around the house. There were two other units to which Carl had not been given access and as usual, he didn't know why. The boss sometimes kept some of the feed to himself. He always assumed that the boss had some kind of developmental work or experiment in progress. Better not to ask. If he was included in the experiment and it didn't work as hoped, he would end up taking the blame. Much better to leave the old man to his tinkering. If it worked Carl would be told in the fullness of time.

"Carl. Have you got any idea what these idiots are up to?" The shout came from the other office.

"Not really, I can't see anything, and the sound is very quiet."

"That's what I thought … they are in, aren't they?"

"Yes, they're in. Perhaps we should move one of the units to an upstairs window, see if we get a better view?" suggested, Carl.

"That's a good idea, but you better get ready to cover your eyes. If they are in the bedroom, they could be up to anything."

"OK, got it. Cover the eyes. Check."

Mr. Köhler was standing next to the bedroom door with a suitcase at his feet, Mrs. Köhler appeared to be packing. Her suitcase was open on the bed and she was folding various items of clothing before placing them carefully in the suitcase.

"Looks like they're going away." said Carl, down the corridor to the other office.

"Yes, I can see that now. It looks like Gunther is ready to go."

Over the next half an hour they watched as Mrs. Köhler finished packing and both suitcases found their way to the bottom of the stairs and they both ended up in the back garden with a bottle of wine. Apparently, they had about half an hour until their taxi was due to arrive. Carl thought they looked like a couple going on holiday.

"Carl. I think we've got plenty of video and sound for demonstration purposes."

"I agree, looks really good. Just as good as I expected, but it is nice to have them out in the real world rather than our testing facility in Germany."

"Oh, completely. They navigated straight there, no problems, the system's working very well. I think we should all give ourselves a pat on the back."

After a few more minutes of surveillance the boss called down the corridor to Carl again.

"Carl, why don't you head off home? I've got all of this under control. I'm going to recall the units soon anyway, once their taxi arrives. I've got plenty of evidence for our buyers."

"Oh, ok." Carl didn't need asking twice. "I'll see you in the morning, then?"

"Yes, see you tomorrow, Carl."

He gave Carl a few minutes. That way he made sure he wouldn't be interrupted by forgotten house keys, or the like.

Once he was sure there'd be no interruptions, he ordered his units do their terrible job.

He observed their video feed. Each unit had been given a target by the computer and each unit performed a flyby to confirm the target's identity. He observed the screaming panic on his screen which brought a smile to the corner of his lips. "Bye, bye."

The video feed from the other units around the garden couldn't see the individual killer units but could certainly see the effect they were having on the victims. Gunther appeared to recognise the insect immediately and understood the reason for the flyby. He knew kill shot would be next. The sound units were too far away to capture it, but he was shouting something to his wife, and she was shouting back. They captured the screaming and the panic, but not the actual words being shouted.

Moments later Gunther's knees buckled, and he dropped, straight down to the ground. Mrs. Köhler had managed to get hold of a tennis racket from somewhere. She swatted at the unit that had dropped Gunther. She then noticed that she herself was a target and began swinging the racket at her own attacker, but it was all for nothing. In the middle of her swing, she herself dropped.

He nodded and smiled to himself, proud that his design worked so well. He ordered the killer units to land. He wanted the units to keep themselves hidden, to stay out of sight. The killer units were efficient and even fairly quiet, if not silent. If they had attracted any unwanted attention, he didn't want to compound the problem by having his unit's all take off and leave the scene of the crime. Once he'd ascertained that no one's interest had been aroused, the bees could fly home one at a time. Even if people had noticed them suddenly dropping dead, the units benefited from their unique camouflage – no one would be looking for insect murderers. They simply had to sit still until any investigation was over.

After ten minutes it was apparent that no one had noticed, so he began recalling the units, leaving about 15 seconds between each command.

From the initial concept to the delivery of a working weapon, he had nurtured the project like his own child. So many people had told him that his idea was simply not possible. It couldn't work. You simply couldn't compress all of the technology and weaponry he wanted into such a small package. They had also told him that his ideas about the units working together was beyond the capability of even much larger computers, let alone his ideas of miniaturizing everything to the scale of an insect.

He had kept developing and improving his concept and as time went on, improvements in materials and computing allowed for smaller and smaller technology. Video cameras went from being the size of a briefcase to the size of a grain of rice. The big leap forward that changed everything had been the advent of the smartphone. Suddenly miniature cameras, microphones and GPS were everywhere.

The exponential increase of processing power combined with unbelievable miniaturization during his career had meant that computers that used to be only a dream could now fit onto the end of his pencil. Combined with the advent of artificial intelligence the underlying computer code that ran his bees had transformed into something truly amazing. A whole new method of killing.

10.

The right rear wheel of the trolley wobbled and fluttered as it progressed along the brightly lit white corridor. It seemed as if it was destined to travel its perpetual chicane, where the other wheels had been allowed to glide unwavering in a straight line, making smooth steady progress towards their destination. The curved lines and smooth welds of the stainless steel structure had been built to minimize difficult corners and grooves where dirt and bacteria could gather and to make cleaning and sanitizing easier. This once elegant design had mostly stood the test of time, but now wore the marks and scars of decades of quiet service. Dents, bruises and scuffs all conspired to hide the former elegance of such a simple tool.

Eduardo's right foot didn't hurt as much anymore. The operation 2 months ago had improved its alignment and mobility, and the pain and swelling were reduced. It was easier to walk now, but it would never look or perform like his left foot. He had been born with what his mother called a "blessing from god". Apparently, his head had been blessed too. The other kids at school had ridiculed him and his foot, calling him names. They used to mock him by imitating his awkward limp and his speech impediment. He was easy to confuse, and the stress of their goading only made things worse.

It wasn't all of the students that treated him this way. Most of them spoke to him as any other school kid. They could talk to him and sit next to him in class without mentioning his blessings at all. They were able to study together in the library, hang out at break times, and walk to and from school without any fuss or special treatment. Most of the time he was just a regular kid, but occasionally one of the nasty-crowd would take it upon themselves to pick on him and his gifts. Sometimes it would last for a morning or a day, other times it could last for a couple of weeks before they got bored and moved on to someone else.

Eduardo sometimes wondered if the trolley was mocking him. That wheel marking itself out as different just like his foot. It only behaved like this when the trolley was empty. Once he had a corpse on board the wheel would go back to behaving itself like the others, as if playtime was over and work had begun.

Having arrived at the chiller room door, Eduardo swept his identity card through the reader producing a green light and a positive sounding beep. He shoved the door open with his behind before pulling the trolley in after him.

He brought it to a rest under door 318 and applied the brake. He lifted the clipboard from the cold, hard metal surface and double checked that he had parked in the right place. He usually collected the correct body. As long as he was calm nobody was rushing him he was able to think clearly. There had been a time when Dr. Martinez had been in a bad mood which seemed to rub off onto everybody else in the coroner's office. On that day Eduardo had felt flustered. Even though he concentrated really carefully and double checked, he had still managed to take the wrong cadaver for post-mortem. Once Dr. Martinez had realised, he really started shouting. He called Eduardo some nasty names. Eduardo was frightened. He had to run away.

He opened door 318 and checked the identity tag attached to the left big toe. His eyes moved back and forth between the tag and the clipboard – Gunther Köhler. The names matched. The case number matched. He checked again. He smoothed his moustache with his thumb and index finger. After a few moments he was happy that this was the correct person. He pulled the shelf out all the way and tugged on the body bag heaving the body onto the trolley. Gunther was certainly bigger and heavier than the average corpse that Eduardo dealt with, but not more so than the average German.

They left the chiller room together and followed the corridor towards the examination room where Dr. Martinez would be waiting. As they floated along Eduardo once again observed the wayward wheel which now steered a steady, even course under the pressure of its silent passenger. Whenever he happened to use this trolley, it was this point in the journey that caused him to wonder. The thought appeared in his head, a question which he was never able to answer. Why was it that the wheel performed better under pressure, and he performed worse? Under the weight of its charge the wheel seemed to stand to attention, to step up to the plate. No more messing around or goofing off, it was time for action.

They arrived at the examination room door. The perpetually unanswered question slipped from Eduardo's mind as he examined the clipboard, checking once again that he had retrieved the right person. He pushed his thick-rimmed glasses onto the top of his head and again smoothed his moustache as he interrogated the paperwork. Everything was in order, but he still would have liked somebody else to double check his work before he handed the body over to Dr. Martinez. He slipped his key card through the lock and shoved the door open. They rolled through the door into the examination room, where he saw the doctor getting ready for his gruesome work. Upon hearing the door the doctor turned expectantly.

"Ah, Eduardo, there you are."

"Yes. Hello, Doctor Martinez." Eduardo's voice sounded nervous and higher pitched than he had intended. "I've brought your next ... v-v-victim. For you." Eduardo didn't like the way some of the staff disrespected the dead people with their casual use of the word victim. They called it "gallows humour", but he didn't think it was funny at all.

He wheeled Mr. Köhler over to the examination table applied the brake. He handed the clipboard to the doctor and took half a step back. He didn't know if he was giving the doctor more room to work or pre-empting the bellowing attack that sometimes happened at this point. Dr. Martinez examined the toe tag and compared it to the paperwork. The doctor nodded.

"Thank you, Eduardo. Would you like to stay and help out?"

He hadn't expected that. Occasionally, Dr. Martinez was in a good mood and seemed to want to include Eduardo in the post-mortem. This unexpected warmth also made Eduardo nervous. He would have preferred the doctor to be more constant, more predictable. These rapid changes in mood always caught Eduardo off guard.

"Well. I can stay if you want me to." said Eduardo.

"I'm sure we can use an extra pair of hands around here this morning. We are going to be quite busy. We've got this man here," the doctor's eyes returned to the paperwork, "Gunther Köhler. Then afterwards we have his wife as well. They came in together."

That was very unusual. A husband and wife in for post-mortem examination together. Eduardo had never seen that before and he didn't know how he felt about it. It made him uncomfortable, but he didn't know why.

Dr. Martinez started with the forehead and the obvious wound and spoke to the microphone.

"There appears to be some kind of penetrating wound in the middle of the forehead. It's about 4 or 5 mm in diameter with the surrounding tissue showing signs of haemorrhage. It could be powder burns, but it's appearance is inconsistent with others I've seen." The doctor took some photographs of the wound.

Dr. Martinez continued with his external examination of the victim. Once he had finished his observations of the front of Gunther's body, he asked Eduardo to help to turn the body. The doctor hefted the body with its shoulders, Eduardo always seemed to get the hips or, as he called it, the bum. Whenever he spoke about his work with friends, they would screw up their faces when he mentioned that he sometimes had to touch the corpses. They said it was weird or freaky. Eduardo usually didn't mind. For the most part, people behaved in a completely predictable manner. They did nothing. Being around them was peaceful and non-threatening. None of them tried to scare him or make him jump. They didn't play jokes on him or embarrass him in public.

Touching them was also uneventful. He didn't hurt them if he pushed too hard or did it wrong. He didn't accidentally tickle them when he had to help the doctors to lift or turn them. The only thing he found uncomfortable about being around dead people was the job he had been given here. Turning a corpse by its bottom. Sometimes they leaked.

"Blood appears to have pooled around the victim's back indicating that he was most likely lying on his back after he was killed. There doesn't appear to be any indication that the body was moved after death."

The doctor's findings were consistent with what the officers had observed at the scene of the crime.

"Thank you, Eduardo. Let's lower him back down. So it looks like it's just this wound on the forehead."

Eduardo didn't know if the Dr. was talking to him or the microphone. After a moment he noticed that the doctor was looking at him. Was he supposed to respond?

"Um," Eduardo flustered.

"Come around here and have a closer look."

Eduardo shuffled towards the head end of the body. He pushed his glasses up on top of his head and leaned in for a closer look.

"It looks to me . . . like, um . . .a single bullet wound to the forehead." Eduardo was trying hard to get the wording right. He copied phrases that he'd heard Dr. Martinez use before.

"That's right Eduardo. What else do we know about this bullet?"

That stumped him for a moment, but then he had a moment of revelation. He knew what the doctor was talking about.

"There is no exit wound. S-s-so the bullet must still be inside Mr. Köhlers's head."

"Exactly. Well done Eduardo. We will confirm that with an x-ray. Do you want to wheel the machine over?"

He felt lifted by his success and couldn't stop himself from smiling a little as he retrieved the x-ray machine.

They set up the machine to take an x-ray off the head, but for safety reasons had to stand in the doctor's office while they took the picture. The machine instantly sent the image to the computer in the office. The Dr. did a few clicks and the image appeared on the screen.

"Interesting," said the doctor, " what do you see? Eduardo? "

"Well. Um, it looks like there are five bullets inside Mr. Köhler's head, but there was only one entry wound. Um. Does that mean the bullet has broken up?"

"It does. Sometimes bullets are designed so they will deliberately break up after impact. We call it spalling."

"Oh. Why would you design a bullet break up?"

"Well, it does more damage that way. When it breaks up, the single bullet effectively turns into multiple bullets, each of which go off and cause more damage."

"Oh dear. That's horrible. Why would people do that?"

"I know, Eduardo, it is horrible. But, at the end of the day, bullets are designed to kill people."

"And this one has."

"It has. Very efficiently. Those fragments of bullet have torn through large amounts of brain tissue. In this case, two of the fragments have penetrated the medulla." Dr. Martinez pointed at the two fragments near the bottom of the brain. " The medulla is at the top of the spinal column. It's where the spinal cord meets the brain, if you like. It's the oldest part of the brain, in evolutionary terms, and is responsible for the body's most basic functions, such as heartbeat, breathing and oxygen regulation. Brain injuries here are almost always fatal."

"So Mr. Köhler would probably have died instantly?"

"That's correct, Eduardo. Although we can't say for sure, it's very likely that the victim didn't know anything about it."

"Well, at least he didn't suffer."

They walked back out of the office to where the cadaver waited patiently. The doctor selected a scalpel from the tool tray and made a large Y-shaped incision in the torso, stretching from the shoulders to below the belly button. Dr. Martinez began removing organs and examining them individually. Their appearance, colour, size, weight, etc. Having already identified the most likely cause of death, he worked methodically through the rest of his examination, before returning to the brain, which was always examined last.

Having determined that the specimen was overweight and had signs of liver and heart disease, the doctor turned his attention back to the head.

"Do you want to give me a hand opening, Eduardo?" The doctor asked.

"Yes, Ok. I'll come round now."

He watched as the doctor used a scalpel to make a long incision from temple to temple around the back of the skull. The doctor then peeled the scalp away from the skull, pulling it forward so that it covered Mr. Köhler's face.

Eduardo shuffled back around to the head. He had helped out with this procedure many times. He quite enjoyed it. Dr. Martinez handed him a face shield, which he donned. He checked that his gloves were still intact, and his sleeves were tucked in. The next bit could get a bit splatty.

The doctor picked up the rotary saw from his tool tray and switched it on. It whirred and spun into life and the doctor gently offered the blade up to the right temple of the body and pushed. The blade sliced easily through the bone, reaching its predetermined depth with ease. After a few minutes of gentle manoeuvring, the doctor had completed a lap of the skull and returned the saw to the tool tray. With a little leverage, the skull cap came away easily. Eduardo held out the tissue tray for the doctor, who placed the domed bone towards the left side.

After some prodding, cutting and pulling the doctor lifted the brain from the skull. Eduardo once again held out the tissue tray. After the doctor had placed the brain in the tray Eduardo could clearly see several damaged areas on the surface of the brain. They looked a bit like bloody bruises.

"What are these bruises, I don't think I've seen those before?" Asked Eduardo.

"Those are where the bullet fragments have bounced off of the skull, then continued tearing their way through brain tissue."

Eduardo shook his head. He couldn't believe the lengths people would go to design new ways of hurting each other more. "This bullet is really quite horrible. I'm glad we don't get many people with bullets in them."

Dr. Martinez nodded. "Me too, Eduardo." He was very pleased to live in a part of the world where you didn't get bullets in dead bodies. Except that there was another one next on the agenda. He also suspected that this could be the tip of the iceberg. "Let's get the brain over to the examination bench."

Eduardo stood ready to assist as the doctor cut into the brain tissue in search of bullet fragments. The scalpel cut easily through the soft, pliable tissue. The first fragment was recovered within moments and was placed carefully in a petri dish which Eduardo had prepared. It was about the size of a grain of rice, maybe smaller. It looked bent and battered from its violent, ugly journey through Mr. Köhler's skull and brain.

As the doctor continued to cut deeper into the brain he recovered more fragments, occasionally referencing the x-ray image for guidance. Eduardo watched as each fragment was removed from its resting place in the brain, then carefully placed in the petri dish. The complicated folds and curves of the soft pliable tissue revealed one cut at a time.

Having recovered all five fragments Dr. Martinez placed the brain in a preserving jar. He carefully poured in formalin until the tissue was completely submerged, its pungent distinctive stench hit the back of Eduardo's nose. It always made his eyes and nose screw up tightly closed and made him hold his breath. He heard the lid being placed on the preserving jar and after a few seconds was confident enough to emerge from his defensive hold. Dr. Martinez wafted the last of the smelly air away.

Eduardo began tidying the benches, bagging up, discarded disposables and collecting tools for cleaning and sanitizing. Busy day today. He wanted to get everything cleaned up and ready for the next autopsy.

Having finished making notes on his clipboard, doctor Martinez handed it to Eduardo.

"Can you run this over to Lina in the office?"

"Of course, I'll do it right away."

"Great stuff, Eduardo. I'll be finished here by the time you get back, then you can take this one back and get our next victim."

"Oh, Ok. Victim. Do you mean Mrs. Köhler?"

11.

Sarah wiped the sweat from her forehead with her wrist. The whole point of moving out here had been to get away from the grey skies and the rain, and in that respect the move out to Mallorca had been a great success. But it was the summer heat. No one had told her how oppressive and interminable it was, or if they had she hadn't been listening. Life seemed so much more agreeable with the benefit of rose-tinted spectacles.

The house she was working at today was enormous, very nicely designed and immaculately presented. These people clearly had money. It was hidden in the middle of endless acres of olive groves at the end of their very own private driveway. There was something about having your own driveway that she craved, particularly one that was over half a mile long.

The entrance hall, which she was currently mopping, was bigger than most normal people's houses. It was finished with a beautifully polished white marble floor. Regular, gently mopping. That was the way to keep these marble floors looking their best. Never allow them to become dirty and people's feet wouldn't have anything to grind into the delicate surface.

Not only was it hot, but there didn't seem to be any air movement. She mopped her brow again. Only another few minutes and she'd have worked her way to the front door, where she could have a few minutes to cool down. She was mostly left to her own devices and was trusted to manage her own time. Anyway, a few minutes to recuperate could only improve productivity in this heat.

She stepped out through the oversized doors and found a cool spot to sit on the doorstep. She watched David as he went past, guiding a lawnmower over the lush green. Lawns were a luxury that most people went without here. In fact, even the idea of having a lawn in these conditions was a folly. The constant need for water in such heat flew in the face of the green brigade, keen on preserving the island's precious and dwindling water supply. But these folks could afford a lawn, so a lawn they had.

He did a half-wave kind of half-salute which confirmed she'd been spotted. No doubt the fact that he'd caught her literally sitting down on the job would be mentioned in the van later. She waved back with a kind of 'up yours' motion.

After a brief cool-down she took the bucket and tipped the dirty water down the drain. It didn't seem to be as red-brown as usual, and she wondered how many feet had actually come through that enormous front door since she'd last mopped.

A quick ten-minute clean in the kitchen should be all that was needed. There was a solitary glass left next to the sink. Apparently, someone had been here since their last visit after all. Ten minutes later she has cleaned and dried all of the work surfaces and other dust-collecting apparatus and replaced the glass in the correct cupboard. Finished.

She looked out of the window looking for David as she could still hear him mowing somewhere. As she headed for the front door, she glanced around the house for details that had been overlooked or needed correcting. She checked that she had her key and the security fob before pushing the button that armed the alarm system. It began its slow-beep countdown. Having closed and locked the door she walked along the pathway to where the van was parked on the driveway.

Even the perfectly aligned stones underfoot seemed more grandiose that was necessary. Their gravel path at home worked just as well, it just didn't shout about itself. Actually, it did; it crunched with every footstep. Maybe it was this one that was understated.

The door to the van groaned as she pulled it against its will. She opened their cooler and removed a cold bottle of water. Its icy liquid almost froze her brain as she swallowed a few mouthfuls.

The distant noise of the mower had stopped, which usually meant that she had five minutes to herself. David would be using the leaf-blower to disperse errant clippings, then they would be finished.

David's door also complained. "Someone should put some grease on that," he remarked.

"Babe, maybe one day you should do it rather than say it."

"Yeah, yeah, yeah. No rush. How's my girl? Everything Ok in there?"

"All good, yeah. But it looks like no one has been here since last time we were here. Seems like a bit of a waste of time."

"Except the bit where we get paid, and that it'll look great if they do ever visit." He started the engine. It took a few turns to catch, but eventually it fired into life. He'd been servicing it well enough, but the fact was that it was just too old and tired. They needed a new van but, of course, the budget didn't really allow for that.

Sarah's phone pinged. "It's Theresa. She'd like us to stop in at her place on the way home."

"Ok. We can do that."

Theresa's house wasn't really on their way home. The short diversion off the motorway leading them away from the mountains. They didn't travel that area very often, its narrow roads through wine country made progress slow and inefficient, so they usually avoided it. Some of the houses and wine bodegas were huge which certainly made for interesting viewing along their way.

12.

The old man watched the telephone in an expectant manner. Of course, he knew the old adage, but he had no other work with which to distract himself. He shook his packet of cigarettes in an attempt to gauge the remainder, then extracted a single stick and pressed it between his lips. He lit his proclivity in his customary manner and felt the internal rub of the smoke.

He checked his watch which confirmed his suspicions. The call was already one minute late. Having satisfied himself of his buyer's inefficiency, he toked again.

One and a half minutes late, his telephone began vibrating and dimly illuminated the room in its blue glow.

"Guten abend, Dmitri", said the old man.

"Good evening." Replied a Russian sounding accent.

"I trust you've received my email?"

"I have, and I have watched the videos you attached. It looks like your product performs exactly as you described."

"Of course. I'm very proud of my babies. I knew you'd enjoy the video."

"I particularly liked the completely hopeless attempt at defence. It's not often that a weapon demonstration amuses me." The Russian stifled a laugh.

"I certainly hadn't anticipated the tennis racket." Said the old man, "They were really designed to be used individually. A single unit resulting in a stealthy and indefensible killing. I hadn't really thought too much about what happens when you attack two people."

"Tactical problem. The weapon itself performs exactly as you described. One shot, one kill."

"I'm glad you like it."

"I do. We are all very pleased. There's just a few loose ends we need to talk about."

"Oh, what's that?" The old man knew full well what was coming next. It didn't mean he had to like the idea, but he felt better being told he had to do it by his purchasers, rather than admitting to himself. He knew what had to be done.

"The rest of your former team are a risk. Gunther knew too much about our little arrangement, so of course he had to go. But it's not just about our anonymity. We are very keen to make sure we are the only people who have this weapon. I want to make sure we've got all of the design schematics, all of the materials specifications, everything we might need to be able to reproduce your weapon in the future. And we want to make sure, not just that no one else has it, but that no one else could build it. For that reason, I'm afraid, your entire former team will need to be disposed of."

The old man gave a sigh. "Well, I suspected that ultimately it would come to this. It's not something I'm looking forward to, but I understand your position."

"I understand. It's not something I would ask if it wasn't completely necessary."

"I'll get it done. Is there anything else you require?" Asked the old man.

"I'd be very interested to see the coroner's report that will be associated with your video. I realise it could be quite difficult to access, but I'm fairly confident that a man of your calibre might be able to get hold of a copy."

"It's certainly possible, but I couldn't make any promises."

"It's not a deal breaker. I'd just be interested, that's all."

"I'll see what I can do. Perhaps we can set a date on the place for our exchange?"

"I'd like to see the loose ends get cleaned up first. We can complete the purchase as soon as that's done."

"Ok. I'll keep you updated."

13.

"Good morning, Theresa. How are you?" asked Sarah, kissing Theresa's left, then right cheeks, as was the local custom.

"I'm very good, thank you, Sarah. And you, David, how are you?" More kissing. "How did you get on over at The Mansion?"

This was what they were calling it now. Most places were 'Sally's flat' or 'Mrs. Watson's house', but this one stood out from the others. Firstly, its size was on a different scale compared to everyone else's houses. Then there was the constant cleaning just in case it was needed by the owners. Theresa didn't care either way. Her company still got paid and then, by virtue of their employment, so did David and Sarah.

"Is everything Ok? What did you want to talk to use about?" asked Sarah.

"Well. Come on through and have a drink. Water?" They both said yes and followed her into the kitchen. "You know I've been thinking about going back to England?"

"Yes, we've spoken about it a few times. You couldn't make your mind up, a lot of pros and cons, as I remember?" asked Sarah.

"Exactly. The long grey winters. The lack of sunshine. Well, my sister called and there's a flat for sale in the next block over from hers. We'll be neighbours."

"Nice." Sarah thought she hated her sister.

"Exactly. I went to see the flat last week, and my offer had been accepted."

"Oh, wow," said David. "This is all moving quite quickly."

"I know, David, but if you know something is right, you have to grab it."

"You do," he said, "if it's right then it's right."

"But it does leave me in a bit of a pickle with the company."

"Oh?"

"I won't be able to run it from in England, and it's too much to expect to ask you guys to run it for me. I'll also need someone to look after this place until I get a buyer. And there's the sheep farm up the road."

David felt the disappointment heading his way, fearing that they were about to lose a valuable source of income, but decided to put a brave face on it. "I'm sure we can keep an eye on the properties until then."

"We could buy it from you." Sarah interrupted.

"Buy it? Oh, gosh. How would we figure out how much it's worth?" Asked Theresa.

"I've no idea," said Sarah, "but that shouldn't stop us." She was fully aware that she hadn't consulted David on her offer for them to buy the company, but the positive look on his face suggested he agreed with her.

"Well, we don't need to decide immediately," said David. "We can have a think about it."

"Indeed. I wonder how much paperwork would be involved. I hate to imagine with these Spanish. They do like a bit of paperwork."

"A friend of mine has just been through the same thing. I'll see what he says."

They said their goodbyes and headed home to discuss Theresa's offer.

"Are we stopping at the bar on the way home?" asked Sarah.

"We can do. I'll call Jose when we get here, see what he says."

"What do you reckon it'll cost?"

"I have no idea I don't know how these things work. There aren't really and assets – no vehicle or equipment. All the expensive bits we already own, or we use the customer's."

"Yeah, like the floor polisher and the van."

"All the chemicals and cloths are hers, but they're not expensive."

Sarah went into the bar and found a table. A nod to the barman being all that was needed to place her order – the usual. David called Jose and was very glad that he did, before reporting back to Sarah.

"Firstly, the paperwork is a nightmare. We'll need a solicitor to do it, and it'll be a couple of thousand for a basic company like this. But. We talked more about what it is that she'd actually be selling us."

"Right,"

"Well, we are the staff, so we aren't really part of the company. So, we aren't being sold. The main assets we already own. The consumables aren't worth anything. All of which leaves…" he left the sentence for Sarah to finish."

"Um," she thought for a couple of seconds, "Um … the contacts. The client list."

"Exactly. And we already know who they are."

"Yes, but we don't have all of their contact details. And that would be effectively stealing Theresa's customers from her."

"What does she care. She's moving back to the UK."

"It's not right, we can't do that. I think we talk to her and get her to see that what she's actually selling is some phone numbers and a good word. If we can get her to come around to that way of looking at it, then she can't want too much money for it."

"Ok. Let's see what she says to that. I think she'd be more receptive to hearing that from you than from me."

"I can do that."

"So, how much do you think the client list is worth?"

"Good question. Well, how much does she charge the customers? €25 per hour per person and she then pays us €15. That means that she makes €20 per hour off of us from sitting on her behind."

"Well, she does have to 'do lunch' with clients sometimes." He said.

"I'm sure that's all just BS, she's just lunching with her mates while we sweat at The Mansion. Maybe we should just take over the list. We could leave a note in each house saying that the company is closing so David and Sarah are starting their own company."

"Come on, we aren't going to do that. You're going to make her see sense. How much?"

"I don't know … I mean, if she said ten grand I tell her to get lost. Ten for a client list?"

"Agreed. If she asks for that then we'll just start our own thing and market to our existing customers. What about five?" he suggested.

"Mmm. It still a bit too much, but it's getting closer."

"Ok, so that gives us our ballpark figure. We should also think about getting a newer van and getting it sign written by a pro company. It is a giant moving advert, after all."

In her head Sarah did a fist pump. She had been on at him to get a new van for years – well, it seemed like years. She didn't really know that much about them, but one that didn't complain when she opened the door would be a bonus. "Sounds like a great idea. What kind of van do we want?"

"I was thinking of a proper sized van, not another little one. It means we can write our name and phone number in bigger letters. It also means that we can carry furniture and other bits. How many times have we been asked and had to say no? Each of those was a missed opportunity."

Sarah felt like Christmas had come early but kept it to herself. "How are we going to afford all of this?"

"We need an easy way to get rich quick … no, seriously. We have a little bit saved up. That and an overdraft might pay Theresa. The van we could get on finance. I know we usually try not to do that, but it's all quite short notice."

"If we are really going to earn more then it'll pay itself off in no time anyway. I think it's a goer. We just need to talk Theresa into giving it to us for almost nothing. Even if she wants ten for it, we'll get that paid off. The only thing is we'll need to go to the bank first, and they will want business plans and figures…"

"We'll make it work, babe. You just need to turn on the charm with Theresa."

Six months later they'd come to a fair deal with Theresa, and she had moved back to England. She'd appointed an estate agent to sell her properties and David and Sarah had taken over the client list.

David drove their new van slower everywhere he went, but especially around groups of people. He wanted to make sure everyone had plenty of time to get a good look at it and, more importantly, the company name. The email address and phone number were largely irrelevant on their giant mobile business card. 'Paradise Cleaning and

Maintenance' had been Sarah's final choice. Straight to the point and in English, their primary customer base. As long as people could read the name, they'd be able to find the contact details on the internet.

He pulled up carefully near, but not outside, the flats where he'd left Sarah earlier. Instead, he parked neatly in a spot with plenty of passing traffic – no point in hiding it away from potential customers. The driver's door closed without complaint or resistance, a pleasing improvement over the old van. He then pressed the 'lock' button on the key, another new feature to which he'd already become accustomed. He noted the van's reflection in a window as he walked towards the entrance for the flats.

"So, how is it then?" asked an excited Sarah.

"She's a babe. Looks great with the new graphics. We might need to start parking it on the main road instead of the driveway."

"Ah, bless. You're like a kid with a new toy," she teased as she cuddled up to him. "If you help me get this place finished you can buy me lunch somewhere nice. Assuming we can afford it, now that we've given all of our money to Theresa and the van sales place."

"Yep, deal. The company has already got money coming in – it'll pay itself off in no time. We should go up to the golf club, then all the well-heeled folks from Portals Nous will be able to see it."

"Christ, you and that van. Is she your new girl now?"

"Oh, babe. I'm just thinking of business. I wonder if I can expense lunch if I'm out trying to pick up customers?"

"Jesus," she said, letting the cuddle go. "Come on, this floor isn't going to mop itself."

14.

The most complicated aspect of accessing the postmortem report had been identifying the building where they performed the autopsies. The rest of the process had been like taking candy from a baby. After a little trial and error, a bee had simply been flown in through an open window and waited on top of an air conditioning unit for the medical examiner's secretary to access her computer. Once her username and password had been obtained, the system could be accessed remotely whenever the old man needed.

He sat in the relative dark of his office, waiting for the phone to ring. He found people's lack of manners frustrating. If he made an appointment with someone, he would endeavour to ensure he was ready early. His father had instilled in him the importance of time keeping. According to him, if you were on time, then you were actually late. He insisted that people should arrive at work early. If you are supposed to start work at 08:00, then you should arrive at 07:45, so that you are ready to start at 08:00.

This time his buyer was over an hour late. It was simply rude. For a moment he wondered if they were trying to keep him busy while they broke into his house, looking for the bees. Perhaps they were trying to steal them from him rather than go to the trouble of having to pay. But he knew he had that covered. If anyone was trying to get into his house, he'd have received an alert by now.

He lit another cigarette, but his seven minute self-indulgence did little to recover his wasted evening. He crushed it out, leaving a glowing ember bright enough to illuminate the inside of the ashtray. It burned his finger, which he quickly withdrew. He cursed it, and the ember, and the Russians.

He had packed everything up for the night and locked the office. He had been sitting in his car when the phone finally showed signs of life.

"Dmitri," he said, in a business-like manner, disguising his frustration. After all, buyers with this much money were few and far between.

"Good evening." Not even a hint of an apology for keeping him waiting.

"You received the report?"

"I did, thank you. I was also able to access their computer system for myself. This is far more than a weapon."

"It is, that's correct. I'm sure you'll find it very capable in many ways. I've also begun to eliminate more of my former colleagues. I'm sure if you give it a few days you'll find post-mortem reports for them on the system too."

"Ah, good. I'll have a look. What about the remaining members of the team, when are you going to deal with them?"

"I have one in the office here and I'll deal with him last." He wondered if there was any way that he could get away with not killing Carl but suspected that there wasn't. "The others sometimes visit the island about this time of year, I'll be able to do it then. Otherwise, I'll arrange for a trip back. Get it done in Germany."

"Good. Then we can think about a date to complete our purchase."

"Yes, exactly. Get this whole thing wrapped up and move on." He wasn't looking forward to the killings but, under the circumstances, they were necessary. "I'll let you know when the rest of the team have been dealt with.

15.

"Actually, I think it's safer if we talk outside." Simon nodded towards the garden.

David looked towards Sarah, who shrugged then started walking towards the door, "Ok, fine." Said David, heading outside.

Sarah pulled the front door closed behind her and they both followed Simon into the garden. Having strolled part way around the house, Simon stopped them and beckoned them closer and spoke in a hushed voice. "Look, I'm sorry about all of this paranoia stuff, but it's a security thing. It's safer if we treat your house like it's bugged until we know otherwise."

"What? You mean people might be listening to us in our house?" Slammed Sarah, almost containing her frustration. "First of all, this guy imposes himself on us - again - and then it turns out that there might be other people involved as well."

"I'm just saying it's possible. The people who build these little bees probably want it back, might be interested in who took it."

"There's no way they could know that it was me that took that bee from the garden!" Said David.

"Are you sure about that? I mean, that's a pretty firm conclusion that you've come to, given that you have very few of the facts." Said Simon.

David cast a look at Sarah and shook his head. "Ok, Mr. Wise guy, maybe you can fill me in on some of these facts."

Simon then cast his gaze around the garden suspicious of bees, or anything else that might be watching or listening. "Why don't we go for a walk up the road where no one will be listening? I can tell you about it then."

"Go for a walk?" Sarah interjected, positioning herself between the two men and squaring up to Simon. "What makes you think I'm going to let you take my husband for a walk? A few weeks ago you bullied your way into our lives, and now here you are again."

David smiled to himself - secretly he loved it when she got like this. He would be able to calm her down and she'd probably even hide her aggression quite well for the rest of the day. But he loved the way she didn't take any crap from anyone. At this point she was probably two or three sentences away from swinging a punch.

"Ok, ok, easy." Said Simon, showing his empty palms and raising his hands in surrender. I'm on your side. I'm here to learn. This bee was sent to spy on me and I don't really know anything about it." He said, indicating the pocket where the bee now resided in its tin.

"Ok," said Sarah, "empty your pockets. Let's see what you're going to be leaving behind as collateral."

It took Simon a few moments to go along with her suggestion, but then reluctantly started pulling items from his pockets, placing them on a nearby wall. Wallet, car key, gun.

"You've brought a gun into my house?" Sarah boomed.

"Standard issue and standard practice in my line of work."

"So it's not yours, it's *theirs*?"

"Correct."

Sarah picked up the wallet and thumbed through it. 200-ish Euros, driver's license, ID card, bank card. She placed it back on the wall and picked up the gun, by its grip, like she was ready to use it. Simon visibly flinched, but stopped himself from reacting. Sarah slid the barrel back and tilted the gun so she could inspect the firing chamber, which was empty. Turning the gun back upright, she then pressed the release for the magazine which fell into her left hand. She kept hold of the gun and placed the magazine back on the wall. Her proficiency with the gun was noted by both men, with Simon approving of her familiarity, while David was left slightly open mouthed. He had no idea where she'd learned about handguns.

She used the empty weapon as a pointing device.

"All of this stuff stays here while you go for your walk," she said, circling the muzzle of the gun around the items on the wall, "that way I know you're not going to run off with him."

"We're just going for a short walk around the block, you can join us if you want."

"Oh, I'll be coming with you. I'm going to follow you in our car with the gun. Any funny business …"

"And I get shot then run over?"

Sarah gave Simon a big smile, "I'll get the car keys and lock up the house then."

Moments later she returned, "ready when you are, boys." She picked up the magazine from the wall and slid it into the gun's grip, banging it home with the heel of her left hand. She then pulled back the slider to cycle the loading mechanism then let go, loading a bullet into the firing chamber. David looked worried. Simon took it that this demonstration meant she was now ready. "Shall we get going?" He suggested.

Sarah climbed into the car and placed the gun on the passenger seat, while David and Simon walked out of the gate and down the road.

"Maybe it'll help if I tell you my story first." Simon suggested.

"Ok. Where did you get your bee?"

"Probably about a week ago I became aware of this new buzzing sound that seemed to happen near my apartment. I think I was on my balcony one evening with a glass of wine. I heard this deep buzzing noise, I mean, we have some big insects here but this was different. Much deeper."

"It's actually quite an impressive noise for a small object." David interjected.

"Yes. It's like the Chinook helicopter version of the insect world."

As they walked a little further, they both noticed the engine noise of Sarah's car join them. She continued following closely enough to ensure her presence was felt.

"Anyway, I saw one of them take off. It couldn't see much detail, but it was close enough to know that it wasn't one of our native insects. Over the next few days, I saw and heard more of them. A couple of days ago I was outside, having my morning coffee, when I saw one at the other end of the balcony, outside my bedroom window. I watched it for a few minutes, and it just sat there on the window sill. Normal flying insects don't usually do that. They're normally moving around, keeping themselves busy. Looking for food or whatever it is that they do. This one was completely still, so it was either dead or it needed investigating. I slowly went back into the apartment and snuck around into the bedroom. I could see the damn thing through the window. Now I was closer, I could see it wasn't natural. That meant it had to be artificial and that it was there for a reason. I didn't know if it was looking at me or listening to me or just sitting there daydreaming. So, I decided I was going to catch it."

David nodded sagely. After all, he'd been there and done that himself.

"I didn't want to just use my hand," Simon continued," because the damn thing would probably get away between my fingers, or sting me, or whatever these things do. So I grabbed the first thing that came to hand."

David noticed that Simon seemed to have deliberately stopped his story, which he took as a prompt. "Oh, what was that?" He asked.

"A dirty pair of underpants from the laundry bin."

They both giggled and David shook his head. "Moving slowly, I unlatched the window. I then kind of launched myself through the window covering it with the underwear. Once I'd secured it, I put the whole bundle in a plastic food container. But then I remembered you. For whatever reason, you had yours in a metal tin, so I searched around and eventually found one. I'd no idea why you used a metal tin, but I figured you must have a good reason, so I copied you."

"It was just the first thing that came to hand." David found the irony amusing. The metal tin genuinely had been the first thing that came to hand, anything to transport it in. But in the end, it turned out that its ability to contain GPS signals was paramount.

Simon shook his head at the unnecessary effort he'd put into finding a suitable container. "So, then me and the tin kind of looked at each other for a while, and then I had to go to work."

"Ah, yes. Your work, perhaps you should tell me a bit more about that and how it led to our first meeting."

"Yes, well. I suppose the first thing to say about that is that it was work, it was nothing personal."

"I'll take that as you skirting your way around some kind of apology."

"Anyway. I was part of a team tasked with watching a property at the other end of the village, I think you know the one I'm talking about. It was all very boring until one day this cleaning company turn up," Simon left a deliberate pause. "The next thing you know there are police and ambulances everywhere.

"That was a pretty awful day for us. We were just going about our day, minding our own business. It's not every day that you discover one and a half murder victims. And then it turns out that you were sitting there watching our crappy day unfold."

"One and a half?" Asked Simon.

"Ingrid was still alive, barely. I think she made it through most of the night ... hold on. You were there watching the house?"

"Not the house, technically. We were there watching the Köhlers."

"Nice little retired German couple? What could you people want with them? Anyway, who are you people? MI5?"

"MI6"

"Whatever they are all about." David had no more idea about the distinctions between British spies than he did of the distinctions between Spanish spies, or Spanish police forces.

"That's exactly how we like it. Basically, we look after British interests abroad."

"Ok. So what do the British government, looking after their interests abroad, want with a nice, retired German couple from Lloseta?"

"In his younger days he worked on some pretty top-secret weapons, which normally would be absolutely fine, being retired and all that. In this particular case, we've got inside information that somebody has managed to steal the weapons system and is now trying to sell it."

"Gunther didn't really strike me as an international clandestine weapons dealer."

"Careful. You should never judge a book by its cover."

"True. But even so, he's more of a mad scientist or a back-office boy. He's no criminal mastermind."

"And our team agree with you, but at the moment we don't know much more than that."

"So this bee that killed him? Is that the weapon he's been working on?"

"We knew there was *the* weapon and I watched you remove something from the crime scene. But at the time I had no reason to suspect the two were linked. We were watching for dodgy people coming and going. Weapons, money, you know, that kind of thing. But yes, we are pretty confident he was killed by his own weapon."

"How'd you know we didn't do it - we didn't kill them?"

"You don't look the sort. Sorry mate, but you two are never going to be killers. Your behaviour and your body language throughout this whole thing. You're not involved."

"So if we're not involved, what did you think I'd taken from the house?"

"Again, we didn't. Could have been something dropped by the killer, a bullet or a bullet casing, we had no idea. It wasn't just cash, because you put it into a container rather than your pocket. That meant it also wasn't drugs or jewellery. But whatever it was, you and Sarah seemed ... intrigued? excited? ... so we knew we needed to get a look at it."

"So they sent you to bully me into handing it over?"

"Yeah, sorry 'bout that."

"No, you're not. You were quite happy to bully me into submission when you thought you had the upper hand. But now the tables have turned and you've come crawling to us for help. You've even given your gun to a complete stranger. You must be desperate."

"Look, if this is too difficult for you then I can carry on investigating by myself. I just thought we could scratch each other's backs a bit here."

"Ok, fine. So, scratch my back a bit more."

"I don't really have much more to tell you. Our operations are always run on a need-to-know basis. I'm at the bottom of the food chain. I'm the grunt that sits in the van watching and reporting."

"Sounds exciting."

"You can't imagine," Simon dead panned. "I was sat there for about 2 weeks before your missus turned up and gave me something worth looking at."

David stopped walking and turned to look Simon in the eye, "Winding me up isn't going to help you achieve anything."

"Oh, come on. Don't be like that. You guys turning up, the dead bodies, stealing property, the police. It was like Christmas had come early. It was so good. I even had to phone the squadron leader to report what was happening."

"So that's the headline story you're telling me? Retired Germans selling top secret military kit?"

"That's about what we know."

David knew that MI6 had to know more than that otherwise they wouldn't have committed this many people to the investigation. "Ok, *who* are they selling it to?"

"Usually, I would guess it was the Russians, but you know how it is these days, so it could be anybody. Iran, Israel, it could even be people much further afield than that. South America? China?"

"So you don't know."

"Honestly, no. And that's got the top brass worried, the fact that we don't know." Simon conceded.

"Well, it started off with people being murdered, so my money's on the Russians."

"Ok, how much?"

"5 quid"

"You're on."

They walked in silence for a little while as they walked past one of the locals with his two dogs.

His once-was-blonde gray explosion of curls left Simon wondering if it was natural, or if he deliberately went to the hairdresser and asked for his hair to be done that way. He was wearing his customary pair of white wireless headphones and had a cigar protruding centrally from his mouth. The cigar was never lit. That way, presumably, it would last longer. More for show than for smoking. David wondered what would be achieved by looking like a smoker but not actually being one. David saw this man almost every day. Morning and evening, no matter what the weather, the man would walk. Initially it had always been with one dog, leading David to name him "One Dog Weirdo". When the second dog had been introduced a couple of weeks ago, he chose to leave the name as it was. After all, he knew what he meant.

The lighter coloured of the two dogs squatted and strained. Its upright tail quivered as if fluttering in an unseen breeze. The dog produced. The man walked on. The product left on the pavement.

"Nice." Said David with a slight shake of his head.

"It'll be dry by morning and mummified in 3 days. Not like back in Blighty, where it just stays wet mush forever. So, come on, tell me what you know about these little guys."

"I don't know where they're from and I don't know who's buying or selling them. The one I found, and then had rudely confiscated," David cast a sideways glance at Simon, " was a weapon. It appears to be a one shot, one kill type of affair. We worked out that there were two bees sent to kill them. It looks like Ingrid swatted one of them with her tennis racket and the other one managed to fly away, probably back to their HQ, wherever that is."

"What did you do with it after you got it home?"

"I took some pictures of it and did an internet search - which came up with nothing. Then I sent the pictures to some friends in England, hoping they'd be able to tell me what it was. They had no idea either. It wasn't until a couple of days later than I discovered it was man-made. It has a screw underneath which holds everything together. It's made up of three parts. We've kind of assumed that the wings and legs are the motor and navigation centre and the abdomen is probably a battery. It's the head that's the interesting part. The one we had - the one you took away - the head looked like it had blown up or exploded. It also smelled of a used shotgun cartridge."

"Wow, you guys are all about your guns aren't you? Never judge a book by its cover. A couple of cleaners from a sleepy village in Mallorca."

"I've been clay pigeon shooting a couple of times. Just 'coz I remember the smell doesn't make me a weapons expert. Anyway. So they use the same propellant as a shotgun. No idea what projectile is used. Maybe you guys will steal the bodies so you can have a closer look?"

"Yeah. My life would be so much more interesting if we actually did things like that. Literally, I sit in a van and watch people go by."

"Oh well, your career choice. Maybe you could get a job as a thug somewhere else?"

Simon left the dig hanging in the air.

"We have absolutely no evidence," David went on, "but we reckon the heads might be interchangeable. There could be a video unit and a sound unit, for example."

"Yeah, like the ones that were watching me. We'll be able to confirm that when we have a closer look at the one I've brought you."

They walked in silence for a short distance. David wasn't overly enamoured with the idea of Simon being in their house and workshop. What he was interested in was his bee, he thought most of it would be the same as the one he had in the workshop. It was the heads that he was interested in.

He hadn't even looked at the bee he'd caught at the Faber's house. Knowing his luck it, it would be identical to the one Simon had brought but that didn't stop him from hoping one would be for video and the other for sound, or something else completely. Anyway, Simon didn't know about the bee tucked away in his workshop, and that's the way he liked it. Him being in control of some of the information and hardware made him feel like he had the upper hand in at least one small part of this whole crazy story. Whatever Simon's bee was, David would report it back as such. How it differed, or not, from his own captive would be his secret.

"What else do you know about these things?" Asked Simon.

"There's not much to add, really. We reckon they navigate by GPS, and are either pre-programmed or they receive information on the go. Either way, I want to build a little Faraday cage so I can have them on the workbench without them communicating to their base."

"Sounds like you thought that through already?"

"Yep. And I know I can test if it works with my mobile phone and my fitness tracker." David raised his left wrist showing David his watch.

"Right, of course. Because if they can't get a signal inside the cage, nor can the bees."

"Exactly."

"You know," said Simon," I think we've both got about as far as we're going to at the moment. Why don't we head back to the house and I'll leave this bee with you? Once you've had a chance to look at it and compare it to the other one, we can get together and discuss it."

"The other one? You mean the one you confiscated?"

"Yes, that one."

"Why don't you bring it back? That way I can compare the two side by side?"

"Well, it doesn't really work like that."

"What do you mean? You're working for MI6, just bring the MI6 bug back."

"Well, yes. I am working for MI6. The problem is that I don't know who sent the bugs to spy on me. Was it the Germans, the Russians or whoever, or was it MI6?"

"You mean your own people could be spying on you?"

"You should never rule anything out."

"Right, I get that. That suggests that MI6 knows a lot more about this weapons system than you've led me to believe?"

"Like I said, I'm at the bottom of the food chain. Simon do this, Simon do that. For all I know it could be MI6 selling the weapons to the Australians or the Canadians."

David gave a sideways look at Simon, fully aware that this guy was part salesman and part full-time liar. With all the different possibilities and twists that Simon had come out with there was no way to know what was going on. The British government indeed.

"This guy must think I'm an idiot," David thought to himself. He looked over his shoulder and gave Sarah a half wave. He then circled his index finger in the air indicating they'd be turning around.

"Shall we get back then?" Said David, coming to a stop.

The two men turned around and began retracing their route. Who was this guy Simon really? MI6? Possibly, but also maybe some other organization or agency. David figured that if he just used Simon as a source of information to help him with his own investigation, then it might not matter who or what Simon really was.

"So, we'll treat it like it could be anybody, including MI6, watching you until we can prove otherwise?"

"That's how I'm looking at it." Said David.

"Then we are both on our own. Unless we work together."

16.

He arrived at the usual time. The traffic had been slightly heavier than normal. This was usually due to some kind of mishap on the motorway, resulting in the side roads taking the brunt of the traffic. Eventually the police would have to drag themselves away from their morning carajillo – espresso with a side of brandy.

As he unlocked the main door, he saw Carl approaching with the customary take out coffees. The old man managed a small smile. Shame.

"Morning, Carl. How are you this fine morning?"

"All good here, thank you."

Up in the office he found that he had a notification waiting for him. The missing bee had finally made contact with home. He waited until Carl was firmly ensconced in his office before opening the report. If at all possible, he didn't want Carl finding out about what he was doing to their colleagues. The boy wasn't stupid. If he saw what was going on, he'd know that he'd be on the list too. He was good with the system and the bees. Of course, the old man could cope without him, he'd have to soon enough. But there was no point in spoiling things until it was really necessary.

Certain that he was safe from Carl's prying eyes, he opened the report. The unit was very low on charge – to be expected – and it had sent a GPS location. Within moments it had then gone quiet again. He looked up the coordinates. It was on the other side of Lloseta from Gunther's house, maybe 1km away.

He thought for a moment about the possibilities. It's last check in had been at Gunther's house, when Ingrid had swatted it with a tennis racket. It hadn't worked properly since then.

First, it's feed went dark, not cut completely, it just showed a dark gray screen on his computer. It had stayed like that, recording for several hours. The feed then went brighter, but still with no detail. Annoyingly, the killer units didn't have microphones, so it didn't record any sound. After that the unit had just disappeared off of the system. He'd assumed that Anna had dealt it a fatal blow, but perhaps not. Either it had moved itself over to the other side of Lloseta, or someone else had moved it.

Later, once Carl had gone home, he drove over to see the location for himself.

17.

"Thanks for coming into the office, Burrows." Said the smartly dressed woman opposite him at the desk. She was always well turned out in a business-like suit, or something similar. Simon had also noticed that she kept her jewellery to a minimum. It was there, but there was nothing overly feminine or girly. Never. In fact, nothing about squadron leader Jasmine "Squad" MacMurty was ever girly. She was definitely a lady, there was never any doubt of that. But she never allowed any question of her femininity to get in the way of her professionalism.

Simon thought she was also a little bit too young for the position she'd been given. As squadron leader, she had about 10 people reporting into her, many of which were hardened ex-service personnel, like himself. He thought she looked like she'd just stepped out of her university graduation ceremony and been handed the keys to MI6's Mallorcan branch. Reluctantly, he also acknowledged that it could be him that was getting older rather than the management that were getting younger.

So far, she was doing a reasonable job. That is to say, she hadn't dropped the ball. Yet.

"Morning, Squad. How's things?"

"Same as. What did you manage to get out of David and Sarah?"

"It's mostly David who's interested in the bugs. Sarah seems more interested in looking after her house and husband. Actually, she gets quite defensive."

"Good for her."

"As we suspected, they're not involved in the killings. They just happened to be in the wrong place at the wrong time. He took a bug home, a few days later he had a look at it and discovered it was man-made and that it came apart. He's extrapolated a few ideas from there, like the parts are interchangeable and there are probably different head units. He thinks he's figured out some of the small details. Beyond that, I don't think he knows anything. He certainly has no idea where the weapons came from or where they might be going."

"That's a shame, I was hoping he'd be able to add a few pieces to the jigsaw. Did you leave him with another one to be getting on with?"

"Yes, just like we agreed. And I gave him the whole story about not knowing who was using it to spy on me and me catching it on my balcony."

"And he bought it?"

"Hook, line and sinker. I'm not sure that we will ever be friends but, at the moment he sees me as a source of information so he's willing to play ball. I'll keep checking in with him. Take him to a bar, watch some football, buy him some beer. I'll get him on side."

"Are there any sprats we can throw him?"

"What do you mean?" Asked Simon.

"Any little reward we can give him to encourage him? Get him on side?"

"He did ask if he could have his bug back, the one I took from him."

"Ok. Have a word with Daniels in the lab. If we've learned everything we can from it, and have no further use for it, I don't see why he can't have that back. He's already seen it. I doubt he's going to learn much more from it?"

"I'll double check that there's no security reasons that he can't have it. This could work quite well. His main reason for wanting it back was just because I took it from him."

"Ok. Well that works quite well. It's an apology and a gift. Reciprocity."

18.

Sarah and David had a house to clean. The owners would be returning next week and the house needed cleaning top to bottom as did the garden and swimming pool. Sarah usually left David to do the outdoor tasks as he didn't mind baking in the sun, while she preferred the indoor tasks which helped her to maintain her pale complexion. However, this was one of her favourite gardens of all the houses she got to visit, so she didn't mind making an exception on this occasion.

"You OK doing the indoor stuff today?" she asked, causing David to furrow his eyebrows.

"Um, I guess so babe, whatever you want."

"Just fancy a change today."

"The sun's going to be pretty strong today, want me to help you with the suntan lotion?"

She gave him a beaming smile and produced the bottle of sunblock from behind her back.

"Thanks babe" she retorted and began bunching her hair up into a ponytail.

"Haven't you got an appointment with Chloe this afternoon to do your hair?" He asked.

"I have. The appointment is at 3:00, but I'll probably get there about half an hour early. She's always quite keen to chat and they always give me a glass of fizz. Rude not to, if it's on offer."

David made sure to get the lotion everywhere including the seahorse tattoo behind her left ear. Once he was done covering all the areas she couldn't reach, he snapped the lid closed on the bottle and handed it back to her. She had white trousers and a long white sleeve top. A white wide brimmed hat completed the sun defence outfit. There was no way she was going to get burnt today.

Once they'd got started with their jobs at the house it only took them about an hour to finish, as they had been regularly visiting this house over the last few months while the owners were back in England. After they were finished, they loaded their gear back into the van. Sarah checked her watch - there was just over an hour to go until she wanted to be at Chloe's shop.

"What are you up to this afternoon, babe?" Asked Sarah.

"I've not really got a lot planned, I thought I might head over to the music place over in Son Fuster, I should be able to find someone to jam with."

"Cool. Sounds like fun. Are you going to get a gig there one day?"

"Well me and the boys keep talking about it, but nothing seems to happen. Maybe one day. Are you driving later, or do you want me to drop you at Chloe's?"

"If you could give me a lift, that would be great. I can always get a taxi back later."

David dropped her right outside of Chloe's shop. She closed the door and waved as he drove on up the road. A small bell rang above the door as she entered the shop.

"Hi Sarah, how are you?" sked Chloe.

"Hi hun, I'm good, how are you?"

"Oh, good here babes. Glass of fizz?"

"Ooh. Yes, please."

Chloe produced a glass, seemingly out of nowhere, and placed it on the counter in front of. She then walked over to the fridge and pulled out a bottle of Cava with a resealable pressure cork in the top. It made a satisfying pop as the cork was removed. Sarah lifted the glass once Chloe had finished filling it and went to take a sip.

"Cheers, hunnie," said Sarah.

"Cheers, babes."

They chatted for a few minutes about what Sarah was planning to have done to her hair, when the conversation turned towards the two dead bodies they'd found in Lloseta.

"Oh my god, it must have been awful finding those two in their garden like that." exclaimed, Chloe.

Sarah was a little taken aback by the sudden change of subject. She had almost got to the point where the shock of what had happened that day wasn't the first thing she thought about every morning. Really, she preferred not to talk about it at all.

"Yeah, it was a bit of a shocker - poor people."

"I remember everyone in the village was talking about it at the time, but I suppose I haven't seen you since. Was it really gruesome? Were there, like, maggots, or had their faces been eaten by their cat?"

"Oh, Chloe." Sarah shot her a death stare. "That's not really acceptable, is it?"

Maybe it hadn't been such a smart idea to come here. Chloe wasn't really the sharpest tool in the box, and her conversation could be a bit immature sometimes. In this case, she just seemed to be jangling Sarah's nerves.

"Yeah, sorry babes. Thing is, I've heard all sorts of stories about it from almost everyone around the town, except you. But, of course, you are the one that was there."

"I was, I remember that much. To be honest, it was all very peaceful. They just looked like they were asleep, except for the small wound in the middle of their foreheads."

"So, do you have any idea what happened?"

Well, yes, Sarah had a very good idea what had happened, but wouldn't be sharing any of it with Chloe.

"No idea. The police never told us the results of their inquiries." said Sarah.

"But they were killed? It wasn't like a suicide thing, or whatever?" asked Chloe.

"Oh no, I think the general feeling everyone had was that they had been killed."

"Wow. Things like that never happen around here. Who would have thought? Murder in Lloseta."

Sarah couldn't help it - she rolled her eyes. Chloe didn't notice.

"Shall I sit in the chair, then?" asked Sarah, trying to steer the conversation back towards hair.

"Yeah, good idea babes, right this way."

Chloe led her over to the hair washing station. Sarah sat down and eased her head back into the bowl. Hair washing duties are generally given to the new hire. Sarah had never met this one before, but she seemed efficient in her hair washing and managed not to get any shampoo in Sarah's eyes. She also didn't talk, which Sarah viewed as a bonus.

Within a few minutes Sarah was making herself comfortable in Chloe's hairdressing chair.

"So, how's Dave," Chloe enquired "has he recovered from the shock?"

Sarah regarded Chloe's reflection in the mirror through narrowed eyes. She left a deliberate pause before responding.

"He's fine. Thank you. Chloe. Never better." Sarah thought she'd made it clear a moment ago that she didn't want to talk about the Köhlers. Apparently, Chloe's brain cells communicated at a much slower pace than normal people.

"Oh, Ok," said Chloe. Sarah hoped she might now be back on track.

"So, what's Dave up to today?" asked Chloe.

"He's gone up to the music rehearsal rooms - he's been going there more regularly recently. I'm kind of hoping he's got some big gig coming up, but he hasn't told me anything - yet."

"Do you think maybe he's got a slot at the club next door, that would be really good for him?" Chloe said excitedly.

"I hope he has. He really deserves it. As you know, he's been playing a lot of little bars around the local towns and villages. He puts in so much time and effort. I know a lot of the people who get to see him really enjoy his music, I just feel he deserves a bigger stage. Maybe I'm just being the proud wife."

"His music is awesome. I've seen him play a few times and you're right, he deserves a bigger stage."

"Well, if that's what he's going for then I wish him all the luck in the world. But he's keeping it a secret, and we need to keep quiet about it too."

Chloe pulled her finger and thumb across her lips as if zipping them closed."

"Did those people have any friends on the island, anyone they were close to?" asked Chloe, seemingly unable to keep away from the subject.

"I didn't really know them that well. Ingrid used to play up at the tennis club, so I assume they knew people up there. I guess I don't really know anything about Gunther...." she tailed off. Actually, she did know something about Gunther

Köhler. "Now that you mention it, Mr Köhler used to work with another of my customers, Mr. Faber. I think they used to work together in the German Air Force, years ago."

"And you say those people on Lloseta, the Köhlers, were killed? Murdered?"

Sarah nodded at Chloe in the mirror.

"So, does that mean that the Fabers are in danger too?" Chloe's question hung in the air for a moment.

"I suppose they could be," said Sarah, wide-eyed in mock surprise, "We had realised they could be in danger last time we spoke to them, but then they were flying off to Germany the next day, so we thought they'd be Ok. That was December."

"Have you not heard from them since then?"

Sarah had to think for a moment. All this had happened months ago.

"We did get an email telling us they were coming back to the island. We went to their house and got everything ready for their return, but we haven't actually seen them or spoken to them. I reckon that was two and a half months ago."

There was a long pause as they looked at each other in the mirror. Chloe looked like she had seen a ghost and didn't want to say anything for fear of being chided again by Sarah. Sarah looked at herself in the mirror. They both wore the same open - mouthed expression.

"So," said Chloe and left the word to hang.

"Mmm," said Sarah. She was already getting a pit in her stomach. What if the Fabers were lying there dead in the garden or living room. They could have been there for months. Sarah closed her eyes and tried to block out the imagery.

"Anyway. So, how's Maria doing?" Sarah asked, nodding towards one of the other hairdressers, "how far along is she?"

"Oh," said Chloe, a moment to cotton on to the very deliberate change of subject, "She's due in about two months. She looks like a beached whale." Chloe said, deliberately loudly and in the direction of Maria, who flipped her the bird.

"Seriously though, I don't know what we're going to do around here without her," said Chloe.

"Are you going to be coming back?" asked Sarah.

"I'm not sure yet, " said Maria, "it's my first one, I guess we'll just have to see how it goes."

"Not what you need to hear when you're trying to run a business," said Chloe with her usual tactfulness. Maria responded by shrugging her shoulders and getting back on with her work.

About an hour later, Sarah stepped out of the salon. Now more golden blonde rather than her previous platinum, with a couple of red and blue streaks for good measure. She messaged David as the taxi took her back home.

I'm done, headed back home.
Hope you're having fun. See you later.

David's response didn't come until after she was back in the house.

Hi babe. We're making good progress here.
Room booked until 6
Home about 7
Love you

That left her with a couple of hours before he got home. Initially, she thought about busying herself in the kitchen to stop herself thinking about the Fabers. She had planned to talk to David about the whole situation when he got home, but then she decided to take action herself. She grabbed her phone, ready to text Anna, but then spent ages trying to figure out what to say.

*Just checking if you need us over the
next couple of months,
I'm trying to plan vacation time.*

After a couple of minutes of looking expectantly at the phone, Sarah realised that by sending the text, she had only made herself think more about the situation, not less. Images of what had happened before and what might have happen now kept appearing in her mind. It became clear that texting Anna had only made her more anxious, not less.

Back to plan A - cleaning the kitchen. She put some upbeat music on while she cleaned. Once that was done, she interrogated the fridge for inspiration - not a lot to go on, but she could probably throw together a carbonara. The next thing she knew, David was home. Maybe she had succeeded in distracting herself after all.

"You have a good time?" she asked as he bundled his gear through the front door.

"Yep, good fun. It actually felt like we were making some progress today. Ooh. I like what you've done with your hair," he said, pulling her in for a kiss," All the boys are going to be looking at you, I'd better watch out."

"They already do, hun."

He ran his fingers through her hair, examining Chloe's handiwork. She turned her head to ensure he noticed the red and blue streaks.

"Oh, I see. Daddy's little monster. Are you going to be wearing the hot pants as well?"

"In your dreams, hunnie."

"You already are, babe,"

She walked with him through to the kitchen where everything was prepared for cooking. She produced two wine glasses and an over chilled bottle of her favourite local white - cork already removed and ready for serving. Having put the spaghetti into boiling water. She poured them both an over-generous glass. David clocked the portion immediately.

"So how was your day, babe," David enquired, knowing that Chloe had a habit of rubbing Sarah up the wrong way, " are you happy with what Chloe has done with your hair?"

"I am happy with the hair, I think she's done a great job, do you like it?"

"It's beautiful babe, very sexy,"

David gave her a moment as she stirred the spaghetti.

"Is everything Ok babe, something seems to be bothering you?"

"Well, I do find Chloe a bit difficult to deal with. She's one of those people who constantly have to be talking. Do you think she knows that she sounds completely thick most of the time? Anyway, she kept asking about the Köhlers. She just couldn't seem to leave it alone. But then she came out with a good point. Do you think we should have warned the Fabers that we thought they could be at risk too?"

It was a good point and he had been thinking along the same lines himself.

"You're probably right. Maybe we should give them a ring?"

"Well, I sent Anna a text about an hour ago, there's been no response. The conversation with Chloe had kind of got me thinking that there might already be a couple of dead bodies at their house already."

"Oh, now I see, you're already dreading going around there."

"Well, let's say I'm keen not to put myself through what we saw that day at the Köhler's house."

"If it's only been an hour then maybe she's out or with friends. There's probably a very reasonable explanation. I tell you what, if there's no response by the morning, I will go round to the house and have a look. I will go by myself. You can wait here."

"Thanks babe."

She lifted her glass and took a generous slurp of the white wine. David was impressed that she'd managed to get this far into the conversation before starting. He lifted his glass and tipped it towards her. "Cheers, babe."

She gave him a little smile and wrinkled her nose. He was familiar with this look. It meant she was out of her depth and needed help, but she would never ask for it directly.

Once they'd finished eating, David tidied the plates away and started washing them in the sink. He left Sarah swirling her wine at the dining table and staring off into the middle distance. Once he'd finished, he brought the wine from the kitchen and topped up her glass.

19.

He caught his reflection in the polished stainless steel that had once served as a mirror at the back of the lift. It wasn't good. The unfortunate angle of the lighting only served to make things worse, highlighting each wrinkle and imperfection. It added at least ten years, at least. Or so he hoped. The shadow cast by his glasses seemed to conspire with his eyebrows to join them into a Neanderthal like mono-brow.

Every time he got into this poxy lift it was the same damned thing. The doors slid open and his distance to the scratched surface, along with his less than perfect eyesight, would serve to obscure the unfortunate reality. As he stepped into the lift and got closer to his own reflection, he saw through the mirror's temporary veil, the naked truth now plain to see.

Perhaps the mirror saw things in his soul that the eye couldn't. Maybe it was more honest and saw things that he didn't like to admit to himself. Surely there would ultimately be a price to pay for his sins. He had killed. He still planned to kill. His former colleagues were next on the list.

Some of them hated him anyway, and the feeling mutual. But others he had definitely considered to be friends. The ultimate betrayal, killing a friend. Surely there was a special place in hell, or wherever, for him.

He put the key into the lock and entered the squalid flat that had served as his temporary office. Every time he did, he wondered if the Russians would be there waiting for him. To take from him that which he had taken from the Luftwaffe. To finish him. To put an end to their demand to kill his friends and to his miserable existence. He could just move on and sell to someone else, someone less demanding. Perhaps another buyer would be just around the corner. He could put his feelers out again.

Or send it all back to Germany and be done with it. Give up on his retaliation for betraying his years of work and sacrifice. Those bastards. Give up and face whatever punishment they saw fit for his theft and breach of national security.

He had been testing a new version of the microphone and transmitter. He'd already gone through the standard testing on the desk and then moved on to eavesdropping on small-talk near the coffee machine. At the time he knew it was a stupid idea, but the opportunity had just thrown itself at him. How could he resist?

His section commander appeared at the coffee machine, having left his office door open. As soon as he saw it, he knew he couldn't help himself. Having issued instructions, the bee took off and flew into the commander's office. He found a nice little hide-away on the bookshelf.

Within minutes the commander had returned and it was relaying inside information to him at his desk. It was mostly background noise and administrative minutiae. He only intended to leave the bee in the office until next time the commander left the office, then he'd get it back on the charger in his lab. The signal was strong and clear. It picked up every little noise, from drawers opening and closing to the commander's nervous habit of clicking his pen. Again and again and again. Click, click, click. He wondered if the computer people could write some sort of code to delete annoying background noise. It was all working perfectly. Until the big boss arrived.

He walked through the offices, giving the occasional nod, then went straight to the commander's door. He knocked and opened the door before there was any time for a response. He went in and closed the door. He assumed they'd be discussing something important and would sweep the office for listening devices or transmitters. He was finished. When his little training mission was discovered, he'd be taken out and shot as a traitor.

His shoulders slumped as he listened for the bug to be found and the shouting to start. But that never came. Instead, the two men got straight into a conversation, as if it was a continuation of one they'd started earlier.

They talked about article 79a and what a success if was becoming after years of time and investment. How it was starting to show some real promise. He'd felt an inner glow of pride that his efforts would be talked about in senior circles and that his team were finally achieving on what they had set out to do.

But then the conversation went sour. His heart dropped as he listened to them planning the dismantling of the team. Once finished, it wouldn't need anywhere near the whole team to develop and polish it.

Some of the members would be reassigned to other departments. He wouldn't. As a reward for his time and efforts he was to be removed. Put out to pasture. Early retirement, starting almost immediately. He couldn't believe what he was hearing. It was a personal insult, a betrayal.

He decided right there and then that his bees would be leaving with him and they'd all just disappear. Getting the bees and the computers off site would be easy. Convincing his wife that they should go on the run from the government and the Luftwaffe, that would be different.

The office still smelled of stale cigarettes from earlier in the day. He lit another. He had left the system running, watching for any suspicious activity at his house or at his office. It would have alerted him if there had been, but he checked anyway. The screen showed him his street and his house. She was on the sofa and her car on the driveway. Business as usual with no suspicious visitors.

He instructed the system to send eight bees over to the house in Lloseta, four video and four sound. They'd fly over to the house automatically, but he'd place them manually once they arrived.

He still didn't know if his bee had flown itself to the house or if it was a person that had taken it there, but he was confident that he would get to the truth and get his bee back.

20.

After a long night of debating it with herself, Sarah had decided to come along with David after all. Whether she was there or not wouldn't make any difference to the truth of the situation. The Fabers were either dead and lying unnoticed, possibility for months, or they were fine.

David walked up the driveway with Sarah following closely behind. Their car was on the driveway but that didn't mean anything. Everything looked normal. As they approached the front door Sarah could feel a wave of panic approaching. She couldn't get away from the idea that what they were about to see was much worse than they had seen last time.

David reached over and pushed the doorbell. She could hear the sound of the chime inside the house and then heard it fading quickly down to silence. Which was followed by more silence.

"Have you brought the keys with you, just in case?" asked an increasingly helpless Sarah.

"I have, but I think we need to give them a little while longer. Imagine if he's on the bog!"

Sarah tried to laugh, but it was all getting too much.

"Maybe I should have waited in the van," she said.

Even David had to admit to himself that the silence had gone on a little too long now and things weren't looking promising. He was wondering how much longer they should leave it before letting themselves in when there was a sudden loud clonk from the front door. It caught them both off-guard and Sarah let out a yelp. The door open inwards.

Standing in the doorway was Anna, in the flesh, alive and kicking.

"Hello, David. Hello, Sarah, come on in. Are you keeping well?" she asked.

"Hi, Anna," said Sarah "we are doing fine, thank you. "We have been very worried about you. I messaged you last night. When I didn't get a response, I couldn't help but fear the worst."

"They did the standard Spanish greeting and kissed on each cheek. Sarah wanted to hug her. She was very relieved that Anna was alive and unharmed.

"Go on through, David," said Anna. "Klaus is in the kitchen."

"Ok, thank you." said David, wandering deeper into the house and leaving the girls to catch up. He was glad that they could both stop worrying. As promised, he found Klaus in the kitchen.

"Hello David, how are you keeping?" asked Klaus extending his hand.

"We are both very well thank you, Klaus," said David, as he shook Klaus' hand.

"Can I offer you a coffee, or anything?'

"No thanks. I'm good,"

"So, what is it that brings you here? Anna tells me that Sarah has been worried?"

"Well, we both have. The last time we were in this house, we were preparing it for winter. You remember the Köhlers had recently been killed at their house? Well, something you said stuck in my mind. You used to work with Gunther, for the Air Force in Germany."

"That's correct, we used to work together. It was a long time ago but, yes, we both used to work for the Air Force in Schleswig."

David began pulling his phone out of his pocket and finding a picture of the bee he'd found near the dead bodies at the Köhler's house.

"As soon as we saw them in the garden, it was pretty obvious that they had been attacked by someone or something. They didn't just die, they were murdered. I also found this suspicious "device" at the scene." said David, "turning the screen towards Klaus.

Klaus froze immediately - his eyes wide, eyebrows raised.

"I take it from that reaction that you've seen this before?" asked David.

"Um......", It took a moment for Klaus to collect his composure.

He put his coffee down and looked David in the eye. He brought his index finger up in front of pursed lips.

"Looks like a beautiful day to walk the dog," said Klaus, "perhaps you would like to join me?"

"Um ... yes. Yes, it looks like a wonderful day to walk the dog," said David, eventually catching up with Klaus' meaning.

Klaus led them through to the living room where the dog was fast asleep in its bed.

"Come on, Toto, you lazy dog, "said Klaus nudging the dog bed with his foot, "We're going for a walk."

"Oh, Ok dear," said Anna, "is everything all right?"

"Perfectly fine, darling," he said, casting his eyes around the walls and ceiling of the room, "I think Toto wants to go for another walk and David was kind enough to offer to join me."

"Alright, well, see you in about ten minutes."

Klaus clipped the lead onto Toto, then gave both girls an exaggerated smile. David shrugged at Sarah and followed Klaus.

"Are the boys Ok?" asked Sarah, once the front door had been closed.

"You know, you really should come along to the tennis club with me. There are some gorgeous men there." said Anna, going off and a complete tangent.

"The tennis club?" asked Sarah, "how did…"

"The bar manager, Enrique, does a really mean gin and tonic. I'm sure you'd fit right in."

"I'm sure I would," said Sarah, gradually coming around to the idea that Anna was going to be steering the conversation and that they weren't going to be talking about why Sarah had been worried. "Anyway, I'm glad you guys are OK."

"We are fine, and thank you for being worried, but there's really no need. Can I get you a drink?"

"Coffee would be great."

"Or a glass of whisky, you look like you've seen a ghost."

"I've not seen a ghost, well not really. But there has been something odd going on. Now I'm wondering if it's the same thing that is happening here."

"Oh god, I'm sorry you've gotten involved. Maybe it's something we can talk about when you come to the club? Whisky?"

Sarah turned her wrist to get a better view of her watch.

"Maybe coffee, 9:30 seems a little early for whisky."

David and Klaus walked Toto in silence for a few minutes as they wound their way out of the sleepy end of the village. Eventually they turned a corner and were greeted with a busy main road, which David knew would be perfect for providing background noise, should anybody be listening.

"So, tell me. David, where did you get that picture?"

"It was taken in the Köhler's back garden about two hours after the police removed their bodies."

"Do you know what it is that you're looking at?"

"I don't know exactly what it is, but I've got a pretty good idea. It's a weapon. It's the one that killed Gunther."

"These people that are watching me, are they watching you as well?" asked Klaus.

"Watching me? Why would they do that? I've got nothing to do with any of this. I've come here because I thought you could be in danger, like Gunther."

"But you are involved, David. You've just shown me a weapon that is in your possession."

"Yes, but I didn't kill Gunther."

"Of course not. But that weapon does belong to someone."

"Oh, yes. You're right. What if they want it back? Unfortunately, I have let my curiosity get the better of me. As soon as I suspected it was a weapon, I should have just put it back where I found it and pretended that I'd never seen it."

"Maybe you should. But it's too late for that."

The conversation paused for a moment, while Toto fertilized a tree. Once the dog was moving again, the conversation continued.

"So how did you know I was involved with this weapon?" asked Klaus.

"The last time I spoke to you, we were discussing details about winterising your house. We were in the garden when Anna mentioned something about you and Gunther having worked together in the past."

"Yes, we were old colleagues, we used to work for the military. We had a research facility on some farmland at the north end of Schleswig air force base. I must admit, I was a bit surprised when you showed me that picture. I've not seen a murder bee for a very long time."

"Is that the official name?"

"Humph," Klaus scoffed, " to us it was called article 79a. Top, top secret. I worked on the battery technology. Have you noticed the impressive capacity?"

"Not directly, they do seem to be able to stay switched on for a very very long time."

"They can go into semi-hibernation for about a month and still be able to function as a listening device."

"What about that flying range?"

"Fifty kilometres, no problem."

"I found another one at your house the day after you went back to Germany for Christmas. We were cleaning your house and Sarah noticed it on the outside of the kitchen window. I guess it was there to watch you. In my infinite wisdom - "

"You caught it," Klaus interrupted.

"I did. I was quite pleased with myself at the time, but now I kind of wish I hadn't."

"Do they know you've got that one?"

"I don't think so. I put it straight into a metal tin and wrapped it in kitchen foil."

"Faraday cage," said Klaus, "that should have blocked any signals. And the one you found at the Köhler's?"

"Well. It was in a metal tin most of the time, but I did have it out in the open on my workbench for about ten minutes."

"So, they know where it is then?"

"Well, they did. They sent a British agent around to bully me into handing it over."

"British agent?" asked Klaus.

"Yeah, English guy."

"To retrieve a German top secret military device?"

"Yeah, that is a bit weird, isn't it?"

"Mmm, I'm not sure what that means. I'll have to think about that."

Klaus paused and then turned around and began strolling back towards his house, giving Toto a gentle tug to encourage him in the new direction.

"So, you've only got one device, then?"

"Correct." said David. Of course, he also had the one that Simon had brought around, but David figured that Klaus didn't need to know about that one. He was coming around to the idea that no-one could be trusted. The less he said the better. In fact, he had a nagging feeling that he'd said too much already.

"And we don't think they know about it?"

"It's been sealed in that tin the whole time. I haven't even opened it."

"Well, if you keep it like that then there's no way they can know where it is." said Klaus.

They strolled in silence for a couple of minutes as Toto sniffed his way along the pavement.

"There were seven of us," said Klaus, "six people doing the research and development, and our team leader. Of the workers, three of us live in Mallorca and three in Germany, but they visit the island regularly. I have no idea where the boss lives these days."

"Three of you here on the island? So that's you, Gunther and who else?" asked David.

"Helmut Schmidt, He lives with his wife Heidi over in Port de Pollença."

"Have you heard from them recently?" asked David.

"No, I've not heard from them in quite a while. The thing is, David, Helmut and I seemed to disagree on almost everything. We were colleagues, but we were never destined to be friends."

"Even so, somebody should check on them to make sure they're Ok, to warn them about what's been going on."

"You are right, somebody should." said Klaus, as he patted his pockets looking for his mobile phone.

"Have you got your phone, David? I've left mine at home. Could you give Helmut a ring?"

"Um, yeah sure," said David, extracting his phone from his pocket, "what's the number?"

"Oh, I've got no idea. But they run a boat charter in the port. I'm sure if you do a quick search, you'll find it."

David did a quick internet search which returned several options. He showed the results to Klaus who scanned down the results and indicated the third one to be correct.

"There, that's them."

David pressed the call button next to the result. The call connected almost straight away, but the phone just kept ringing. Eventually the call cut itself off.

"No answer," said David, "maybe they're out, I will try again later."

"Unfortunately, David, the best way to rule out foul play is to go over there and have a look yourself. I'm sure they are going to be fine. You never know, you might be able to sell them your cleaning services."

David raised an eyebrow and nodded. New customers were always welcome.

"I'll try them on the phone again later, but if there's no response, we'll head over there."

"But you will let me know how you get on?"

"Of course,"

Back at the house Klaus opened the front door and the three of them entered.

"Hi honey", said Anna, "how did you get on?"

"Oh, fine. Toto wasn't really that desperate after all."

"So, looks like we're all done here," said Klaus.

"Indeed, it does," said David, as he caught Sarah's eye and nodded towards the door.

"Ok," said Sarah, "I'll just pop my cup back in the kitchen."

Once they were back in the van, they both deliberately avoided obvious conversation. David knew that the van was potentially bugged and Sarah was getting the idea that something weird was going on, and she should just play along.

"Lovely couple," said Sarah, "I'm glad we've had the chance to catch up,"

"Me too. We shouldn't leave it so long next time."

With the engine running and the stereo blazing they pulled away, heading nowhere in particular. After a couple of miles, David pulled over at the side of the road, leaving the engine and music going. He leant over, positioning his lips close to Sarah's ear.

"That was completely crazy," he whispered, "Klaus was part of the team that developed the "murder bees", as he called them."

"Anna kept steering the conversation onto frivolous things, like her tennis club."

"There were seven of them - six researchers and a supervisor. Gunther was one of the researchers, as was Klaus. Another one of the researchers lives in Port de Pollença, and we've been unable to get hold of him on the phone."

"Oh god, here we go. I already don't like the way this story ends."

"Well, we don't know anything for sure.'

"So is Klaus going to go and check on his old colleague?"

"They don't get on, never have done. I think Klaus is a little concerned that if Helmut is still alive, then Klaus will be the last person he wants to see."

"Great," Sarah whispered, "so it comes down to you and me again."

"Well, I can go by myself, if you'd prefer.'

"I don't really prefer either option,"

"Maybe a beer then?"

Sarah again turned her wrist to get a better view of her watch.

"10am, still too early for booze,"

"Still?", asked David.

"Never mind. Come on. Let's get going, it will take us about half an hour to get to Port de Pollença."

21.

Thirty minutes later they parked outside the address listed for Heidi and Klaus Schmitz. They got out of the van and wandered over to the front door. David rang the doorbell, then stood back a couple of paces and waited. After about a minute, he rang the bell again and knocked on the door for good measure. There was still no response.

"Ok, this is working well," said David.

"What else can we try, is there any way of having a look around the back?" asked Sarah.

"Not sure, let's try around here."

Around to the left of the house, there appeared to be a small gate. David pulled the gate, which was unlocked and opened easily. They both made their way down the footpaths towards the back garden.

"If this was our house, that gate would be kept locked,' said Sarah.

"I know. What's the point of a gate with easy public access if it doesn't have a lock?"

The answer became clear almost immediately. They were huge walls surrounding the back garden, to which access was via another gate, but this time a bit more over engineered. And locked. There was no way they were getting in without a key or a ladder.

"Well, that's kind of ruined this idea, hasn't it?" Asked David.

"What we need is a drone so we can see over the wall."

"Well, technically we do have those, but not here. We also have no idea how to control them."

Sarah elbowed him and pressed her index finger to her lips. "Not really the time or place," she whispered.

David had an idea and headed off to the van. Moments later he returned with an extendable cobweb brush, essential cleaner's kit, and a roll of gaffer tape. He extracted his phone from his pocket and taped it to the end of the brush. He set the camera to video mode and pressed record.

"This should do the trick." he said.

He hoisted the phone up so that it was high enough to look over the wall. He panned it around to give a good view of the whole back garden. Having got about 30 seconds of video he lowered the phone back down.

"Right, let's see what we've got," he said, stopping the recording and then replaying it, "this is the bit I'm not looking forward to."

"Oh, God," said Sarah, "what's that smell?"

David took an ill-advised deep sniff of the air.

"Yuck, that's the smell of death."

As the video played, it panned around the garden towards the house. There on the grass, was what they could smell. Two dead bodies.

"I'm assuming that's Helmut and Heidi," said David.

"We don't need to get any closer to tell they've been dead for quite a while," said Sarah, " the question is: what do we do now?"

David began removing the gaffer tape from his phone.

"Well," he said, resigned to what was coming next, "we are supposed to phone the police."

"And then that will be twice that we found murdered people in their gardens. That doesn't look suspicious at all."

"I guess we should have seen that one coming. If we thought this through, we would never have come anywhere near this house."

"And if we leave, and someone has noticed us, then it looks even worse," said Sarah, " I think I'm ready for that beer now."

They wandered back around to the front of the house and leant on the van.

"What if we phone Miquel instead of phoning the police directly?" Asked David.

"We could, but I don't think it's going to achieve much. He's been retired for years, I don't think there's much he can actually do for us."

"It just makes me feel better knowing that someone we trust will cast his eye over this, rather than just leaving it all up to the Guardia Civil.

Sarah breathed deeply and let out a long sigh.

"Well Ok," said Sarah, "but it still seems like we're stuck between a rock and a hard place."

"I couldn't agree more, but we're kind of stuck,"

David pulled out his phone and dialled.

"Hello David, my friend, how are you?" Asked Miquel, in his usual upbeat manner.

"Not good, Miquel. We have found another two bodies. I think they've been dead for some time."

"Ok, Ok."

David could hear him scrambling around for something to write on.

"So, David, don't touch anything. Keep out of the property. Are you both Ok?"

"Not really, no. This is bloody horrible, and I know it doesn't look good, but I swear this is nothing to do with us."

"Ok, David. Just tell me where you are, and I'll come over there immediately. Of course, I will need to call the police as well."

David gave him the address over the phone and then sent him a map location via text. Having discussed it further, they decided that Miquel would phone the original detective in charge of the Köhler's case. Having hung up there wasn't much for them to do except wait for the inevitable.

"Shall we move the van around the corner?" Sarah suggested.

"Oh yeah, good idea. We don't need the company name plastered all over the front of a murder scene. Good job we're not wearing company overalls."

22.

The police car pulled up outside the house and two officers got out.

"Are you, David and Sarah?" asked the first officer.

"We are," replied Sarah.

"I understand you have discovered two dead bodies in the back garden?"

"We have," said David. "They weren't answering their phone, so we came to the house. They wouldn't come to the door either, so we had a look around the back. I've got a video on my phone I can show you."

"Ok, you can show me. Where did you take this video?"

David indicated the side gate, then held up his phone and pressed play. The officer watched as the video played, showing the phone being hoisted up over the wall and then panning across the garden towards the house.

Just as before, the two dead bodies lay unmoving on the grass. It was less difficult to watch the second time around. It was also easier without the stench of death in the air.

"We could smell them from the other side of the wall," said David "I'm quite surprised no one has reported that already."

"David and Sarah, I am arresting you on suspicion of causing death..."

"What, you have got to be kidding me. What the hell is

wrong with you Spanish police officers?" Sarah shouted, unloading her tension.

"You need to calm - "

"I'm not going to calm down, you prick. We are here checking on some people who haven't been heard from for a while, doing our civic duty ... then you pitch up with your badge and your uniform…"

David held up his hands to her in surrender, even though she wasn't attacking him.

"Babe, we need to keep our cool. I don't think having a go at him is going to help."

For a moment Sarah looked like she was going to punch someone or something. David kept eye contact with her and tried to smile. It took a moment, but eventually Sarah's shoulders relaxed and she took a deep breath and held it for a moment.

"Of course, officer," said David "however we can help, we are happy to cooperate.'

The officer pulled out his handcuffs and held them up.

"I don't actually think you're a physical threat, but it's procedure."

"Can I start with you, Sarah?" asked the officer.

She nodded and held out her arms in front, visibly defeated. The officer was careful as he bound her hands, leaving the cuffs quite loose.

"Is that comfortable?" He asked.

"Yep. It's Ok."

During this, another police car arrived, and the officer got out and approached David. He held his arms out in front, waiting for the handcuffs. They were put into separate cars and driven to the police station.

David was sick with worry about Sarah. He knew she would be winding herself up into a state and he wasn't there to calm her. He knew he was in exactly the same situation, but he really wasn't worried about what was going to happen to him. He just kept thinking about her.

David's car pulled into the police station car park first closely followed by Sarah's car. They got out of their respective vehicles and were corralled towards the custody suite. David tried to make eye contact with Sarah to check she was alright, but the two were being kept apart, so no communication would be possible.

Upon entering the custody suite, David could see various police officers going about their duties, but it was the two men dressed in suits that stood out from the rest. They were sitting in a waiting area reading some paperwork, but both men stood up when they saw David.

"Good afternoon ... David," said the first man nodding at David and then examining the officer's name badge, "I am your legal representative. Officer Ramirez, I demand to know why my client is being detained and what evidence you have."

David noticed that Sarah had now entered the room and the second man was giving the same speech to Sarah and her police officer.

Both men launched into machine gun Spanish. From what David could catch, they were repeating the same question. Their volume and cadence increased. After a few minutes of loud conversation, they seemed to reach some sort of agreement, although it had all been too fast for either David or Sarah to follow.

"Sorry David," said the first man, "My name is Aitor Gonzalez, I am your legal representative. These guys haven't got a damn thing on you, so we will have you out of here in a few moments."

"Fantastic, but who called you? I didn't."

"Let's just say we have a mutual friend."

Aitor then turned and directed his next Spanish outburst at the senior officer behind the desk.

There was a lot of passionate Spanish discussion and gesticulation. During the commotion, David managed to catch Sarah's eye. She raised her eyebrows and gave a cheeky smile, David figured she was feeling more optimistic now that it seemed someone was on their side, even if they had no idea who they were or where they had come from.

"Are you ready for that beer now?" David suggested.

Sarah made a bit of an act of looking at her watch despite the handcuffs getting in the way.

"Well, after 5 o'clock somewhere."

David was happy with the flippant response; she was obviously feeling better.

They were required to give an official statement to the offices, but their legal team wouldn't let the situation drag on or get out of hand. Thirty-five minutes later they were both walking out of the police station.

"Ok, Aitor, thanks for your help. What do we do now?" asked David.

"I think our mutual friend is here to give you a lift," he replied, indicating a white nondescript minibus parked opposite them. David could see the driver, but the rear windows were tinted and obscured his view of the inside.

As they approached the side door slid open but they couldn't see who was inside until they were at the doorway.

"Hello mate." It was David's friend, Simon, "got yourself into a bit of a pickle?"

"I never thought I would be pleased to see you, but on this occasion, I'll make an exception. Are we going for a beer or what?"

"Beer later. My boss wants to talk to you both."

That knocked David straight out of his optimistic mood.

David climbed into the minibus closely followed by Sarah, who thumped the door closed behind her.

"So, what have you guys been up to to get yourselves in trouble with the police?" asked Simon.

"Well, it was a bit of a repeat of what happened at the Köhlers's house," said Sarah. "We turn up and there's two dead bodies in the garden. These guys aren't our customers, but it's the same story. "

"Do you know how they died?" asked Simon.

David and Sarah gave each other a quick puzzled look. They thought it was obvious, but Simon was right - they didn't actually *know*.

"No, we don't know. We couldn't get close enough to see. But my guess would be the same method as Gunther and Ingrid. What's your angle here? Why are you guys suddenly interested in what we've been doing?"

"That's above my pay grade, mate. You need to talk to the boss."

"Oh, of course, you're just a courier."

Simon raised his eyebrows and gave a slight smirk, acknowledging another conversation they'd had when they first met.

"She will be joining us in a few minutes", said Simon, " I know she's keen to meet you both and see how we can all work together."

Within a couple of minutes the van was approached by a smartly dressed woman and man. She seemed quite young. The man was almost a carbon copy of Simon, but for a slightly different hair colour. They joined them in the back of the minibus.

"Hello, Sarah," she said, " extending her hand towards Sarah.

"Hi," said Sarah "Likewise, I think,"

"David," she said, shaking his hand. "It's good to finally meet you both."

"Sorry," said Sarah, " and what do we call you?"

"Around here I'm called Squad – short for squadron leader."

"Ok, Squad," Sarah had to force the name out and stop herself from rolling her eyes, "nice to meet you too."

"This is Stephan,"

Stephan nodded at Sarah and David but remained silent.

"I take it your experience with the police was short and sweet?", asked Squad.

"Thanks for getting us out of there," said Sarah, " It was only a matter of time before I punched one of them. "

"You should try to avoid that," said Simon, "It tends to make things worse."

"So, I guess we owe you a favour now?"

"That's a slightly vulgar way of putting it. But yes, I would like us to work together on a little project."

David's eyes flicked between Simon and his boss.

"Ok, I'm listening," he said.

"There's not an awful lot to it. We'd just like you to keep doing what you're doing but keep us in the loop."

"Ok, that doesn't seem too difficult.", said David.

"How is it that you came to be at Helmut Schmitz's house?" Squad asked.

"Oh, that's all my fault," said Sarah, "I was worried about something Klaus and Anna had said last time we saw them. He mentioned that Klaus used to work with Gunther Köhler, the first couple who were killed. I had convinced myself that Klaus and Anna were also potential victims, we hadn't heard from then for ages, so we went to their house to talk to them."

David paused for a moment. What he was about to say next meant there was no backing out. He figured that Simon had already seen the original bee that he'd caught, so it didn't feel like a step too far.

"Then I showed Klaus a picture of the bee that I caught at Gunther's house. Klaus recognised it immediately; he even had a name for it. He called it a murder bee."

"Murder bee?" Squad said, "we know it as article 79a."

"Yes, that too," said David.

"He told me about the team of seven men that worked on article 79a. Six researchers and one supervisor. They all come to the island regularly. Some have homes here, while others have favourite hotels. Klaus is super paranoid that he is being watched, so we had to take the dog for a walk on a main road in order to discuss the situation."

"If he used to work with Helmut, why didn't he go and check on his colleague instead of you?" asked Simon.

"Well according to Klaus, the two of them don't get on. He also said I might be able to sell my house cleaning services to him."

"So, he set you up as the fall guy?" Simon suggested.

"I guess so."

"Yes, that's exactly what he did," said Sarah, "he set us up."

"He has. The question is *why*? What else did he say?" asked Squad.

"He asked me if I still had the bee," said David, "I told him there was some British bloke that bullied me into handing it over to him - seemed to think he was James Bond."

"Damn, that would have been better as a secret. Was he surprised to hear that?" asked Simon, a little smile confirming he'd heard the jibe.

"He said it was a bit weird and that he would have to think about it."

David was now debating with himself whether to come clean about the other bug, the one he'd caught at Klaus' place. He knew he didn't trust Klaus and had already betrayed by him, so David definitely wasn't going to be trusting him again. He now debated whether Simon and his people were any more or less trustworthy than Klaus. On balance, he thought that these guys probably had more to offer him with help and support. He could learn more from these guys.

"So, I kind of caught another bug at Klaus' house just before Christmas." He said.

"Jesus, said Simon, "you're a dark horse, aren't you? You've kept that quiet."

"Well, the whole thing has piqued my interest. I was worried that if I told you, you might try and take that one away from me too."

"And Klaus doesn't know about that one?" asked the boss.

"No, I've kept that one for me."

"So, who put that bug there?" said Squad.

"What? It wasn't you guys?" asked David.

"Well, we are watching him, but not with 79a. What he's paranoid about is someone else. Those are the people we are interested in," said Simon.

"We were being really careful, I don't think we could have been overheard, so I assume it's just Klaus who knows." David paused trying to make sense of all this information. He couldn't get his head around it. Maybe he never would. At the moment everyone else was using him as a chess piece in a game he didn't understand.

"What do you know physically about these murder bees?" asked Squad. "You've seen them up close."

"I have. Very close on the workbench. I don't know an awful lot really. I know they communicate by radio waves of some sort, and probably navigate by GPS. I think some of them are weapons and others are eavesdropping devices," said David.

"Do you know they come apart?" asked the boss.

"Yes. And they are very nicely engineered. They are made up of three parts held together by a single screw underneath. I suspect the parts are all interchangeable so that individual components can be replaced, but I've only studied one on the bench, so that's just a theory."

"Yes, everything you said there is correct. The rear section is a battery pack, which can be swapped out to get the bug back in service quickly. The middle section is all about flight and navigation. The head is the interesting part. We have seen four different versions, but of course, there could be more. There's the eavesdropping version and the video version. You've already seen the results of the explosive charge version. It uses a high explosive to drive several depleted Uranium spikes through the skull and into the brain. Our people tell us it ought to be a very effective weapon. The final version, that we are aware of, is designed to deliver a liquid payload. We've only seen empty ones, but we assume they are designed to deliver some form of tranquilliser."

David sat back into his chair. Tranquilisers weren't the only liquid payload he could imagine. It would be ideal as a bioweapon delivery system. This whole thing had escalated way beyond anything he could have imagined.

"Unless anybody's got anything else to add, we can wrap this up," Squad said.

David shook his head and Sarah gave a slight shrug of the shoulders.

"Ok, in that case, I'll leave you boys to arrange how you are going to communicate. I'm expecting weekly updates, even if there's nothing to report.

"Yes boss," said Simon, who raised his eyebrows at David.

"Yes boss," said David.

"Simon will give you a lift back to your van. If everything's in order, I look forward to hearing from you soon." said Squad as she got out of the mini bus.

23.

Squad closed the door on the minibus, leaving the rest of them to sort out the details of how this arrangement was going to work.

"Shall we go and sweep your van?" asked Simon.

"Yep. Let's get it done so we can get out of here, this is turning into a long day," said David.

The minibus took them from the police station back to where the van was parked, in Port de Pollença.

"So, when are you boys going to meet up then?" said Sarah.

"I've got an idea," said Simon," how about the Tuesday morning spinning class at the gym? I doubt anyone will be able to hear even a normal conversation with the music up that loud."

David was caught off guard for a minute. That was one of his usual classes, how the hell did ... oh yes, Simon knew everything. The gym had also been where Simon had first approached him about the first bee. "Sounds like a plan," said David.

They arrived at the van where Simon showed them the detector. It was a small device about the same size as a mobile phone.

"You switch it on here. The RF aerial is here", Simon said, indicating a grill at one end of the device, "you then move it around slowly while watching the display. I think you'll find it quite obvious when you find something. Get all the doors open, then sweep around the entrances and interior. Don't forget to sweep the open door as well." He handed the device to Sarah, "Ladies first."

Having opened everything up, she followed the instructions she'd been given and within a minute found a bug near the rearview mirror. She continued her sweep and another one hidden in a corner in the back. She closed the van up in case they would be overheard, then walked back over to David and Simon.

"Little gits," she said in mocked surprise. She'd been pretty confident that she would find a bug, but there was no indication of who might have planted it.

David nodded.

"That's them," said Simon, containing a snort.

"That was easy, apparently even a girl can do it," she said, handing the detector to David.

"So, what do we do if we do find bugs then? Do we leave them, so they don't know they've been discovered?" asked Sarah.

"That's exactly what we do. We could destroy them, but then they'll know they've been found. If we leave them where we found them - but keep in mind that they are there - then we have the upper hand.

"Can we use this scanner to sweep the house?" asked David.

"Yes of course, and you need to - as soon as you get back. If you find anything, don't touch it, but keep in mind where it is and be careful what you say when you're near it."

"So, we can scan the house, but is there anywhere else we should sweep as well?"

"If you give it back to me, I'll change the screen, so it looks like a mobile phone. That way you should be able to use it anywhere."

Sarah handed him the scanner and, with a few clicks on the touch screen, it now resembled any generic mobile phone.

"Obviously, it doesn't actually have any mobile phone signal, so the signal strength display is...... bug signal strength. When the signal indicator turns red, you are right on top of it. Other than that, the battery charge indicator is an actual battery charge indicator. You charge it with the USB port on the bottom - just like a mobile phone." He handed the scanner back to David and indicated that he should have a go at sweeping the van. He approached it in a methodical manner, as instructed, and within a couple of minutes had found the two bugs that Sarah had found. He closed each door as he went.

"Great work guys," said Simon, "check your car over when you get home and then maybe a quick sweep of your house? When you're using it, pretend you are on your mobile and texting or surfing social media. That's why if there is a video device they won't see you doing a bug sweep, they'll see you going about your normal business.

"Once you've scanned the house, you can go for a beer, I think you've earned it."

"Good plan," said David, "um, one more thing."

"Yep," said Simon.

"These people breaking into our van and, I'm guessing, into our car and house too."

"Yep."

"Do you guys have some kind of camera system that might help us keep an eye on them or whatever?"

"Yep. Yes, we do. I was just about to come onto that subject because we are quite interested in these people too. I've got a gift from Squad in the minibus for you."

Simon opened one of the rear doors of the minibus and removed a box the size a small suitcase. "This little box of tricks has everything you need." Simon walked the case over to the van where David opened one of the rear doors. Once Simon had placed the case inside David closed the door and they went back over to where Sarah was waiting. "It's got a full suite of cameras for the house and vehicles. "They are all battery powered and will last about a month between charges. There's also a base station, through which it communicates with the outside world and our cloud-based AI. If there are people watching you, it'll find them. It's very efficient."

"Oh, brilliant. Maybe one day we'll get the upper hand on these people. I hate having them sniffing around in our house, grubby little shits." Said David.

"Anything that gives you more control will make you feel much better about the whole thing. Unless there's anything else, I think we are just about done here."

"Ok then mate, we'll get going and I'll see you on Tuesday, unless anything urgent happens."

"Ok mate, Tuesday. Oh, there are two spinning classes. Early or less early?"

"Your usual."

They were both quite excited to get back to the house and scan for devices. David relinquished control of the scanner to Sarah, who began her pretend social media surfing before going in through the front door. David started to unpack their gift from Squad in the living room. It seemed very comprehensive.

"Cup of tea, babe?"

"Yes please ... "

David didn't think that sounded quite like her normal reply, but figured whoever was watching wouldn't notice. Was this how it was going to be from now on? Were they going to be constantly putting on a good performance for the spyware?

David made the tea and placed her cup on the kitchen work surface. "Your tea is ready."

There was no response from Sarah, and anyway, David was too engrossed in his new toys to notice. He took his cup and wandered off back to the living room.

It looked like each camera was similar to a run-of-the-mill wi-fi home security camera, but he thought that was the point. Proper spy kit masquerading as normal store-bought security.

The vehicle dash cams were noticeably smaller than the other units. Each had its own mount which had an adhesive pad attached. There were nine cameras for the house, which he decided should all be exterior, and two for each vehicle. He spent a little time planning their locations around the garden, then began sticking them into place. The adhesive pads were extremely effective, and instant - there would be no correcting any errors in positioning.

It took him about half an hour to get all the cameras mounted, including the car and van. He then braced himself for the technical part of the installation: getting them all to talk to each other. He was thinking about taking another slurp of his tea, which he had left somewhere around the garden, when his phone pinged in his pocket. He retraced his route, looking for his cup as he teased the phone out of his pocket. He saw that he had a message from Simon, which he opened. It was a picture, no – it was live video – of him in the garden. Apparently, the tech stuff was already working.

Simon's message said that it all looked good and to just leave it to do its job. It also said he should stop picking his nose. Satisfied with his handiwork, he went in search of his errant cup then headed back inside. It turned out that his wasn't the only tea to have gone cold - Sarah's cup was still where he'd left it in the kitchen. He went looking for her, very conscious that he was probably being spied on in some manner, and found her upstairs. "What you doing, babe? Are you texting your mum?" he asked.

Sarah couldn't help but laugh.

"Oh," she said, going along with his narrative, "I'll do that in a minute, I'm just looking at videos of dogs being stupid." She was sitting on his side of the bed with the device pointing at the bedside lamp. As he came through the door she looked in his direction and raised her eyebrows and nodded towards the lamp.

"Your tea went cold," he said.

"Oh, well thanks anyway, hunnie."

He walked closer to her and looked at the screen on the device. "Oh," he said in mock surprise, "nice puppies."

She nudged him with her elbow.

"I'm going to go back downstairs, let me know when you've finished up here."

She looked at him with a big smile and winked, "Ok babe, I'll be down in a bit."

Fifteen minutes later she appeared in the living room.

"Come on, babe, I'll let you buy me a beer," she said.

Once in the car Sarah put the music on and tried to make sure it was at the normal volume. They chatted about nothing in particular and began to speculate as to who would be in the bar at this time of day.

"Do you want to stand at the bar, as usual, or shall we get a table?" asked David, once they'd walked through the door and were safely bathed in the background noise of the bar.

"Stand at the bar," she replied, "no need to break with tradition just because of these idiots."

David nodded; she was correct. If they started changing their behaviour, it might be obvious.

Once their beers had arrived, Sarah scanned the area around the bar for bugs. They stood in exactly the same spot that they usually did so she wouldn't have been surprised if she found something - but she didn't.

"Looks like we're clear," she said.

"How did you get on at the house, my guess is that it's not just the bedside lamp?"

"That's correct, it is not," she said, "There is another in the kitchen, one in the living room and one just inside the front door."

"Did you get a look at any of them?"

"The bedroom, living room and kitchen are microphones. The one near the front door I couldn't quite see properly. We might need to find an excuse to go up a ladder so we can get a better view."

"Nothing in the downstairs toilet or bathroom?"

"Not that I could find, but we can always do another sweep to make sure," she said.

"So, these plonkers have been in our house? Muppets."

" I would put it more strongly than that."

"But at least we know where they are, so it does give us some degree of control back."

"Yeah, I do feel a lot better, now that we know. How did you get on with the cameras outside?"

"It was quite straightforward, really. How do the kids call it - plug and pray? Anyway, it's all up and running. Now we just wait for results. I don't know about you, but I'm finding it quite difficult to act normally in front of the bugs." he said.

"I know. It makes it really awkward just to have a normal conversation. Maybe we will relax into it after a few days?"

It turned out that they didn't need a couple of days to help them relax about it, they needed a couple of beers. By the time David was halfway through his third beer he could feel his voyeur-induced stage fright turning into contempt.

"We still need to play it cool around them. I can just imagine us going home and you shouting at the microphones," said David.

"I know, right? Bunch of idiots. Who do they think they are breaking into our house and spying on us like that?"

"Maybe we should head back after this one? Did you say there weren't any bugs in the spare bedroom?" he asked.

Sarah shook her head. "Careful what you wish for mister."

24.

"How did you get on with your bug sweep?" asked Simon.

"Two in the van, two in the car and our in the house, one is a camera." said David.

"Well, at least now you know where you can and cannot talk. Don't forget to scan regularly, just in case any of them move while you're out."

"How would they mov……. Oh, I get it. In case someone goes into the house and moves them."

"Correct. It's a standard tactic, especially if they aren't hearing what they want to hear."

"We'd see that with the security cameras." Said David.

The instructor got louder and more excitable. Apparently, this was the bit where they were supposed to put more effort in. They paused their conversation while they kept up with the class.

It took a couple of minutes for David to get his breath, but Simon seemed unaffected by the strenuous exercise.

"You're not even out of breath." said David.

"No, not really. Back in my days in the regiment, we maintained a ridiculous level of fitness. We could have done two hours in here and then gone out for a run."

"Jesus, I'll never get anywhere near that."

"These days I just maintain my fitness level as *slightly crazy*, rather than *completely insane* as we used to. Sometimes, if I ever get a weekend off, I like to go running up in the mountains."

David could think of any number of things he could do with a weekend off, none of which involved running up a mountain.

"I've got some results for you from the house and car cameras," said Simon.

"Oh, right. Go on", David hadn't been expecting that.

"There's a strong possibility that the lady across the street from you is having an affair."

David raised his eyebrows and shook his head. Now that he thought about it, she did seem to enjoy a change. But that wasn't why the cameras were installed.

"Anything else interesting?" he asked.

"Oh, yes. Your house is being watched by two separate people, blue cars. They are probably working together because they never turn up at the same time."

"Christ, they're like crap in a field."

Simon liked the analogy and burst out laughing. David didn't think he'd ever seen Simon laugh properly before – human after all – who knew?

"So, what do we do with them, then?"

"Nothing at the moment. Just know that they are there and ignore them. We can't really do anything else because they will know that we are onto them."

David kept pedalling as he thought about how this all fitted together. It seemed like no aspect of his life was private anymore, and he wondered how long this might continue. He was either pandering to Squad and her team or being watched by … well, by whom exactly? Was there anyone else? The Russians perhaps? He needed a holiday.

"So, are those the people that broke in and installed the bugs in our house?"

"Maybe, maybe not. They are probably part of the same organisation and if anyone breaks in to move them, it'll be these guys."

"So, you reckon we're in danger of being broken into again?"

"Absolutely, to reposition the bugs, it's standard practice."

David imagined them gaining entry and placing the bugs around the house. How many times have they moved them already? Have they been searching for the murder bee while they were there? They obviously didn't find it, because it was still there - wasn't it? David suddenly realised that he hadn't actually opened the drawer for quite a while. And what would it mean if they found two instead of the one that they were expecting?

"That bug you brought around when you told me they were spying on you," said David.

"Yes...." Simon knew what was coming next.

"Was it really spying on you, or did you just pull it out of a drawer in your office?"

"Sorry......speaking of which, we need that one back. If you're in danger of being broken into then we need to make sure it doesn't fall into the wrong hands. Maybe you should find another home for yours too?"

Ha. If only, the damned thing flew off, probably back home to report into Klaus. David went quiet and nodded his head. This meant that Squad had been keeping an eye on them right from the beginning. Ever since Simon's original contact, they had been pumping him and Sarah for more information.

"Ok, I've got another class here on Thursday, I will bring ..."

"Thursday at 9:30."

David blinked. "Exactly. I'll bring your precious little bug then."

Simon smiled.

"But why are the British so interested in top-secret German technology? Surely, we're all on the same side, aren't we?" asked David.

There was a long pause before Simon answered. It was quite obvious that he was debating whether he should say anything, and if so then what.

"Let's continue this in the café after the class," said Simon.

They had never been to the café together before, but they were both very familiar with it individually. They found a table close to a rowdy bunch of Spaniards. With background noise like that, there was no way they could be overheard.

"This is supposed to be above my grade, and I am certain that you're not supposed to know."

"Ok," said David, impatiently ignoring Simon's misgivings.

"The supervisor of the group that developed article 79a has stolen it. All of it - the technology, the research, the weapons system itself – all of it. He is selling it to the Russians – and of course, we can't let them get hold of it and we'd quite like it for ourselves.

The rest of the research team seem to be dying, one by one. We assume this is to keep the sale secret and to make sure all of those involved stay anonymous. Another researcher that lives in Germany was killed a couple of weeks ago, so that's three."

"Right, I guess that does explain why the Brits are involved."

Simon had a quick look around the room to make sure they were not being overheard.

"Have you noticed that Klaus hasn't been killed?" said Simon.

He left the words hanging while David's brain processed the information. It took a few seconds, then David's eyes went wide and he looked straight at Simon.

"That took a moment," said Simon.

"He's the one who's spying on us. Christ, and we were round his house."

"Which is why we needed to bring you in and talk to you. You guys have got access to the German supervisor. That could be a great source of intelligence."

"Oh, great. So, this hole that I've dug just keeps getting deeper."

Maybe he could just give the bee back to Klaus? With both of the bees being back with their owners, surely that would be enough to put an end to this whole debacle.

Well, he knew that wasn't right. The bugs would be gone, but he himself would still be a security risk. He knew too much. In fact, now that he thought about it, that damned bee was the only thing keeping them alive. Keeping it secret was clearly worth a great deal to Klaus. All of the time that he had it, and Klaus couldn't find it, they'd be safe. Spied on and never really alone, but safe. As soon as Klaus got it back, they'd be dead within a day.

Simon couldn't help but smirk. This poor guy and his wife, a couple of house cleaners from a sleepy village in Mallorca - thrown into the middle of an international black-market arms deal, and the body count was rising.

25.

David tried to concentrate on the road, but it was a losing battle. The entire journey back from the gym was filled with planning the jobs he needed to get done and the short time he had available to do them.

His bee investigation project had suddenly gone from 'all the time in the world' to 'finished by Thursday'. At least that's how he saw it. Simon wanted his bee back immediately, so that would be the end of his opportunities to compare them side by side, and to test his theory that the parts were all interchangeable.

His sudden realisation that they were being watched had also complicated things. Their value as living people might cease if the bees' owners were to remove them from his possession, so he needed to hide his bee and any other evidence that might suggest it had ever been there. That included his Faraday cage, which he now had to build, use and dispose of in less than two days.

"Hi babe, I'm home," said David as he pushed the front door open. Sarah's bag and keys were in their usual place on the dresser, so she was around here somewhere. "Hello…?" He called.

"Oh, hi babe," Sarah called down from upstairs, "I've been changing the bedding. How was your spinning class?"

"It was a lot of blood, sweat and tears. The saddle has cut into my butt, legs have turned to jelly and I've probably lost a couple of litres of water."

"So, you enjoyed it then?" She asked as she bounced down the stairs and planted a big kiss on his lips. She threw her arms around him and immediately felt how wet his top still was from the profuse sweating. She instantly recoiled.

"Eww, that's disgusting. So, you didn't shower then?"

"Of course not, I couldn't wait to get back here and see you."

"Mmm. Nice try. The shower is up there," she said pointing upstairs, "off you go."

"Perhaps you'd like to join me?" he asked in a deadpan tone. His facial expression was blank, apart from single raised eyebrow. It took Sarah a moment - there were things that needed discussing.

In the bathroom, David got the shower going and put some music on the Bluetooth speaker. Sarah casually wandered into the room carrying the bug scanner and swept the room while being careful to look like she was texting or surfing.

"All clear," she whispered into David's ear, she closed the door and put the scanner next to the sink. "So, what's going on?"

"It looks like Klaus is the supervisor, the big boss of the murder bee project. It's him that has stolen it from the German government and is selling to the Russians. It looks like it is Klaus that is the one eliminating the members of his research team - but I suppose it could be the Russians. And it's him that's had these people spying on us."

"Oh my god, we were in his house the other day."

"Yes. And he's the one that arranged for us to go over and find the Schmidts."

"He did, didn't he? And in the process, he maintained his distance from the crime scene, while landing us in the crap."

"Exactly," David nodded, "and after we were arrested, we got out of the police station pretty quickly, with help from Simon and his team. Let's hope Klaus hasn't noticed how efficient the process was, or he might suspect we have friends in powerful places. I'd prefer to remain the image of the gullible cleaner who keeps finding bodies."

"But they actually didn't have any evidence that we had done anything, so they weren't going to be able to hold us for long anyway. We just got out a little quicker because of our new friends."

"I know," said David, "let's pretend the legal help came from Miguel and Angela, He's got contacts all over the police force, it would stand to reason that he has contacts in legal defence as well."

"That sounds good to me. That's our story and we're sticking to it." She paused for a moment weighing up the pros and cons of the story. They'd be able to sell that story to Klaus. "What else did you find out?"

"Um..... we have two cars that routinely park outside, where they sit and watch our house. They are both Seat Leons, both blue, but different number plates and different drivers."

"Little turds. So, it's not enough that they've bugged the van, the car and the house, they have to watch us too?"

"He said that these guys could break into the house, again, in order to reposition the bugs if they aren't getting a good signal, or whatever."

"What?"

"I guess they could follow us around too, with those people in the cars. Oh, and he wants his bee back. And we need to think about what we are doing with our bee - if it's still there, I haven't looked for a while."

"Too much, too fast." Even if he'd only told her half of that, it wouldn't have made much sense. None of this was.

It would take some time to process all of this new information. One step at a time, that's how she usually approached new problems. She would deal with all of these individual intrusions, one at a time, until she could begin to understand what it was all about. "Well, you can do your workshop stuff once you're done in here."

"I also thought that we might get away for a couple of days. Maybe to a hotel or a friend's flat. Somewhere where we can relax, knowing that there aren't any bugs around. I can see this thing was getting a bit too much for us to handle. A little break might help."

"It is too much," she said, "we are now effectively working for the British government, but without getting paid, while being spied on by some German arms dealer. You're damned right I need a holiday. I could do with the whole thing just stopping and going away." She blew out a long breath through pursed lips and took a few moments to think. "Ok, look. We are supposed to be cleaning a flat in Alcudia next week, it belongs to my mate Denise. I think it's just going to be empty for a few weeks after that, until the start of the tourist season. I'm sure she won't mind us saying there a couple of days, I'll give her a ring later."

"Brilliant. Well done babe, that sounds like just the thing."

"Did he say anything else?"

"Oh, well there is one more thing. You know our neighbour across the road, Antonia? We think she's having an affair."

Sarah rolled her eyes and shook her head, "I knew it, dirty little cow."

Sarah messaged Denise, while David took his much-needed shower, who was very happy to lend her flat to them and in return Sarah offering her cleaning services for free.

"Are we still going to the gym tomorrow morning?" Asked David, as he reached for his towel, "Your normal yoga class?"

"I thought," she paused for a moment catching up with David's train of thought - normal routine, "yes, of course. I'll book myself into the class now."

"How's Denise?"

"Oh, it's all sorted, tomorrow afternoon, so that's perfect."

26.

Simon's request – demand? – to return his bug left David with two days to investigate the bugs. He'd repeatedly been putting it off and now he was on a tight timetable.

He had built the desk-top Faraday cage over a week ago. It was a bit lop-sided and there wasn't a single straight line anywhere on it, but it worked. Crude but effective.

He did one last inspection of the cage. He'd spent weeks being afraid of what these bees were capable of doing. After all, they'd already killed four people.

He reminded himself that they were no longer prepared to be the scapegoats in this saga. They were no longer prepared to stand idly by while other people spied on them and even set them up as murderers. This marked the moment that they started to take back control of their lives. This bee was going to be part of the solution and no longer part of the problem.

He removed the pellet tin which contained his bee from the back of the drawer and placed it on the workbench, banging the drawer shut. He was in control this time, this little bee was not going to intimidate him any longer.

He removed the lid and tipped the contents of the tin out onto the bench. It skidded across the surface, coming to a rest on its back.

David placed the bee back onto its feet and waited to see if it would power up. It had been a long time since it would have been last charged and, after five minutes, the bee showed no signs of activity.

He could clearly see a retaining screw where the legs met under the thorax. He grabbed his screwdriver and rotated the screw 90° anticlockwise. As expected, bee fell into three lifeless parts on the bench, head, thorax and abdomen. The legs aligned under the wings. He'd been this far before.

Since his last inspection of the bug, he had managed to find a loupe in a second-hand shop, which would give him an extreme close-up view. He picked up the abdomen with his tweezers and examined it. It had two electrical contacts which seemed to align with two similar contacts on the back of the thorax. They'd seen these in the pictures before, but there also seemed to be similar contacts between the front of the thorax and the head.

They believed that the abdomen was probably a battery of some sort and the thorax the motor and maybe navigation section. He had speculated that there were different types of head. The previous bug that he had examined had been a killer. He now looked closer at this one.

It certainly looked different. It appeared to be a camera of some sort. The lens was quite small, about the same size as the one on his mobile phone. He imagined it would be very effective as a spying device. Being able to place a camera almost anywhere without it being noticed. It could sit for weeks gathering intelligence.

He grabbed Simon's bug from the drawer but was disappointed to see that it was of the same type, the head unit identical to the one he already had. He disassembled it anyway, but kept the parts separate. He methodically fitted different parts together from each of the bees. Having confirmed that all the parts were of a standard architecture, he replaced Simon's reassembled bee, made up of Simon's parts, back into its tin.

He moved on to the battery. The only thing he thought he knew about it was that the battery was probably flat. He had no idea what voltage it produced or would require in order to charge.

He was by no means an expert in electrics or electronics, but he knew not to zap it with too much voltage otherwise he might damage the battery or worse, cause a fire.

He started with a single AA battery which gave out 1.5 volts, and did precisely nothing. Joining two batteries to produce 3 volts resulted in a blue LED illuminating on the abdomen. Within 30 seconds, the LED had gone back off. Either the bee had finished charging or the batteries were flat. He figured it would be the latter and his voltmeter proved his hypothesis.

He gradually increased the voltage eventually ending up with one of the square 9-volt batteries which took a full minute to go flat. Having sacrificed his entire stock of 9-volt batteries he hoped that his efforts had resulted in at least a partial charge. He consigned both batteries to the growing recycling pile.

It wasn't ideal but a partial charge would likely be enough to wake the bug up. He hoped it wouldn't be enough to make it fully operational, but enough for him to learn more. He reassembled it and a few seconds later it vibrated for about 2 seconds. This time he was ready for it, and he didn't jump out of his skin. It then went quiet; David and the bug regarded each other.

David's phone pinged, which did make him jump. He cursed himself for not leaving his phone on silent, but then realised that he shouldn't be getting any signal inside the cage anyway.

He looked at his phone and saw that he had received a pairing request from a Bluetooth device. His eyebrows furrowed - there shouldn't be any signal inside the cage. David's eyes then moved from his phone back to the bug. Surely not. Was the bug asking to pair with his phone? He figured there was nothing to lose, so in the name of further research he accepted the pairing request.

His phone pinged again. He was almost afraid to look at the screen.

Input 12v

There was no way any exterior signals were getting in, this had to be the bee. Was it asking or telling?

The only 12 volt supply he had was his car battery. "Ok 12 volts it is, but I'm not stupid enough to take you to the battery, so the battery is going to have to come to you."

He left the bee on the work surface and took some spanners with him to the car. Five minutes later he was back with the battery which he hefted up onto the workbench.

"So how do I connect this battery to you?"

To David's surprise, it appeared to respond by attempting to fly up onto the battery. It almost made it, but then toppled onto the bench. He picked it up gently with his tweezers and placed it on top of the battery where it crept over to the positive terminal, placing its left rear foot on the terminal. "So you can charge through your feet? Of course you can. You don't want to be taken apart every time you need a top-up."

David grabbed a spare piece of wire and twisted one end around the negative terminal, leaving the other end close to the bug. David couldn't believe what was going on. They were communicating. Firstly, through its actions in order to get recharged but secondly, David realised, he had been talking to it. He was as certain that it didn't speak English as he was that he was being recorded. As he moved the free end of the wire near the bug, it lifted its right rear leg. Was this actually for real? This thing has asked him for power and once it that had been provided, it plugged itself in. The blue LED illuminated and it sat motionless.

David sat, mesmerised by the charging bug. He had completely lost track of time, but at some point Sarah stuck her head around the workshop door.

"Oh, there you are! I've been looking for you everywhere."

"Yeah, I'm in here. I've been having a look at our little friend."

"Oh, right. How are you getting on?"

"Um, well….. It asked me for 12 volts."

"It did what, are you crazy? It talked to you?"

"Not exactly. It sent a message asking for 12 volts."

Sarah cast an eye over his workbench. "And, by the looks of things, you have provided 12 volts."

"Well, yes."

"Oh great, and then once it's charged, is it going to bring all its friends over to kill us?"

"Oh babe, I've got no idea. I just thought we could learn more from a charged bee than a flat bee."

"Ok, Ok. Can it escape? I mean, it can't get a signal out, can it? But can it physically get out of that cage?"

"I don't think so, but you're right, I need to keep a close eye on it. It probably couldn't fly through the chicken wire, but I guess it could crawl."

"Maybe if we keep this door closed." She said, pulling it closed tight. "I'll see you later, when you're finished." She said through the door.

David and the bee looked at each other across the workbench. After about an hour of inaction while the bee was charging, David's boredom, thirst and numbness in his behind were getting the better of him. He stretched his arms over his head. And gave a long yawn. Perhaps a cup of coffee would perk him up.

He got up from his stool and made his way carefully out of the cage. The double door system had managed to contain mobile phone and radio signals during testing, so there was no reason to doubt it would work now. He made certain that both doors were closed before he headed towards the workshop door. Keeping his eye on the bee. He opened the door as little as was needed for him to slide out. He closed the door gently but firmly behind him.

It couldn't have taken him any more than a few minutes to make the coffee. He arrived at the workshop and entered through the door with one smooth action. Open, through and closed. He had even managed to avoid spilling his coffee, at least, up to the moment when he noticed the bee was missing.

"Holy crap!"

Within seconds he was inside the cage looking for the bee. It hadn't fallen off the battery, it hadn't managed to fall behind the bench, it wasn't crawling on the floor. David stood with his eyes closed. Gently shaking his head at his own stupidity. Even worse than losing the bee was the fact that, at some point, he was going to have to explain this to Sarah.

He slumped down onto his stool and thumped his coffee cup down on the bench. What an idiot. Ok, so it could probably crawl out of the Faraday cage, but he couldn't really see anywhere that it could have gotten out of the workshop. After taking a slurp of his coffee, he went out of the cage and started looking around the rest of the room. After a few minutes his panicked, frantic search began to slow into a more logical considered approach.

He realised it was broad daylight outside, but in the workshop the lights were on. Maybe if he made it dark in here the bright daylight might show him the point of escape. He flicked the switch casting the room into sudden darkness. And there, under the door, the daylight shone in through a half inch gap. More than big enough for a bee to creep under.

So that was it, the bee had escaped and would surely report back to base on where it had been and with whom. All of his planning, effort and research wasted.

27.

On Thursday David was up bright and early, eager to get to the gym and give Simon his bee. He also decided not to tell Simon about his little escapologist. Once that was done, he hoped that he'd feel a little more free of everything that had been going on. On the way, David dropped the remains of the Faraday cage off at the local recycling point, before carrying on to the gym. Simon took the bee, but David couldn't be bothered to do his usual spinning class. He had a coffee in the café and went home.

That afternoon Sarah and David dumped their overnight bags in the bedroom of a client's apartment in Alcudia. It wasn't in an ideal location, but it didn't really matter. It was quiet at this time of year and that was what they needed. In a couple of months, it would be full of drunken Brits with sunburn and unfortunate clothing choices. But that would be then.

"Wow. This apartment is beautiful," said Sarah, "I'd always thought this part of the island was a bit trashy."

"Look at this view over the bay," said David, opening the blinds, "loads of other buildings in the way, but I can see over them."

Sarah began sweeping the apartment for bugs, as David began unpacking his overnight bag. He brought the essentials: a bottle of red and a bottle of white - which he put straight in the fridge - and went on the hunt for glasses.

"All clear, honey," said Sarah, "now we can finally relax."

David returned from the kitchen brandishing two small glass jars of herbs.

"I found these bugs in the kitchen," he said, placing one on the coffee table in front of the sofa.

"Really? I thought we were here to relax and get away from this crap?"

"We are, but I thought we practice in a safe environment,"

"There's no escape, is there?" Asked Sarah, "And I'm not sure if I'm escaping from them or from you. Where are you putting the other herb jar?"

"Maybe on the little table near the front door?"

"Good idea," said Sarah, "you do that, I'm going to lie down in the bedroom."

"Why don't we start our mini holiday with a walk on the beach and maybe a drink or two?" David suggested. There was no reply, so he stuck his head around the bedroom door. She was fast asleep with her mobile phone in her hand. David crept into the room. He teased the phone from her fingers and placed it on the bedside cabinet.

He retreated from the bedroom and decided to sit on the balcony overlooking the bay. The view out into the distance, where the sea met the sky was mesmerizing. He found himself lost in a cloud of memories. Old friends, old colleagues, family he hasn't seen in a long time. He always found that looking out to sea somehow pulled memories from deep within him that had become covered over time.

David had no idea how long his memories had held him captive, but the shrill blast of a car horn brought him back to the present with a jolt. He checked his watch, but then realised he didn't know what time he came out here or what time Sarah had fallen asleep.

He extracted his phone from his pocket and began surfing social media. He scrolled through a few posts, but he didn't find anything interesting to explore. He put his phone down on the side table and made himself comfortable in the reclining chair. Within moments he was drifting off to sleep.

Sarah came around from her slumber and checked the time. She figured she had been asleep for 45 minutes or so. She grabbed her phone and sprung out of bed, expecting that David would either be at a local bar or halfway through a bottle of wine, giving him an unfair head start. As she came into the living room she could see him through the window, fast asleep on the balcony.

She decided to let him wake up in his own time, and within moments had found where David had put the red wine. After a quick look through the drawers in the kitchen she found the corkscrew and set about opening the bottle. She extracted the cork with a pop, which seemed to rouse David from his slumber. She pulled two generous glasses and took them out to the balcony.

"Hey babe," she said," have you been asleep too?"

"I guess so, I must have drifted off. Thanks babe," he said as Sarah handed him his glass of wine. "This view of the bay is so beautiful; we should see if we can borrow this apartment more often." She leant on the handrail, looking out at the view of the town and the bay beyond. He looked over at her, raising his glass.

"Cheers," he said, but Sarah wasn't listening, her attention was somewhere else. She was now looking down at the road outside the apartment.

"Isn't that one of those damned cars that sit outside our house?" She asked.

"Where?" asked David, getting up out of his chair and looking down at the street. Sarah pointed at a dark blue Seat Leon parked opposite, with the driver at the wheel. David took a long slurp from his glass.

"It does look like the same car," he said, "but we'll need to see the reg number to make sure."

Sarah had pulled out her phone and was scrolling through images from the surveillance system results. She found an image of a Seat Leon and showed it to David.

"This is one of the cars from the surveillance system." The image and the number plate were very clear.

"I've got an idea," said David. "How about we finish this wine then get freshened up? We can head over to that little Irish pub that we went to last year."

It took her a moment to remember where the bar was. Sarah cast her gaze around streets and walkways in front of the hotel, imagining what route she would take to get there. A moment later she knew what David was talking about. The best route to the bar involved walking straight past the surveillance car.

"I could do with a nice pint of Guinness," she said, giving him a knowing nod.

"Thought you would."

Ten minutes later they were strolling out of the front door of the building. They held hands and boldly strode across the road in front of the car, deliberately making a show of it for the benefit of the driver. It took all the will in the world for them to avoid looking directly at the driver, but they steeled themselves and carried on. David let go of her hand and gave her a pat on the bum.

"Come on chica, I'll let you buy me a beer."

"I'll let you buy *me* a beer, Mister."

It was literally 100m to the bar, just around the corner and out of sight of the surveillance car. Having ordered two pints of Guinness, they found a table and waited for the barman to bring the Guinness when it was ready.

"Come on then, let's have a look at the footage," said Sarah, impatiently.

He played the video and she watched. "Come on chica, I'll let you buy me a beer." And right there was a crystal-clear shot of the number plate. He paused.

"There you go, clear as day." he said.

Sarah placed her phone next to his with the image from the surveillance system at their house.

"Same car. Little tosser."

"So how have they managed to find us so quickly? Maybe those bugs in the car have locator beacons?"

"That must be it," she said, "either that or they overheard us in the shower, which I doubt. Or maybe they followed us."

The Guinness arrived at the table which, unusually for Mallorca, had been poured perfectly.

"Thank you mate," said David.

"You're very welcome guys, enjoy." Said the very English barman.

Sarah waited for him to get out of earshot, "so what do we do now?"

That was a very good question, to which neither of them had an immediate answer.

"We drink Guinness. We'll will think of something."

Sarah was about halfway down her pint when David saw her eyes go wide. She put her pint down a little more forcibly than intended and pointed at their phones on the table in front of them. David knew exactly what she meant straight away. He had been thinking about the bugs in the car, conversations being overheard and what other common denominators were present.

"You enjoying your pint honey?" He asked.

"Yes I am, thank you," she said circling the two phones with her index finger.

"Oh, I see what you mean, you're going to need another pint soon."

He got up, grabbing his pint, and began walking towards the bar, beckoning her to follow. She arrived next to him and they propped that bar up together.

"I wondered what you were on about then," she said.

"Yeah, sorry, but I think we were both thinking along the same lines. I wanted to get you away from the phones so we could talk about it."

"So, what do you think it is about the phones then?"

"Well. They have GPS,"

"They've been hacked? What else, intercepted messages and phone calls?"

"There's that, and also they have microphones. Actually, they're pretty perfect, when you think about it."

"Those little gits. I'm going to go around to that car smash his windscreen."

"Babe, keep calm. Let's think about it over another pint."

"Excuse me mate," Sarah half shouted across the bar, "can we have two more?"

"Of course, love. I'll bring it over to your table."

"Can we have them up here at the bar, mate?"

"Yep."

Sarah went back to the table and put the two phones into her bag, which she brought over and placed on the bar right next to a speaker. It was playing background music, but it would be loud enough to drown out their conversation.

"I've got an idea," said David, "there's got to be a mobile phone shop around here where we can get a disposable mobile phone."

"At least then we'd be able to call people without being overheard or followed."

"Exactly. We have plenty of clients around Alcudia. One of them has got to have a flat going spare for a few days?"

"Yes. Emily has got one, we were supposed to clean it on the same day as Denise's flat."

"Right. I'm going to go and get a phone now."

David pecked her on the cheek and hurried out of the door. While he was gone. Sarah got her phone out of her bag and opened her contacts list. She was part way through scrolling down to Emily's name when she realised that all of her actions on the phone were potentially being watched. She realised that she couldn't just look up Emily's number, she'd need to look at quite a few in order to hide Emily's number among useless data.

She found a pen and something to write on in her bag, then perused the contacts list, randomly clicking on names then counting to fifteen in her head. She thought that should be enough time to write a phone number down. Having looked at several random people, she clicked on Emily's name and wrote her phone number down. Sarah kept looking at other contacts from the list, continuing to cover her tracks.

An alert came up on her screen. She recognised the symbol but couldn't place it immediately. She clicked on it anyway. It opened up a new window where she could see a video of the front of their house. She could see a man entering the front gate and walking towards the front door. She shook her head in disbelief. She could feel anger rising but then had a light bulb moment.

She opened the app for the alarm system on her phone and watched expectantly as the alarm system was disabled. The status on the app clearly changed from armed to disarmed. *Little shit.*

By the time David returned she had packed her phone away again and was halfway through her second pint. He placed the new phone on the bar in front of her with a beaming grin. She showed him the phone number.

"Our friends are in our house," she said in a matter-of-fact tone. Guinness was beginning to have the desired effect, She was beginning to care less about the idiots watching them.

"Didn't take the bastards long," he said," I guess the guy here gave them confirmation that we were at a safe distance."

David had been fully expecting that they would be going into the house. They'd be moving there surveillance devices around or maybe adding more. He wondered how long they would spend looking for the murder bees.

"We should run a sweepstake on where they're going to move their bugs to. I reckon the camera will be watching the bed in the spare room."

She shook her head, nudged him with her elbow then showed him her scrap of paper.

"Well you get on with that," he said indicating the phone and phone number, "I've got a job to do,"

He lifted the pint to his lips and took a deep gulp. Sarah went outside to call Emily, leaving her bag and its contents behind with David.

He'd barely had time for a couple of sips when Sarah bounced back into the bar grinning with victory.

"Anytime we like," she whispered in his ear, "there's a key safe outside the door and I have the code."

"Perfect."

They both looked at her bag, wondering what to do with the contents. They spent a little while making sure they'd drained their glasses of their ridiculously expensive contents. David picked up Sarah's bag and handed it to her. As she took it, he paused and deliberately aimed his voice at the bag.

"Back to the room for a quickie then?"

"Oh my god," She was actually speechless for a moment, " I can't take you anywhere."

28.

About half an hour later they entered the code into the key safe and walked into the flat. The layout was almost identical to Denise's.

"Are you going to put pretend bugs out here too?" She asked.

"Not this time babe, I'm done."

They had left her bag and the two phones at Denise's flat. They'd packed as light as possible for their one night of freedom - wash bag and wine – which Sarah poured while David ensured the blinds were closed. They put the TV on, but didn't really care what they watched. As long as it provided some distraction from recent events.

At some point, David snuck out onto the balcony and had a quick look around to see if they were being watched. He couldn't see the Seat, but that didn't mean there weren't other cars.

"Anything interesting out there?" Asked Sarah as he sat back down on the sofa.

"Not that I can see, we might actually have given them the slip."

"Well, we can have a peaceful night here, but we'll have to go back to the other flat and pretend everything is normal tomorrow, otherwise they'll know we are on to them."

The idea didn't really fill David with enthusiasm, but he knew that she was right.

The next morning they snuck into Denise's flat - It was probably paranoia, but as they looked around the flat they got the feeling that some things might have moved. Had somebody else been in there?

"Oh, there's my bag!" said Sarah with enthusiastic fake excitement, "I must have left it here last night."

"Actually, I found it quite refreshing having an evening interacting with people rather than phones."

Sarah pulled both phones out of the bag, neither of which had enough power to make it through the night. She put both phones on charge in the bedroom then closed the door before heading to the kitchen where David was making coffee.

As they sipped their drinks out on the balcony in the cool morning air David's attention was again drawn to the view out to the horizon. Sarah couldn't help but watch for visitors, and it didn't take long either. She had finished her cup and was just about to find somewhere to put it down when she noticed the blue Seat Leon come around the corner at the end of the street.

"Looks like your mate is back," she said quietly without looking at David.

"When will the fun ever stop?" He dead panned without moving his gaze from the sea.

The angle at which his cup was hanging from his finger suggested it too was empty.

"Do you want another coffee?" Asked Sarah.

"Go on then," he said, handing the cup to her.

When she returned with the coffees he was still staring out to sea.

"That view has really got you, hasn't it?"

"Yeah, something about the sea. Don't know. It's completely timeless. It's like the view gives you access to the whole world, the past, everything."

"Maybe you should write a song about it,"

David turned and looked at her as he took his cup out of her hand. "That's exactly it. You should have brought my guitar."

"Well, there's nothing stopping you. This place is probably available until Easter. All we have to do is cross Denise's palm with multi-surface cleaner."

"I could just sneak in anyway, she'll never know."

"But that's not how friends behave is it?"

"No, you're right. Speaking of breaking and entering, when do you want to head back to our house?"

"Well, we might as well get it over with. The cameras only showed us what was going on in the garden, but I'm assuming that they've been back inside."

"That's what I'm assuming too, but I'm prepared to be pleasantly surprised."

29.

Their heart rates were already beginning to rise as David eased the car up onto the driveway. As he brought it to a gentle halt, he saw that Sarah's eyes were wide and she was breathing harder then usual. He grabbed the bags from the boot as Sarah closed the gate across the driveway. David could feel his adrenaline level increasing too as they approached the front door together.

David grabbed the key from his pocket and inserted it into the lock. He eased the front door open and stepped inside to disarm the alarm. Sarah held the door open and immediately spotted some white powder on the floor. She'd never seen white powder there before. Leaves, dirt, even squished olives from their tree outside, she had cleaned all kinds of crap off of that floor over the years, but not while powder.

She had mopped that floor yesterday before they went out, so she knew immediately that it was the result of their visitors. The powder had to be plaster or paint from above the front door. Someone had moved the covert camera.

She grabbed David's attention and looked up indicating the prior location of the bug. David gave a slow, knowing nod.

Strangely, knowing that they had been in the house seemed to diffuse the tension. There was no longer the unknown of what might be. They had thought that these idiots would come into the house while they were away, and that's exactly what happened. Sarah felt that being able to predict the actions of their observers almost gave her a level of control over the situation.

"Well it was lovely to catch up with your friends last night," Sarah deliberately boomed across the room.

"Yeah... it was good fun, wasn't it?" Said David, reintroducing himself to the concept of being on stage in his own house.

"Man, those guys are really good fun. I can't believe we've left it so long. We'll have to do it again soon." Sarah pulled the bug scanner out of her bag and began sweeping the hall on her way to the kitchen.

"Cup of tea?" She asked.

"Please, babe."

David went upstairs and unpacked his wash bag. It was quite subtle, and if he hadn't been paying attention he wouldn't have noticed, but things had moved in the bathroom. There were a couple of drawers under the wash basin. He opened the top drawer where they kept what they called 'midnight medicines' - headache tablets. The contents were sort of in their normal places, but someone had gone through this drawer looking for something.

It was the same in the bedroom. In his sock drawer David noted that, while his socks were paired and folded as they should be, they were not facing in the correct direction. He wasn't quite OCD, but he was close on some items. He didn't have control of most aspects of his life, but sock direction was his domain.

And again in his underwear drawer. They were supposed to be in colour and frequency-of-use order. Everyday pants at the front, the posh ones that Sarah liked - for special occasions - further towards the rear. David shuddered at the thought of one of these greasy little pricks going through his underwear drawer. Then he remembered that they'd probably gone through Sarah's underwear drawer as well. Eww, gross.

Having thought about it, David decided not to tell Sarah about the drawers in the bedroom. If she noticed, she noticed. But if he could avoid putting her through the emotion and weirdness of some random bloke going through her underwear, then he would.

He didn't need to inspect the drawer in the workshop. He already knew that would be empty.

Back downstairs the kettle had boiled and David made the tea while Sarah continued her sweep of the house. As she came into the kitchen she was putting the bug detector back into her bag. She approached David arms out stretched and wrapped them around his waist, pulling him in for a cuddle.

"The camera is now in the smoke detector in the living room," she whispered close to David's ear, "bedroom the same place as before, microphone under the tea and coffee cupboard behind me."

"Oh, that's a shame, I thought I'd pulled there for a moment," David whispered back, kissing her ear.

"You want to do it here? Where you know they're listening?" She had to admit she found the idea quite exciting, but hoped she was calling his bluff. She hadn't really thought about it before, but they probably got up to all sorts before they became aware of the bugs.

"Well, if you play your cards right,"

"Mmm. We'll see. We've got a busy afternoon - two houses in Inca." She said.

"Really? Oh, I guess we do."

They were wandering around the supermarket near their gym having left their mobile phones in the car.

"Have you noticed that our friends outside the gate have a semi-regular pattern?" Asked Sarah.

"I thought they might," said David," but I knew you had been keeping a closer eye on their timekeeping."

"And I have. It's the same car every morning. He turns up just after 7 and leaves around 10. The other car is there from 4:00 till 8:00 p.m."

"So, what's that all about then?"

"I think those are the times when we are usually coming and going from the house. They can already see and hear us in the house, so I don't really understand why they need to see us walking to and from the van."

"Maybe he can't get enough of you," said David.

"Or maybe he can't get enough of you," she retorted.

"The thing is, there's not enough information to make an educated guess."

"So we need to get more … " Sarah suddenly twigged where he was going with this idea.

"Wait, no, not again. Don't you think we've poked at the hornet's nest enough?"

"Last time you did something like that you caught a bee, and Klaus has been watching us ever since."

"I'm not suggesting we do anything too drastic, but I don't like feeling that we are on the back foot. What if there was a way of following these idiots back to wherever they go after they finish spying on us?"

Sarah paused, facing him, looking up at the sky for inspiration as if caught in the middle of her longest ever eye roll.

"So, I take it you don't approve?" Asked David.

"You're damned right I don't approve. These idiots are already making my life hell and the last thing I need is to provoke them and make the situation worse."

"I know, babe, but they already break into our house anyway. Last time they had a good search around as well. It just seems like we are sitting here and letting them do it to us. I just want to do something. "

"They had a good search around? And exactly what were they looking for, that stupid bee of yours?"

"Well yes probably, but they didn't find it."

"Yes, because it's already escaped. Oh my god. You're absolutely impossible." Sarah paused for a moment to try to understand David's logic. "Ok, so once you've followed these idiots back to their secret spy office, or wherever they go, then what are you going to do? Break in?"

"No, nothing like that, well I haven't really thought it through that far. It's just for information, I suppose. Maybe we could tell Simon or Squad, or just file the information for future use."

"Squad." Sarah almost spat the name out. "Ok, I do agree that knowledge is power. The more we understand about these people watching us, the more in control I feel. So let's say, theoretically, that I'm on board with this. How do we make this idea work?"

"Well," said David, knowing that this could be a hard sell, "Emily has a car."

"What?"

"Our friend, Emily. She has a car in the garage under her flat. It could probably do with a short run to charge the battery."

Sarah shook her head again. If she could just go back to England and stay with her mum for a while. Maybe all of this crap would go away.

"So how's that conversation going to go? 'Oh, hi Emily. We've got some crap going on in our lives and we need to go on a secret spy mission. Can we borrow your car?'."

"You don't need to word it quite like that," said David.

"Oh, Ok. How would you word it?"

"Well, we don't have to ask. We could just *borrow* the car."

"You mean steal it?"

"That's a bit harsh, isn't it?"

"I don't think so. If this idiot idea of yours goes wrong, as everything else seems to be at the moment, then you'll need to explain it to the police. And you know what they call borrowing without permission, don't you?"

David had to concede, she did have a point. If he did get stopped, for whatever reason, he'd have a hard time explaining.

In the back of her mind, Sarah thought she remembered that Emily kept the car for her customers to use while they rented her flat. David didn't seem to need any further encouragement, so she decided to keep the idea to herself until she could dig into it a bit more. She had to be in the same area as Emily's flat tomorrow for work. She'd pop into the flat and see if she could find out about the car. Whatever she found out, she'd let David stew for a few days.

"Ok, Dave. Why don't we say that we're going to think about it for the moment?"

"Yeah, of course. I wasn't suggesting we do it today or tomorrow. Just an idea. Get one over on these idiots."

"I know, they piss me off too."

"I just want to go out there and punch one of them." He said.

"I have to stop myself from smacking one of them every day."

Sarah entered the code into the key safe outside Emily's flat. She inserted the key into the lock and eased the door open. There was nobody in the flat and it was still tidy, just as they left it. This was what she expected to see, but these days you could never be sure.

She seemed to remember that the visitor's information pack was in the first drawer as you entered the kitchen. She slid it open revealing an A4 folder inside.

Having flicked through a few pages of *Welcome to my flat* blurb, she landed on the page regarding the car. Apparently, the car was insured for anybody to drive, as long as they had the owner's permission. Inside the glove box was a letter confirming that the driver had permission to borrow the car, along with all of Emily's insurance and identification information.

Well, technically she had given them permission to stay at the flat...... so it wasn't too much of a stretch for that permission to include the car, was it?

David had smartened himself up as he usually did for a night out. He was patiently waiting in the living room. Sipping a glass of water when he heard Sarah coming downstairs.
"Wow," he said, and wolf-whistled as she walked into the room. "I'd better watch my step tonight, I reckon I'm going to have some competition."

She'd really gone to town on her look for the evening, dressed to kill from head to toe. This either meant she was in a good mood and was feeling bright and confident, or it meant he was in serious trouble. There was no way of knowing which.

"Evening sexy," she said as she came over and air kissed him, so as not to mess up her makeup. "Where do you want to go tonight?"

"One of the wine bars in Inca or maybe over to that place you like over in Santa Maria?"

"Oh, Inca. I'm guessing neither of us wants to drive home and a taxi from Santa Maria will be impossible."

"Inca it is, madam. Your carriage awaits," he said, showing her the way to the door with his left arm.

Once in the wine bar they left their phones in Sarah's bag, with his phone gently serenading her phone with some rock and roll. Having said the usual hellos to the staff and some of the regular punters, Sarah chose a table. After a few minutes the waiter came over and Sarah pushed the boat out a little more than usual and ordered a nicer bottle of red and two glasses.

David knew his days were numbered. She was dressed to the nines. She'd picked the bar, table and the wine; he knew it was only a matter of time before she verbally smashed his face in.

Once she was getting towards the end of her second glass of wine, David hoped she would be more suggestible. If he was going to bring the subject up, now would be the time, but he just couldn't start the conversation that would kill their evening.

As David topped up her glass, Sarah figured she had let him simmer for long enough.

"So, I had a look over the guest information pack in Emily's flat." She left the sentence hanging in the air.

"Ok?" he inquired.

"It clearly states that the car is insured for anyone to drive provided they have the permission of the owner. The car is for people staying at the flat and, technically, we have stayed at the flat."

This was going smoothly, suspiciously so. David wasn't sure if she was being genuine or leading him into a bigger trap.

"So, are we saying that I can borrow her car and do some investigating, as long as I'm not a complete pillock?"

"Ok, do some investigating. The more information we've got, the stronger position we are in. But I want you to go softly, softly. We don't want to dig this hole any deeper than it already is."

"I promise, babe, I'll take it easy. You're right, if I get seen then the whole game changes."

"Yes, it does, and I already don't like the game as it is. Look, we are supposed to be cleaning a flat near Emily's on Monday morning. Why don't we go over there in separate cars, then you can park up at hers and borrow her car?"

On Monday evening around 7:30 pm, David pulled up at the side of the road in a 20-year-old Opal Corsa. It had squeaked, rattled and complained the whole way back from Emily's flat. He got out to stretch his legs and admire the bodywork. The thing was covered in dents and scrapes from front to back. At no point was there any more than a hand span between battle scars. But, despite its appearance, it started, drove and stopped. It was the perfect camouflage for the streets of Mallorca.

He had parked it up about five minutes walk from home on the route that, he assumed, the spy cars were taking out of the village. Sarah had driven back to the house earlier, taking both their phones, so he had been without internet based entertainment for several hours. Normally, he'd be bored without his media feeds, but the anticipation of playing them at their own game kept him alert. He got back in and waited. Patiently. With no phone or radio.

At about quarter to 8:00, a blue Seat Leon rounded the corner behind him. He recognised it instantly. He'd spent enough time looking at it from the garden, the bedroom and on CCTV. He checked his watch.

"Pedro's early," he said to himself.

He turned the key and the engine started first time, luckily. He let it get a little way ahead before pulling away. Turning out of the village and onto the main road he had to wait for a couple of cars before proceeding. His target was now a good hundred meters ahead and David felt confident that he wouldn't be spotted. Everything was going to plan.

Initially David assumed they were heading towards the motorway, but before getting that far the target vehicle turned right on the old main highway towards Binissalem.

"Uh oh, I wonder where we're going?"

Klaus and Anna Faber's house was in Binissalem. David figured it wasn't a coincidence. He began to hang back even further, thinking that he knew where the blue car was going. It didn't disappoint. Within five minutes it pulled up outside the Farber's house. The driver got out and walked up to the front door. He was obviously expected as the front door opened before he could get to it.

David had expected it would be Klaus greeting the spy, but to his surprise it wasn't. Even at this distance David could clearly see Klaus' wife Anna greeting the driver and ushering him inside.

So, it wasn't just Klaus, Anna was also a fully paid-up member of this conspiracy. David had no way of knowing whether this guy meeting Anna without Klaus was significant, or not. Maybe she was going behind his back. Maybe it was just regular business. Anyway, just because

Klaus' BMW wasn't there didn't mean that Klaus wasn't there.

He had a sudden attack of paranoia and moved the car further up the road. Having made sure that he could see their front door, he slid down in the driver's seat, hoping it would make him invisible.

After about half an hour the same man appeared out of the front door and was waved off by Anna. He got back into his car and drove away. David followed, keeping a safe distance so as to ensure that he continued to go unnoticed. Fifteen minutes later the car pulled up outside some non-descript flats in Santa Maria and the man went in. Two hours later, nothing had changed. Eventually, David crossed his boredom threshold and went home.

30.

David looked at the display on his phone then waved to attract Sarah's attention.

"It's Klaus," he said, raising his eyebrows.

"Oh god, well, good luck."

He pressed answer and raised the phone to his ear.

"Good morning, Klaus."

"Good morning David, well are you well?"

"We are both very well, thank you." *Very well, despite your attempts to get us arrested.* "How can I help you today?"

"I've just got word from my friend Kristoff. He used to work on article 79a with me. He's coming over to Mallorca with his wife, Lina. I think they would have liked to buy a house here, but they have too many toys keeping them in Germany. They usually come over about this time of year."

"Oh, that's great." David replied, mostly for Sarah's benefit. "They're coming over for a holiday?"

"Yes, they usually rent a villa near Port d'Andratx. They also have Johann and Amelia Maya joining them. Johann used to work on the project as well."

Let me guess you want to set Sarah and me up as fall guys at a murder scene, again?

"Are they aware of what's been going on with Gunther and Helmut?"

"I'm not sure," said Klaus, "somebody does need to tell them."

"Perhaps you could pop over and see them? It sounds like they're having a bit of a company reunion?" David suggested, already knowing what was coming next.

"Well I'd really like to, and I know it would be good fun but, unfortunately, I need to go back to Germany for a couple of weeks. I don't think I'll have the time."

"Maybe Anna then?"

"Well, of course she's coming with me." Klaus chuckled.

"Well, of course." David let the moment hang in the air for longer than seemed comfortable. "Maybe Sarah and I could go over?"

Sarah mouthed an obscenity at him.

"Well, that's a great idea David. I understand they're planning a pool party and barbecue. Maybe that would be a good time to talk to them?"

Good time to talk to them? It's like we will all be standing in the same killing-field together. Sounds ideal. For you.

"That's a good idea. We do like a party."

"I'll find out when the pool party will be, and I will let you know."

"Ok, great. Call me or send a text."

"Ok, great. Thanks David. See you soon."

"Ok, bye."

"Please tell me you didn't just arrange a time and date for our own murder." Demanded an exasperated Sarah.

David pressed his finger to his lips and looked around the room reminding her that the walls have ears.

"It's going to be a lovely barbecue, sure. We'll make all sorts of new friends."

Sarah sliced her index finger across her throat simulating a knife.

"Oh, come on honey, it'll be fun." he said.

Two days later they were working at a flat in Inca when Sarah received a text message from Anna:

Kristoff and Lina Schneider and their friends, Johann and Amelia Meier, are arriving on the 15th of April. Pool Party is on the 22nd starting at 4:00 pm. They are expecting you. I've told them all about you. Dress for swimming even if you are not.

Ok, thank you Anna.

"Are we actually going to this party?" Asked Sarah.

"Somebody needs to tell them what's going on, preferably before they are dead. I'm not really that enthralled at the prospect either. We can always back out of the whole thing and just let them get killed."

"Well, you know we can't do that. If we just let it happen then we are as bad as Klaus and his friends."

Sarah thought about the situation for a few moments. What they needed was some fresh ideas about how to deal with the situation. If the two of them walked into that party surely it would be just like sending lambs to the slaughter?

"Maybe we need to call Simon?" She suggested.

"Yes. That's exactly what we need to do, we need to get that gang involved. In fact, I'm a little disappointed they haven't been keeping in touch. We are doing the dirty work for free, after all."

On the way home David dropped Sarah off at a cyber café while he headed to one of their regular bars with both of their mobile phones.

He was just in the middle of ordering his second beer when Sarah walked in, and he changed his order to two.

"It's all arranged, 5pm, Lloseta. Train station," she whispered in his ear.

"You or me or both?"

"Either. I don't suppose it really matters. Maybe just you then. They didn't say who they'd send, but if it is Simon you can have a catch up and pretend to watch football."

31.

Sarah dropped David off near the station in Lloseta. As was the local custom, she stopped the car so that it was blocking pedestrian crossing. It wasn't the only available space, but it made the stopping and pulling away easier. She had always assumed that actually parking on pedestrian crossings had a negative impact on road safety but, when in Rome …

David strolled under the shade of the trees. He was certain there was a local name for them, but to him they had always been London Planes, with their flaky bark. Springs warm kiss welcomed those who sauntered away from the direct heat of the sun.

He walked up the pedestrianised thoroughfare which served as the village's High Street. All of the essential services were available there. The bank, the tobacconist, estate agent, jeweller, one barber for the men, and two hairdressers for the ladies.

Two bars stood like gatekeepers, one at each end of the street. The whole street was in permanent shade, except for one hour around lunch time. The ideal place for local sun-dodgers to gather like partial vampires; able to come out during the day provided they avoided direct exposure.

The embrace of cool air conditioning greeted David as he entered the mini supermarket. His customary lap in search of inspiration was interrupted by a small bottle of chilled water, the actual reason for his visit. At the checkout he spoke to the girl in Spanish while she replied in English. It seemed that, at least here in the village, anyone who'd attended college within the last five years was keen to practice their English, while older generations stubbornly refuted its existence.

David leant against a shade bathed wall opposite the station and sipped his water. He surveyed the area for any suspicious looking cars or people that might be watching him. He glanced at his watch.

The arrival of the train was foretold by vibrations and sounds transmitted along the rails and overhead power lines, and with a fanfare of automated whistles breaking the quiet of the otherwise sleepy village.

He was easy to pick out in the crowd. The taller and lighter-coloured male wearing a Barcelona football top contrasted against the melee of shorter, darker locals all of which seemed to support Real Madrid.

Simon was always intrigued by the automatically folding rear view mirror that stuck out of the driver's cabin. Why did it need to fold? Was space really at that much of a premium on these narrow gauge Mallorcan railways that an extra 20 cm of mirror would need to be tucked in whilst on the move? Perhaps it was for aerodynamic reasons. Perhaps it was a safety concern.

Either way, Simon was pretty sure that whatever effect the mirror had would be minor compared to the bulk of the train to which it was attached.

As he made his way towards the ticket barrier the train's automatic whistle blasted in his ear. Every damned time. Mental note - travel on the last carriage next time. That way the driver could blast his whistle while Simon was still walking up along the platform at a safe distance.

Having negotiated the electronic-but-ultimately-inefficient ticket barrier Simon made his way across the tracks towards the village.

David timed his crossing of the road to coincide with Simon's arrival.

"Hello mate, how are you?" asked Simon.

"Good, thank you. How are you?"

David fell into step beside Simon. They made small talk about the weather and such things, while they walked through the busier part of the village. Simon was on the lookout for suspicious people and vehicles, David's main concern was spotting dog eggs before they became a hazard underfoot.

"What have you been up to?" David asked.

"I've been on a short holiday back to England. Good to catch up with old friends. What have you been up to?"

"We found out that they can track our phones and probably use them to listen in on us."

"Interesting."

"I didn't think it was interesting, it really annoyed me. We had gone way for the night, to get a break from them bugging the house, and hey presto, there's a blue car outside the hotel." David didn't feel he need to give Simon the whole truth. There was still no way of knowing if this guy could be trusted. He felt better about keeping their supply of alternate accommodation to himself, at least for the moment.

"But, now that you know, you can decide what you're going to tell them, and what you're keeping to yourselves."

"True. And we have already been doing that."

"Have they been back in your house again?"

"They have. They went through everything."

"Did they find what they were looking for?"

"No. That's hidden somewhere else. Nice and safe."

"Good man. You hid the faraday cage too, that might be a giveaway?"

"Long gone. In a bin near the gym. As far as I know they never saw it. Well, it only existed for about 3 days."

"Anything else?"

"Well. Sarah really didn't like me doing this, but I kind of borrowed a car and followed one of the guys from outside our house."

"Oh, really?"

"Followed him back to Binissalem, where he met with Anna Farber."

"Where did he go after that?"

"Dunno, I chickened out and went home."

"You've been a busy little ... bee ... haven't you?"

"Then we got a phone call from Klaus. The remaining members of his team are coming to the island for a holiday. They have rented a villa near Port d'Andratx and are having a pool party on the 22nd. We both agreed that it sounds like an ideal opportunity for a murder bee attack."

"How many people are going to be there?"

"I've no idea, but it's a party, so ten, twenty, fifty?"

"Oh Jesus. It'll be like shooting fish in a barrel."

"Exactly. And Klaus has suggested that Sarah and I attend so we can talk to them about what happened to Gunther and Helmut, to warn them about the danger."

"So, you're targets as well?"

"That's what we are assuming. He'll be able to clean up all of his loose ends at the same time."

"Look. Don't panic yet, you've got over a week until the party, so that gives us plenty of time to prepare."

"What do you mean prepare? You think we should go?"

"Oh definitely. It's not every day that you get to meet members of the project team. Anyway, they seem to be a dying breed. This could be your last chance to get inside information."

"The way things are going I'm sure you're right, but what concerns me more is the danger to me and Sarah."

"We need to come up with a method for you to protect yourself."

"We reckon Ingrid used a tennis racket."

"That's one method, but I was thinking more along the lines of protecting the area that they like to attack."

"The forehead?"

"Exactly. If you think about each individual bee, they are just a small drone with a small targeting algorithm. It can't be anything too complicated because they're not carrying around a big processor. So, what do you think they are targeting?"

"The forehead."

"Yes, but to them its the big patch of skin between the eyes and the hair."

"So, we need to protect that?"

"Either that or disguise it; camouflage."

32.

They dumped the car in an underground multi-story car park leaving their phones and Sarah's bag in the boot. Having wandered around the old part of town for a while admiring the narrow streets and old architecture, they'd settled on a little bar off of the beaten track. They'd seen this place many times in passing and often thought it looked like a quaint old café. This seemed like the ideal opportunity to try it out.

David poured a little more wine into each of their glasses and prepared himself for what he was about to say.

"So, Simon thinks we should go to the party."

"Of course he does. Whose side is he on? Is he trying to get us killed?"

"Hold on. Wait a minute. What he said actually did make sense. These guys are the last of a dying breed, this could be one last chance to get inside information."

"And if we die, we die. And if we don't die, we can be sure the police will be waiting to ask us more questions."

"Oh, good one. Three murder scenes with identical injuries...."

"And us, the suspects - means motive and opportunity." She interrupted.

"Wait. Opportunity, sure. But what's our means and motive?"

"Oh, I'm sure they'll make up a plausible story."

David picked up his glass.

"So, are we hoping to die at the party or hoping to survive?" He took a sip and waited for the fallout.

"I'm still hoping we don't go."

Sarah could picture the scene perfectly. A sunny Mallorcan afternoon around the pool with the sun gently heading towards the horizon. The harsh light of day turning to golden and then to orange as the end of the day and beginning of the night drew closer.

Then she got the image she didn't want to see. David lying dead with a tell-tale red dot on his forehead. Murdered by Klaus and his cronies, even though the two of them knew what to expect and could have simply not gone to the party.

"Ok, Sarah couldn't quite believe what she was about to say, "so we can decide not to go at any point, up until we walk through their door. In the meantime, we can plan for how we might......defend ourselves?"

"That reminds me, Simon said something about how the bees identify their target. They always seem to go for the forehead, or as he called it, big area of skin between the eyes and the hair."

"Right, Ok."

"So, we either need to protect that area,"

"Or disguise it. Hide it so they can't identify the target zone. Big hat and sunglasses."

33.

The invite stated that the party would start promptly at 3pm, so David and Sarah rolled up outside the large, doubtless expensive and very well-maintained villa at 3:30, fashionably late.

There was nowhere to park anywhere near the villa, so David carried on further up the road and, to his amazement, found a parking space in the shade.

They walked from the car hand in hand, David carrying a bottle of fizz and a card, while Sarah carried her handbag which matched her new outfit. And very glamorous it was too. A polka dot dress finishing just above the knee, with a hat and shoes to match. Large dark sunglasses completed her suit of armour.

David's outfit was quite smart, though slightly less glamorous and definitely less new. A smart short sleeved shirt with contrasting formal shorts. David had treated himself to a new pair of flip-flops, but the crowning glory of his outfit was his slightly battered but still perfectly serviceable trilby. And dark sunglasses, but not as large as Sarah's.

They approached the front door through perfectly maintained grounds. David noted that the grass had been cut that morning and all of the bushes and olive trees were perfectly manicured. But then, if you're paying this much to rent a villa for a couple of weeks, it ought to be perfect.

The door was already open and the party well underway. Bubbling laughter spilled from deeper within the house inviting them to venture inside.

They had just about made it to the kitchen when a tall, blonde, slightly older lady gave a bellowing greeting across the room.

"Hallo! Ah, you must be Sarah und David. Come, come in. Let's get you both a drink."

"Yes, Hi. I'm Sarah, this is my husband David. It's good to meet you, Lina?"

"Yes, I'm Lina. Kristoff is outside somewhere with Johann, doing men things, and this is Emilia," she indicated a tall, darker haired lady who was painfully thin. They waved and said 'hi', nodding and mouthing "hello" to others in the room.

Lina handed a glass of fizz to each of them in turn. "Here you go, my new friends," Lina bellowed at them, even though their range would be measured in fractions of a metre not multiples.

They both noticed the size of the diamonds in Lina's jewellery. She had a really quite impractical engagement ring nestled alongside its less showy neighbour. But it was the tennis bracelet that really shouted 'money'.

They took the champagne glasses and raised them in Lina's direction.

"Salut." David and Sarah said in unison.

"Prost" said Lina

"Yes, *prost*." Sarah corrected herself. Well, you know, when in Spain, do as the Germans do.

Lina then continued to be her over bubbly self as she went around the kitchen introducing each person in turn. Neither of them had any hope of remembering any of their names. A raise of the glass and a nod to each would have to suffice for the moment.

They gradually filtered their way towards the garden and the swimming pool. Again the greenery was perfectly kept with neither a stray leaf nor clipping anywhere to be seen. The grass was a lush, verdant shade of green.

David approached the pool and saw that it was designed for much more than just swimming. At the shallow end, before getting anywhere near the pool, was a paddling area. Not even ankle deep, it's aim was to cool the feet on those warm summer days. The pool then dropped down a couple of steps to a seating area, where David imagined the water would come up to mid torso. Venturing deeper was the pool proper. Perfectly clean. David knew, without even checking, that the pH and chlorine levels would be spot on.

They spent the next hour or so talking to various guests around the pool area. They turned out to be a fascinating mix of people from various parts of the world, most of which had houses in the area. They were asked for their business card several times, which they were happy to provide, but had to explain that they didn't cover this part of the island.

David spotted a couple of men who seemed to be doing the rounds together. They appeared to be of the right sort of age to have worked with Klaus and his unfortunate colleagues.

"Hi, are you Johann and Kristoff, by any chance?" David asked.

"We are, yes." Said the slightly taller of the two, "I'm Johann, and this is my good friend and former colleague, Kristoff." He said indicating the thinner of the two.

"Oh yes, I'm David and this is my wife, Sarah."

It was at that moment that a large bee buzzed past. The hair on the back of Sarah's neck stood up and goosebumps ran down her arm. She became aware that she could feel her heart beating. They both turned to look at the source of the sound as it trundled past. Johann noticed that their attention had been distracted by the insect.

"It's just a carpenter bee, minding her own business - she won't hurt you. Yes, Klaus said you would be coming. You used to work for Gunther and Ingrid, is that right?"

"Yes, we did. Terrible business, what happened there, in fact, that's what I wanted to talk to you about today." Said David.

"Oh, really? I thought it was just some horrible accident." Johann enquired.

"Oh no, not at all," Sarah interrupted," quite the opposite. They were murdered."

Kristoff and Johann both sucked air in between their teeth.

"But Klaus told us there had been an incident with a ladder?"

"Not quite. There was an incident with Article 79A. And it was the same with Helmut and Heidi." She said.

Sarah could still feel her heart pounding as Kristoff and Johann looked at each other in horror. They spoke to each other in rapid fire German for a couple of moments. Sarah figured that penny was about to drop.

Kristoff and Johann stopped talking and both started looking around at the air around the garden. Sarah cast a sideways glance at David who was doing the same to her.

"We need to go inside to find Lina and Emilia."

"Good idea." Said Sarah, although her input was unlikely to have any effect on their panic at this point.

As the two men walked hurriedly towards the house, David and Sarah watched them go.

"You know, neither of them is wearing a hat or sunglasses." said Sarah.

"I know, but then I guess they weren't expecting bees as uninvited guests.

They both took a moment to cast their eyes around the guests gathered in the back garden. The cava had been flowing, and the conversations were getting more animated. Everyone seemed to be enjoying themselves, regaling each other with stories of times past and future plans. Some people were German, but most seemed to be from other European origins. A cosmopolitan mix of people. Some people were wearing hats, some people were wearing sunglasses. Sarah wondered how many of these people might be on the kill list. Just the former colleagues and wives? Them too?

"They could kill everybody here if they wanted to," said Sarah.

"But I don't think they have that many bees. Well, I guess I've got no idea. What I mean is, they're not all killers. A lot of them are just for eavesdropping and spying."

"Well, they could be. It depends how they've been configured for today's mission." She said.

David had to admit that she was right. Not all of the bees were necessarily killers. The one that had escaped was a video unit and it hadn't tried to kill him. Yet.

For David it took a moment to sink in. There were about 35 people in the garden plus another 20 inside. He had no idea how the bees performed as killers in an indoor setting, but outdoors they had a 100% kill rate. 35 bees would equal 35 victims. Then he realised that he hadn't included Sarah and himself. He grabbed the rim of his trilby with index finger and thumb. He pulled it down a little more snugly to ensure there was no gap between the rim and his sunglasses. Sarah noticed and did the same.

The sun was definitely getting lower in the sky, casting its golden, flattering warmth onto the faces of the party goers. Sarah noticed that more and more people were having to shade their eyes.

"This would be a good time to do it," she said to David, who was shading his eyes with the rim of his trilby.

"Exactly. An attack out of the sun."

They shuffled around a little so the sun was shining on the left side of David's face and the right side of Sarah's. Hopefully this would give them the best visibility in difficult conditions.

"All four of them have just come out of the back door," said Sarah, "and I think they're heading this way."

"Hello, hello. Look, I need you to go over what you told me again for the girls." Said Johann.

"Oh, ok," said Sarah, "we were talking about Gunther and Ingrid."

"Yes, and you said it wasn't an accident?"

"That's right. They were murdered by those bees that you used to work on. And it wasn't just them. Helmet and Heidi Schmidt from Port de Pollença were also murdered by them."

"By them or with them?" Asked Kristoff.

Sarah was a little puzzled by the question. "Does it make any difference?"

The conversation stopped abruptly as they all heard the deep humming of a swarm flying overhead. They all looked up and saw a large cloud of fast moving bees criss-crossing the garden. It was difficult to count numbers, but there must have been at least 50 of them. All together they produced quite an impressive noise. They all seemed to be staying at least 10 metres in the air.

"What are they doing?" Sarah asked with a raised voice.

"Reconnaissance," said Johann, "identifying their targets." He seemed to be mesmerised by the sight of the bees criss-crossing the sky, caught somewhere between awe and nostalgia.

"Shouldn't we be getting the hell out of here?" She shouted.

"Yes, run," shouted Johann, "everybody run!"

34.

Sarah grabbed her hat to ensure it stayed in place and started running towards the house, but of course everybody else had the same idea. She saw Emelia trying to swat a bee. It circled around her head a few times. It then seemed to pause, to stop and hover before flying straight into her forehead with a pop. It wasn't as loud as Sarah had expected. Emilia slumped straight down to the ground, as if a puppeteer had cut her strings.

David was trying to make his way to the house but was getting blocked by the panicked crowd. Keeping his attention upwards and being ready to swat any approaching bees, he didn't notice that his path was leading him directly to the now dead body of Emilia lying on the grass. He tripped over her leg and fell face first to the ground, his hat and sunglasses coming off of his head and tumbling to the ground in front of him.

The sunglasses were immediately crushed by an errant foot of some other party-goer trying to escape with their life. Similarly, the hat was kicked out of reach. As he lay on his front, watching the hat disappear with the crowd, he suddenly felt completely exposed - a sitting duck.

Sarah watched as another bee swooped in and struck Kristoff on its first pass. Another pop that sounded like an over-done child's toy gun. Mid-run, he fell face forwards - dead before he hit the ground.

She realised that none of the bees appeared to be interested in her. Either her disguise was working or she was not one of the allotted targets. There was, of course, no way to tell which.

She looked around the crowd to see where David had got to but couldn't find him. Panic was setting in again, adrenaline rising. She kept looking but couldn't see him. Maybe he'd already gone. And then she noticed him lying on the ground, propped up on his elbows with no protection against the killer bees. Her panic worsened when she noticed a bee was circling his head.

Lina and Johann had headed towards a side gate instead of the overcrowded back door, figuring that it would provide a quicker means of escape. This wasn't the time to be hanging around. As they approached the side gate they heard the approach of a few bees which zipped past them like miniature, low pitched racing cars. Four of them. Johann struggled with the lock while Lina watched in horror as all four of them did a U-turn and headed straight back towards them.

She brought her arms up in a failed attempt to protect herself from the oncoming attack, swatting at an enemy that had a clear intent and a clear target.

Pop, pop. They both dropped dead where they stood.

Sarah hurried over to David to see if she could help protect him from the bees, or at least their targeting mechanism. She was making good progress but her shoes weren't ideal for running.

David watched in horror as the bee orbiting his head slowed and eventually came to a stationary hover less than one metre from his head. The adrenaline had gotten the better off him, and what should have been a flight or flight response now had him frozen in place. Unable to move, think or seemingly breathe, he looked at the bee as the bee looked at him. They regarded each other for a moment. Was it the same bee he had in his workshop?

The bee seemed to be enjoying looking down the barrel of its gun towards it's hapless and helpless victim. It seemed to be deliberately drawing out the attack to ensure David's ordeal was maximised. It wasn't just going to kill him, it was going to ensure that he suffered first.

He seemed to have a million thoughts all at the same time. He was also aware that this rush of thoughts was happening. This was what they said happened at the end, the moments before death. The replay of his life raced through his mind, yet he was aware that he was very much still present in the moment. The bee torturing him. Or was it Klaus tormenting him vicariously through his murderous creation?

The bee then seemed to nod or bow at him and then flew away vertically. Gone. David was frozen in place, pinned in place partially by the adrenaline and partly by his mind still thinking through the reasons why the bee had let him live. Maybe it couldn't confirm him as a target, maybe it had identified someone else as a higher priority or was it low on power. Was it more likely that its orders had been changed? Had Klaus had a change of heart, or was he just scaring the crap out of David, sending a message? What about Sarah? Jesus, where was she, was she Ok?

"Babe, get up." Sarah bellowed as she approached him en route to the door.

David shook his head and forced himself to forget about the bee and all of the other ideas whirling in his head. To Sarah it seemed to take him an age but eventually he got his footing and accelerated towards the house.

The bulk of the guests were already inside and flooding out of the front door. Sarah and David forced their way through the crowd bottle-neck at the door. The flow of panicked people then carried them through the house and out into the front garden.

"Are you still keeping up with me babe?" Sarah shouted over her shoulder.

"I'm here. Keep going."

"Towards the car?"

"I guess so."

Within moments they were clear of the panicked melee. Most people seemed content to hang around once they'd spilled outside, perhaps assuming that the swarm would only attack in the back garden and wouldn't bother to fly over or around the house to the front. Sarah maintained an energetic pace towards the car, with David almost keeping up.

"Are we getting in?" Sarah gesturing towards the car, hurrying him to catch up.

"Yes. Get in." David thought the car might offer some protection, both from targeting and from attack. "We've got to be safer in the car rather than out in the open air," he said as he fumbled for the keys in his pocket, eventually retrieving them and pushing the button. The locking system gave a dull thud and he pulled at the driver's door handle.

Sarah entered the car more quickly than was elegant or sensible, given her attire. She thumped the door shut and checked her hat and glasses were still in place. She had no idea if they were still needed, but it was better not to risk it.

David started the engine. The air conditioning gave a welcome blast of cool air and the radio came on filling the air with happy music, a complete contrast to the events of the last five minutes. Sarah reached for the volume control and turned it down.

"Christ, I didn't think they'd actually go through with it," she said, still shocked and still recovering.

"I guess they've shown us before that they're capable of killing. I just didn't expect it to happen so brazenly in front of a crowd."

"And were we targets as well, or not? I'm still not clear about what exactly happened in that garden."

"I thought your disguise was working very well and, so was mine…"

"Until it got knocked off when you tripped over Amelia."

"Oh, is that who it was? I didn't get a chance to see. I just went down and the next thing I knew someone had stepped on my glasses and kicked my hat away."

"And what was that bee doing?" she asked.

"I have no idea. I thought I was a goner, for sure. It was circling me, I assume identifying the right part to hit. And then it stopped and looked at me. It was actually looking at me. Then it felt like it nodded at me and then flew away."

"What, like it said goodbye?!"

"Yeah, or something like that." He couldn't quite believe what he was saying, but that was what it looked like.

"Look, I don't want to wait here until the police arrive, shall we sod off somewhere else?"

"Yeah, good idea. Do you remember that German café we went to a couple of years ago?"

"The retro 70s place? Sounds good. And it's inside, out of sight in case of your airborne artillery put in another appearance."

The café hadn't changed a bit, neither in the time since their last visit, nor since it was originally outfitted in the 70s. They grabbed a table at the back of the café while their phones sang to each other in Sarah's bag.

"So, I'm guessing we were on the hit list. Klaus seems to have gone out of his way to make sure we were going to be there." She said.

"Absolutely, we were targets. Then you managed to outsmart them, and…. I don't really know what happened with me."

"Was that the same bee you've been charging in the workshop?"

"I suppose it's possible, but they all look the same. Well, I mean, the three that I have seen all look the same."

"Apart from whatever payload is fitted at the front, the head."

"Each bee is made up of three components. Head, thorax and abdomen." He said.

"Right," she said, impatiently. She already knew this.

"So, if the abdomen is just the battery and the head is the payload, does that mean that the thorax is the processor as well as the motor?"

"So, when we say 'bee' we mean as a thorax?"

"Exactly. I think. Anyway, I don't think there is a way of identifying individual bees."

"So, let's say that it was *your* bee. Does that mean that it now … what, sees you as a friend?"

"Maybe."

"And if that wasn't *your* bee?"

There was a pause as they mulled the question, and the barman took their order. Unusually, given the situation, they ordered water.

"If that wasn't *my* bee, then…"

"It has been told that you are off limits?"

"Possibly, but it's a bit of a stretch, don't you think?"

"I guess so. But, if you think of it in terms of bees, you are a source of nectar."

"But they're not bees, they're drones."

"Either way, it was very low on power, and you refuelled it."

Their water arrived and they poured the sparkling liquid over the ice cubes in the heavy, old school German glasses. David chugged most of his water on his first gulp. Sarah likewise.

"I'm not sure this water's cutting it." She said. David nodded.

It was at this point that an older gentleman across the room interjected.

"You've got to be careful with bees, you know. You're not using them to make honey, are you?"

Sarah and David both looked at each other with furrowed brows, wondering where this old man had come from, what gave him the right to butt into their conversation. Had he been sat there all along, or had he snuck in while they were deep in conversation?

"No," said Sarah, "We're not making honey."

"Just as well, my dear. People around here grow a lot of o-le-an-der," he stretched the name, as if he was instructing them on its pronunciation. "Highly toxic, I'm afraid. The pollen gets into the honey and, you know. You've got to be careful." he shrugged his shoulders and pushed out his bottom lip, which seemed to be its natural resting place.

"Oh, believe me, we intend to be careful!" Sarah chuckled, and then, directing her comment to David, "Maybe a glass of wine somewhere else?"

"Mmm, good idea."

He grabbed the bar man's attention and rubbed an imaginary note between his thumb and first two fingers. The bill came promptly, which David covered generously with a €5 note, preferring expediency rather than financial efficiency in their exit of the bar.

"Where the hell did he come from? And anyway, I didn't think oleander attracted bees." asked Sarah as they paced towards their car.

"I have no idea, but also he was clearly able to overhear our conversation."

"Thank God he's not one of theirs."

"You know that for certain?"

"Eh?"

"Poisonous honey? Are you sure that wasn't some kind of threat or warning?"

The drive home was a solemn affair. The once green landscape was turning brown under the heat of the imminent summer and its inescapable sun, but as night fell it was cast as monotones. Each passing kilometre putting them further from the horrors of the party, but no closer to the truth.

They'd finally witnessed the bees in action, rather than just seeing the results. Efficient. Very efficient. The swarm circling overhead until all intended victims had been identified. Then swooping in for the kill, one after the other in rapid succession. Almost instantaneous. As long as the targets didn't know that the attack was coming, there didn't seem to be any method of defence.

"That method of attack is pretty unstoppable." Said Sarah in a dull, monotone voice, staring aimlessly out of the passenger window. The rush of the adrenaline high had been replaced by mild shock.

"It was quite impressive." He conceded.

Their minds kept wondering back to the precision of the attack. Clinical. No collateral damage. All intended victims dispatched. A single headshot. Except David.

David put some music on but kept the volume low. Sarah was obviously spooked, but was holding herself together for the moment. He decided to leave her as she was, at least until they got home. The headlights pierced the darkness as they rounded the corner into their road and David's attention suddenly turned to their house and its potential visitors.

"I wonder if our watchers have been here, or if they've been working over in Andratx?" he asked.

"Good point. Have we been broken into again? They knew we'd be out all day."

These thoughts didn't help the sombre mood as they turned into their driveway. David brought the car to a gentle stop. Nothing seemed out of place in front of the house, or as they entered through the front door. Sarah surreptitiously scanned for spying devices, and found them all where they ought to be. No new devices had been added. After a few minutes of creeping skeptically around their own home, they concluded that no one had been in, and nothing had been touched.

"Looks like we're alone, then." She said to David, still sounding down. He cuddled up behind her, put his arms around her waist and pulled her in close.

"Shall we get out of these clothes?" He suggested.

She left her response for a few moments. "Good idea, but I'll wait until you've finished snuggling me first."

While they were getting changed, Sarah suggested going to the usual bar for a glass of wine. Within fifteen minutes they were perched on their usual bar stools.

"I think I'll have a glass of water first," said Sarah.

"Really?"

"I know, I'm just not feeling it at the moment."

"Ok, I'll have one too."

The barman looked at them quizzically. He rattled off something in Spanish, which sounded a bit like "are you feeling Ok?". David gave a slight chuckle.

Sarah checked that the music was loud, the punters were Spanish and that the phones were talking to each other in a bag out of earshot.

"So why haven't the police caught up with us on this one?" asked Sarah.

"Oh. Good one. I hadn't even thought about that."

"Exactly. It's like they're always there, soon as anything happens with these damned bees."

"Well, to be fair, we are the ones that keep calling them." David conceded.

"I know, but they've just got four new victims, killed with the same weapon. You'd think they'd have put two and two together."

"You're right, but Andratx is miles away. Definitely a different police force. It'll probably take them a few days to investigate and do a report. They'll then send it by snail-mail to Palma."

"And that's when our friend Miquel will phone." Said Sarah, nodding as she spoke.

"Exactly."

"Today is Saturday, tomorrow is Sunday. With four dead bodies even the Spaniards will have to work tomorrow. Two days for investigation, one day for report writing, one day for the report to land on the right desk in Palma."

"So, Miquel will call on Thursday?" he asked.

"We'll see. So, if your bees have added you to the good guys list, what about me?"

"I'm not sure what you mean."

"Am I on the good guys list?"

"How do you propose we test that?" He chuckled.

She narrowed her eyes at him – she knew exactly what he meant: stand there in front of a bee with no hat or glasses. See if it wants to kill you.

35.

He sat sipping his coffee and watching the world go by on the terrace of his favourite venue in Inca. Perched at the end of the busiest avenue, it was a great vantage point for people watching. To his left was the old manor house, surrounded by mature palms, cycads and cactus. It gave the place a feel of luxury, of richness, of indulgence. To his right the inadequacies of the Spanish road and drainage systems made themselves felt, through the sights and sounds of congestion and, perhaps more pressingly, through the nostrils.

People were starting to arrive for the lunch time rush, which was usually Simon's cue to settle up. On this occasion, however, his day was about to take a different turn. As he tried to catch the waitress' eye someone walked past him from behind and sat down at his table, straight opposite him.

"Good morning. Simon, isn't it?" Asked Klaus.

"Who the hell are you?"

"Now Simon, let's be civil, shall we? My name is Klaus and I have a job offer for you."

"You should take more care, Klaus. You might get hurt sneaking up on people like that."

"I tell you what, Simon," he said, reaching into his pocket and pulling out a small plastic container, "why don't we start again?" Klaus tipped the contents out onto the table.

Simon didn't break eye contact with the old man. He had a pretty good idea of what he'd just shown him, which was confirmed when he heard that familiar deep throb of the bee's wings starting to beat. Only at that point he did look away from the old man and at the object on the table. As expected, it was an article 79a bee. And this one was a killer.

It flew upwards and landed just over the window, a few metres up the wall of the main building. Its presence was supposed to be intimidating, but Simon knew how these things worked and knew they could be defended against – if you knew it was coming.

He decided that it was smarter to play whatever game Klaus was planning rather than make an initial move that might well turn out to be an over-reaction. "I see you have me cornered. I'm going to assume you have more of your little friends dotted around."

"Several. More than sufficient."

"Now, look. You didn't need to go to these elaborate extremes. It you wanted to talk, you could have just said."

"I've seen you at work. You seem to tend towards violence, you're easily provoked. I wanted to make sure we started out on the same page."

"Ok then, Klaus. What can I do for you?"

"I have a job opportunity for a man of your talents. The project that I'm working on requires someone to take care of ... security. It's a position for which, for various reasons, you are uniquely qualified."

Simon sat back in his chair and lent it back, raising the front legs off of the ground. He thought about what he meant by 'uniquely qualified'. Klaus couldn't know about his former military service, nobody did in truth. So Klaus either meant what facilities or people were currently accessible to him.

"Let's suppose I am."

"Exactly. And that puts you in a position to help me. All we need to do now is discuss your requirements."

"Compensation for giving up a promising career with the British Government?"

"Oh, you don't need to worry about that. You can keep working with them - if you must. I just need someone to help me to tie up a few loose ends."

"Like MI6?"

"No, you won't need to do anything with them. This doesn't directly conflict with your current role. It's more of a little side-line. Moonlighting, I think you call it?"

36.

It didn't take until Thursday for Klaus to phone. As David's phone rang in his hand, Sarah and David looked at the screen and then at each other.

"Oh, here we go," said Sarah, with a shrug.

David pressed answer and reluctantly raised the phone to his ear.

"Hello Klaus," said David.

"David, I heard something went wrong at the party. Are you both Ok?"

"We're both fine. A little shell shocked, I guess."

Sarah started to gesticulate what she thought of Klaus, but then remembered that people could be watching.

"But you're Ok, that's the main thing. So, tell me David, what the hell happened?"

"Your bees happened. I've got to congratulate you, they are very good at what they do."

"Oh, David. They're not my bees. I was just one part of a much larger department. While I was working on the project, we never killed anybody. We only got them to attack mannequins, you know, dummies."

David noted that Klaus hadn't mentioned the killings *after* he had left the project. It seemed like a politician's answer, not technically a lie, but it was *economical with the truth*.

"Anyway, they did a fantastic job. Very impressive. Very efficient. They managed to kill both of your ex-colleagues and their wives. Well, I say kill, I mean, I didn't exactly hang around to check for a pulse."

"I suppose not."

"There was a big panic with everyone trying to get out of the back garden. Too many people to fit through the door. I tripped over and ended up on the ground, then one of the bees started showing an interest in me. It kept circling me."

"Oh my god, that's terrible. But then you managed to get away? Or you swatted it?"

"Something like that, yeah," said David, this being his turn to keep the truth for himself.

"But you've managed to get back home safely now?"

You know I have, you idiot, you're watching me with the cameras.

"Yeah, we are home. Maybe a nice cup of tea."

"Look, David, if there's anything I can do, you'll let me know?"

"How are you feeling, Klaus?"

"Mm?"

"Well, two more of your ex-colleagues have just been killed. You must be quite upset."

"Yes, well. I am of course. I must have worked with those guys for about 5 years, but it was a long time ago."

"So, is that everyone on the team dead except for you and the boss? Aren't you worried?"

"What do you mean?"

"Well, it seems to me that the boss is killing off all the members of the team. You're the last one."

"Christ, I hadn't thought of it like that."

"And you said you thought your house was being watched? Who do you think that is?"

Although he had no evidence, David was pretty convinced that nobody was watching Klaus' house. Had it all been an elaborate ruse to pull him and Sarah into Klaus' web of deceit? Drawing them in so they could help to do Klaus' dirty work.

Having initially discovered Ingrid and Gunther quite accidentally while going about their day-to-day work, they had then been conned into discovering the bodies of Heidi and Helmut.

This party in Andratx had been a gift to Klaus and his cronies. An opportunity too good to miss. Two more ex-colleagues and their wives, complete with David and Sarah. All standing close together at the same time in the same back garden. Despite Klaus' reassuring words, David was now more convinced than ever that Sarah and he were both supposed to be lying dead in that garden.

"I suppose what you're saying does make sense," said Klaus.

"Look, whatever is going on, I think we all need to be a bit more careful."

"You're right, David, of course."

Sarah elbowed him and gesticulated that he should wind the conversation up. All of this talking to the enemy was just giving him free information that he'd probably find a way to use against them. "Klaus, I've got things I need to be getting on with, like drinking a lot of gin and forgetting about what we've been through today."

"Of course! Sorry. I've taken up too much of your time already. Be careful, David. And, let's keep in touch."

"Ok. Thank you, Klaus. Goodbye."

David didn't wait for him to say goodbye, he just hung up and gave Sarah a wide-eyed look, as he returned his phone to his pocket.

"I don't think we should be drinking, we need to be alert." Said Sarah.

"Oh, I agree completely. If we need to drive, or run or whatever, we're going to need a clear head."

"Exactly, but I don't want to just sit around here either. I need to do something, keep my brain busy, or I'm going to go crazy."

"I was thinking about going down to the studio, see if anybody wants to jam. But that doesn't really give you anything to do."

"I can play the cowbell......" Sarah half joked.

"Babe, if you want to play the cowbell, then you come and play the cowbell. I'm sure no one at the studio is going to object to having a chick around for a change. It's usually just unwashed kids."

They both had to giggle at that, and for one brief moment everything felt normal again.

"Ok, cowbell, it is mister. Pack your bags."

Minutes later they emerged from the front door looking like a comedy cross between ill-advised tourists and wannabe rock stars. Anti-bee baseball caps and sunglasses, biker jackets and jeans, his Vans and her DMs. With his guitar, his amp and his chica loaded, David started the car and reversed out of the driveway.

As they pulled into the car park at the studio David recognised a couple of the cars. He nodded to himself as he remembered jamming with these guys before. They had been great to play with and he was now quite excited about the musical possibilities that lay within. As he was unloading his guitar and amplifier from the car Sarah's phone rang.

"Hello?" Said Sarah, pressing the phone to her ear.

"Oh, hi, is that Sarah? I'm Veronique," a voice replied with a European accent which Sarah couldn't immediately place. I'm friends with Pepe and Marta from Alcudia."

"Oh yes," said Sarah, "how are they doing?"

"Oh, they're fine. But I've called to talk about my mother. She has a flat in Port de Pollença, but she's quite old and needs to come back to France to live with us. She's not really safe living on her own anymore."

"Sorry to hear that. How can I help?"

"I guess, really, we need someone to help us sort the flat out and sell it. I'm afraid it's not been looked after very well for a few years. We are planning on taking mother and some of her more important possessions next week. After that I was hoping you would be able to arrange for the flat to be emptied, decorated and then sold."

"That's quite a bit more work than we usually take on, but I guess we could think about it."

"I'm expecting to have to pay. I'm quite aware of the fees that estate agents charge on the island. I'm happy to pay that. I'm also happy to pay for your time organizing removals and decorators and whatever."

David had stopped unpacking the car and was listening to her conversation. To him it sounded like a project they'd be managing rather than doing themselves but, more importantly, it was another empty property that no one else knew about.

"Perhaps we should meet to go over the details?" Sarah suggested. "I'm actually free now, if you want to meet for a coffee?" She knew David didn't really need her to play the cowbell. He gave her the thumbs up and then wafted his hand at her as if to get her moving.

"Oh, Ok. I hadn't expected that but, sure, I can meet for a coffee." Veronique said.

"Great. You know the road from Palma as it gets into Alcudia, there's a roundabout near the Yamaha dealer, where the road goes either to Alcudia or Port de Pollença?"

"Yep, I think I know where you're talking about."

"There's a few cafés around there, some of them have easy parking. Are you on WhatsApp, I'll send you a map pin?"

"Yes, I am."

"Ok, I'll send you a map. If you could reply so I know you've got it?"

"Yes, of course. Any problems and I guess we'll be talking on the phone again."

"Brilliant. It will take me about an hour to get there."

"Ok, see you then."

Sarah held out her hand for the car keys which David pressed into her palm. He knew this was exactly what she needed. She'd be much better off focused on work and in this case, a new project, rather than sitting around hitting a cowbell with him and the boys.

"Have fun with Veronique."

"I will. I'll text you after the meeting, see how you're getting on here."

"Yeah. Look, I'm going to keep a close eye on my phone in case you need me. Can you get a picture of her and send it to me, just in case she's working for them? And you call me if there's any problems."

"Babe, come on. You're being a bit paranoid."

"Yeah, maybe. I'm supposed to be here for the music to relax me, but now I'm worrying about you."

"I'll get a picture. Any indication of any Klaus crap and I'll be out of there straight away."

"Maybe I should come with you instead?"

"Oh, no. No way. You stay here and have fun with your boys. I'm going to go and have a coffee and talk to a new customer about a lucrative project. It could earn us a lot of money."

"Ok, babe, if you're sure. "

"I am. I'm not going to let this Klaus idiot interfere with everything in our lives."

She realised that they both said too much, given that people could be listening. The fact that she'd stopped talking and not launched into a torrent of abuse reminded David that the walls have ears.

"Look, I'll talk to you in a bit," she said, giving him a hug and a long kiss.

"Yep, Ok. Be careful."

He watched her as she got into the car and adjusted things the way she liked them. The stereo blew up with the din of a track that he half recognised but couldn't place. After a bit of careful reversing, she zoomed off out of the car park. Much quicker than he would have, but probably under control.

He just hoped that the recent attempt on their lives and sudden appearance of this new customer weren't related.

37.

When Sarah pulled up outside of the spartan but functional café, the only person who could possibly have been Veronique was already sitting outside with a coffee and reading a book.

"Hi, you must be…"

"Veronique, yes. You must be Sarah?"

"Pleased to meet you," said Sarah. "I just need to get a picture of you, for our records. It's so my husband and will recognise you in the future. And also, just in case you're a serial killer." Sarah gave a slightly embarrassed giggle as she snapped the picture.

Sarah caught the eye of the waiter and ordered herself a coffee. Taking the picture felt a bit weird, but Sarah understood David's paranoia. Maybe he was right.

She wondered if perhaps she ought to be more worried about safety herself. Perhaps surviving the slaughter at the party had unbalanced her normal feelings of self and self-worth. She certainly knew she wasn't bulletproof. Maybe she knew they were going to get her in the end and there wasn't any point in thinking that she could stop them.

"So, tell me about this flat."

"Actually, it's just around the corner from here, we can walk there after our coffees."

"And how is Mum?"

"Well, you know. She's been slowing down for a long time, but now we're getting concerned. She's got very thin, we think she's forgetting to eat, or maybe can't be bothered. Either way the family is agreed that she'd be better back in France where we can make sure she's getting the proper care."

"I'm so sorry to hear that."

"She's been living her dream out here for twenty years, and I think she's enjoyed every minute of it. If it were up to her, she'd stay. But I think she knows she needs a bit more help now."

"The flat is full of 20-year-old furniture?"

"And probably hasn't been decorated in 20 years either."

"Are you in a rush to sell it, or would you prefer to hang on and get a better price?"

"At the moment nobody's in a rush, so we don't need to give it away. But you know how families are… maybe we'll wait, think about marketing strategy once the flat's finished. Let's get it looking great and then we'll see."

David's phone pinged and he picked it up. The jam session was providing him with a welcome distraction, but not to the extent that he'd hoped. Everyone had paused for a comfort break, which meant most of the boys were getting stuck into another beer.

He had a notification about a new picture added to his shared folder. It was a picture of a North European looking lady outside a coffee shop, which he took to be Veronique. But something was a bit weird. There were other pictures in the shared folder that he didn't recognise.

He tapped on a thumbnail which opened up into a bigger picture - a picture of the inside of what had been his Faraday cage. Odd. He hadn't taken any pictures in there, had he? He could only remember trying to call Sarah and get GPS signals as his means of leak testing the cage. Taking pictures to see if they uploaded onto the shared drive? Did he do that?

The next picture was of him holding a pair of tweezers, seemingly pointed towards the lens of the camera that had taken the picture. He didn't take any selfies, certainly none at such a creative angle.

"Oh my god." He looked around, but no one had heard him. Either that or talking to himself had become so commonplace that everyone ignored it.

He looked through the other thumbnails, which included the car battery, a picture of Sarah, and a short video in which the camera escaped from the cage and under the workshop door.

So these were pictures taken by the bee that he'd had in his workshop? The next thumbnail seemed to confirm that theory. It was a video of the bee arriving at a block of flats and landing on some kind of charger or base unit on the balcony of a flat on the second floor. David recognised the building. He had followed one of the blue Seat Leons there after he'd followed it to Klaus' house.

He stopped himself for a moment, stopped his brain forming the impossible narrative that he thought the pictures were giving him.

He locked his phone and stuffed it back into his pocket. This was ridiculous. The day's events had obviously been too much for him. Coming out to play music with the boys had been a mistake. They should have dumped the car outside their local bar and diluted the day's stresses with a bottle of wine, or two. Instead, they both remained sober so they'd be ready for any more surprises that Klaus and his bees would throw at them. And now his bee was sending him pictures.

He wandered off to find the boys and a beer. The bottle was served to him with ice frozen to the outside of the bottle. Even the one mouthful seemed to push the horrors of the party further into the past. The second mouthful confirmed that all musical activity had ceased for the evening. He messaged Sarah saying he was finished and was ready whenever she was.

As he watched the message go, his mind went back to the series of images and videos. What were they supposed to mean?

He quickly decided that it must be Klaus sending them to him. Somehow he'd hacked David's cloud account and was uploading content. He immediately assumed that the eventual aim of this new tactic was to get David to paint himself into a corner. The only other explanation was that it was the bees talking to him.

Sarah messaged to say she was finished at the flat and would probably be with him in about 45 minutes. He replied with a thumbs up.

He then noticed that there was a notification, another file had been added to his shared drive. David took his phone and beer away from the noise of the bar and found a quieter corner. Somewhat reluctantly, pressed the thumbnail revealing a video and pressed play.

The video seemed to have been taken from the webcam on top of a computer monitor. A somewhat plain man sat facing the screen in a small bedroom or office. Judging by the expression on his face, whatever he was looking at on the computer screen was a cause for concern.

"No, that can't be. That's not right. Nothing. It's not possible," the man on the screen said. After a couple of minutes, the man's attention was suddenly distracted. It seemed like someone else had entered the room.

"Damn it, Carl, you idiot. Move out of the way so I can see." The man got up from his chair and made way for the new arrival. Moments later their old friend Klaus sat facing the screen.

The video appeared to be an insider's view of Klaus' office. It went on, showing them bickering about some impossible loss of data. David watched the video a couple of times. He still wasn't sure whether this was a setup or a communication attempt.

What was apparently not possible, according to their conversation, was that the bee had turned up with no data from the entire time it had been away. Time it had spent in his workshop. But he knew this wasn't true - he'd already seen video from that time.

He stuffed the phone back in his pocket. This latest video wasn't helping. The only thing he knew for certain was that if he told Sarah about any of this, he wouldn't hear the end of it. This had all started the moment *he* had captured the bee at Klaus' house, and everything that had happened since then was because of that stupid action. Without that bee, nobody would be watching them or breaking into their house. Nobody would be sending them to discover dead bodies, and then get implicated in their murders. Nobody would be sending them to a party to die.

He decided that, for the moment, the safest course of action was to do nothing. He brought the beer bottle up to his lips and tipped it expectantly, but somehow it was empty. Sarah would be at least half an hour, so he rejoined the boys at the bar.

David was ready and waiting with his guitar and amplifier at his feet when Sarah pulled up. During the drive home they tactically avoided conversation about the new flat, other than there was a new customer that needed their cleaning services. Between them they already knew that this flat was another bolt hole they could use to avoid being spied on, so there wasn't any need to risk anyone overhearing them.

When she asked about how his evening had been he glossed over most of the details and avoided all discussion of shared drives and possible communication attempts. A moment of dread came over him as he realised that Sarah's shared drive might also contain the pictures. He couldn't ask her, and going through her phone wasn't his style. After all, they had nothing to hide from each other, usually. The only thing he could do was wait and see.

Later, when they were sure no one was listening, Sarah told him about the flat. The emptying, the decorating, the selling and the car in the garage that was insured and which they had permission to drive. At least something was going right today.

The next morning David was up early, his mind racing with possibilities about the shared drive. It had been a night of broken sleep and half remembered dreams in which various bees seemed to be attempting telepathic communication.

He was no further towards deciding if any of this was real, or a setup. Other than the images themselves, there was no evidence to support anyone or anything as the source. The more he thought about it, the more he realised he was getting nowhere.

"Morning babe," said Sarah as she walked into the kitchen, "crap night's sleep again?"

"Yep, rubbish. Too much going on. How about you?"

"I didn't think I slept at all, but then every time I looked at the clock another couple of hours had gone."

David placed her coffee in front of her.

"Do you want any breakfast?"

"Not at the moment, I'll just drink my coffee for now. Maybe brunch somewhere in Port de Pollença?"

"Oh, yes." he said, remembering the new flat, but not telegraphing it to the world. "Haven't we got another one to clean there today as well?"

"We do. It's in the town, not the port, but it's fairly close. What time do you want to get going?"

"After we finished these," said David, lifting his cup, "no point in hanging around."

The plan was to park where Sarah had done yesterday then walk to the flat again, hopefully keeping under the radar. David patted his pockets confirming that his phone and wallet were present.

"Hang on a minute," he said, "where's the car key?"

"Dunno babe, you had it … oh, wait, I had it last," admitted Sarah.

He checked the key hooks under the shelf in the hallway. Van keys, yes, but no car keys. How was this possible? They had two keys for each vehicle, and they lived right there, on the hooks.

"What were you wearing yesterday babe?" He asked.

"Ok, give me a minute, I'll check."

A couple of minutes later, Sarah returned holding the car key out towards David. Her body language was half victorious having found the keys, but also half guilty for being the one to misplace them.

"Ah," he said.

"Sorry babe, forgot to hang it up."

"Any idea about the other key?"

"It'll turn up."

"Mmm."

The drive to Alcudia and then around the bay to the port was beautiful at this time of year. The motorway was lined with countless oleanders flowering in an endless sea of pink, red and white flowers. Sarah chuckled as she thought back to the man in the café - highly toxic, I'm afraid.

Having parked the car and then walked to the flat, Sarah grabbed the key from her pocket and inserted it into the lock. David counted eight letterboxes outside of the door which presumably correlated to the number of flats in the building.

She pushed the door open, and David followed her through.

As they continued to the back of the hallway, they passed stairs that zig-zagged upwards into darkness. Sarah pressed the call button for the lift and within moments the door opened, revealing an older but relatively clean interior. Sarah pressed the button for the second floor. There was a short delay before the doors closed and the lift got underway.

One wall had a mirror with obligatory finger marks, and there were a few loose scraps of paper on the floor. Screwed up receipts or maybe sweet wrappers. It hasn't been cleaned recently, but at least it didn't stink of urine, cigarette smoke or worse.

The interior of the flat was dark. The dark furniture, dark curtains and heavy external shutters, all conspiring to eliminate virtually all light. David flicked the switch illuminating a bulb in the hallway then another in the living room. Neither had any discernible effect on the level of brightness in the flat.

"There's a lot of clutter in here," he said.

"Isn't there? It's difficult to believe you can get so much furniture into one room."

"Perhaps the kitchen light will help us to see our way around."

David flicked the switch in the kitchen causing the fluorescent tube to grunt a couple of times followed by several pings as the feeble starter coaxed the mercury vapor to arc in the tube. It hummed as it was reluctantly forced into giving off its dull glow. It did help with the light levels in the kitchen, but its influence didn't spread far.

The French doors to the balcony opened inwards. Having opened both, Sarah then unlocked the exterior shutter doors and pushed them outwards, allowing a flood of light to enter the room. David extinguished the largely ineffective and now also superfluous kitchen light.

"You could get a four-seater dining table out here," said Sarah, poking her head out and admiring the balcony's generous proportions, but not wanting to risk being seen.

"And a couple of comfy chairs down that end." Said David, also remaining mostly inside.

Sarah headed for the bedroom, where she opened the shutters, again allowing light to flood in. It was a good size too, but was full to the brim with twenty years' worth of trinkets and nostalgia.

"You know," said Sarah, "once we've got this place empty, it's actually a really nice flat."

"Have you noticed the marble floor under all of these rugs and dust?"

"It'll need a good polish, but we can handle that. First, we need to get a house clearance company in."

"Am I doing the decorating, is that the plan?" Asked David.

"Well, yeah. If you do it, or we do it, then we're not paying someone else."

David nodded in agreement. "Perhaps we should keep one of these tables as a work surface, until the painting is finished."

"Good idea. Do you want to go and have a look at the car in the garage?" She said, handing him the keys.

It was an older Volkswagen Golf, with a different battle scar on every panel. He hopped into the driver's seat and inserted the key. The dashboard lit up. At least there was enough power for that. David held his breath as he twisted the key to engage the starter. Click. Nothing. He would bring his charger next time and get the old girl up and running.

On the way back to the car they decided the order in which the work needed to be done but didn't tie themselves down to a schedule. After all, the longer it took to prepare and sell the flat, the longer they'd have it as an off-grid base it they needed it.

"I'll call the house clearance people on our spare phone. The one that Klaus doesn't know about," said Sarah.

"Actually, maybe it's time we got a new one of those. That one's been hanging around for a while and you just never know."

"Ok. We can sort that out on the way home. I'm sure there's a phone shop just around the corner from here."

Half an hour later the house clearance company were booked, using the newest phone, for the following Monday. Having gotten back into their car Sarah grabbed their phones from the glove box and saw that, amongst the other message and email notifications, there had been an alert from their home CCTV.

It was one of their observers letting himself in through the front gate and walking towards the front door.

"Looks like the house has had another visit from our friends," she whispered into David's ear and showed him her phone.

"We'll probably be home in a quarter of an hour," he said to the hidden microphone.

Sarah shook her head. She knew they would be gone by the time they got home. She shook her head and smiled at the thought of their visitors having a mild panic because of their imminent arrival.

Thirty-five minutes later they pulled up onto the driveway, both keen to know where the eavesdropping devices had been moved to now.

David opened the front door and deactivated the alarm. He wondered if there was any point to the damned thing, given the circumstances, but it amused him to play the game. They walked into the house with familiar discomfort knowing that their privacy had once again been violated.

"Cup of tea?" he asked, walking towards the kitchen.

"Please."

Sarah scanned the house for listening devices. She retraced her route a few times to double check, but ten minutes later she had found none and went to find David in the kitchen.

"Looks like they've taken the bugs." She said, in a hushed voice just in case she was wrong. She didn't quite trust her results.

"What, all of them?" He asked, sliding her cup towards her.

"Well, all the ones in the house, at least as far as I can tell. And, I guess the van has been parked here while we've been out."

A few minutes later Sarah returned with a spring in her step.

"The van is clear too," she said, grabbing her cup.

David pulled her closer so he could whisper in her ear.

"Do you think they've really gone, or have they been replaced with new ones that our detector can't find?"

"That's why I wasn't certain. This scanner says they're gone, but ..."

David brought his index finger up to his lips to quieten her. They were both on the same page. If there were new listening devices, there was a danger of telling Klaus everything they knew while their guard was down.

"Just in case they're listening," he whispered, "can we go for a walk or something?"

Closing the gate and walking up the road, they both noted that the car scheduled to be there watching them was absent. Its favourite parking space was still vacant, and it wasn't anywhere else up or down the road.

"The way I see it," said Sarah, "they've removed their spying devices, even removed their little shift-worker here." She indicated the vacant parking spot. "Their level of interest in us has definitely changed."

Something has changed: their search came up blank and their bee came home with amnesia, he thought.

"Assuming they have removed their equipment, not replaced it with an upgrade."

"There's no evidence for that at the moment, but you're right. We know all of their usual hiding places, so we know where to look for these spying devices."

"I just want to make sure we're not walking into a trap. Maybe we should still treat the house like its bugged for the moment."

"That's a good idea," she said, "but just for the sake of argument, let's say they have lost interest in us. Why now? Did the deaths at the party really put an end to Klaus' interest in us?"

"He said there were seven people working on the project."

"I'd take that with a pinch of salt." Said Sarah

"Probably, but let's say for the moment that's correct. With Gunther and Helmut, then the two at the party -"

"And their wives," Sarah interrupted.

"Yes, and the wives. That's four project workers accounted for. That leaves two others and the team leader."

"I'm going to assume that Klaus lied to us from the beginning. I think he was the team leader all along."

"I think you're right, and he's killing off his old team one by one. Helmut might not have been the first, maybe there were more deaths in Germany. He might have killed them all, we just don't know."

David thought about the other worker he'd seen in Klaus' office. Carl. Wasn't that what Klaus called him? He looked a bit young to have been part of the team back then, but maybe he was the intern. The office new-boy, fresh out of university. In any case, he was part of the team. Whether or not he was part of the original development was largely irrelevant. Surely there was no way Klaus would leave him alive.

"Your bee *escaped* as well", she said.

David noted how she'd emphasised *escaped*.

"But that was ages ago, it can't have taken him that long to notice it was back." He said.

"Who knows? Maybe these are all just parts of a jigsaw, and Klaus is now happy that all the witnesses are either dead or know nothing."

"He thinks we know nothing? We did manage to leave the party alive."

"Well, maybe nothing worth worrying about." She said, hoping that she was right, but knowing it couldn't be that easy.

Their conversation paused as they turned into a new road, their route around the block having passed the half-way point, they were now heading home.

"So, at the party, when that bee put the frighteners on you and then let you go... was that Klaus telling you he could kill you at any time?"

Or was it my bee telling me it can disobey orders.

"Could be," said David, "they don't need to bug the house because they've got mobile surveillance and murder on demand."

"Ok so. We assume we're still being watched, either by undetectable bugs in the house and car or we can be watched by your little buddies. Either way we still need to watch what we talk about and when."

"Exactly."

"But if it's not that, if this is a de-escalation, or even an end to his interest in us, then we should also not be interested in him or his activities. We just go back to our normal lives and try to forget about all of this."

David knew she was right. In Klaus' eyes they needed to be *seen* to be disinterested in him and his project. The idea of letting it all go and forgetting about it, provided it did actually go away, was quite appealing.

38.

The next few days were very busy with work. The peak tourist season was starting, which meant they'd both be putting in a lot of hours over the next few months. October, the end of the season, seemed a very long way away. They needed to hire a couple of extra workers to help out for the summer. For the moment they could look after their properties with just the two of them, but they needed to split up to cover the geography. Sarah covered Alcudia and Pollença, while David took care of the middle of the island from Santa Maria to Inca.

The longer days and stronger sun meant the algae was starting to proliferate in the swimming pools. Around Sarah's patch the flats that had swimming pools were shared access and were looked after by the residents' association. There were a few properties that had their own private pools, but Sarah could handle those. David's patch had a lot more private pools, which meant each of his properties took longer to service.

He was in the middle of checking the pH and chlorine levels at one of his regular properties when his phone pinged. He put his water sample down and retreated from the edge of the pool. There had been accidents before, so David's phone being in his pocket was a breach of their own company rules. No phones within five metres of the swimming pool.

A file had been added to his shared drive. He clicked on the thumbnail. The video played. It showed the outside of the block of flats where Klaus' office was. After a moment it showed Klaus closing the external door behind him then crossing the street and getting into his car. As the car drove away the camera followed for a short distance before stopping in front of a pharmacy. The sign outside the pharmacy, as well as displaying a bright green cross, also showed the temperature. 25°C. The sign's multi-purpose display then cycled to show the time, 20:36. Then the date 26th April, yesterday. Then the video stopped.

David shook his head. He placed his phone on a chair, away from the swimming pool, and returned to his water sample. The video, he supposed, showed what time Klaus left the office yesterday, but it didn't tell him who had sent the video. It didn't give him any more real information, so he pushed the video to the back of his mind and carried on with his work.

Once he'd finished the day's houses he messaged Sarah:

I'm done. You need a hand?

Just started last flat. Home in 1.5 hours

OK. See you at home.

OK

He was just about to pocket his phone when it pinged again. Another file had been added to the shared drive. He clicked on the thumbnail and it was another video of Klaus leaving the office, the same format as the one he'd watched earlier. This time the sign on the pharmacy said 18:35, 27th April. David checked the current time at the top of the screen. The video had been filmed 5 minutes ago.

Another ping and another file added. He clicked and it played. Again, it was Klaus leaving the office, but his time the sign on the pharmacy said 4pm last Friday. This piqued his interest. Tomorrow was Friday. He figured he had a method of testing who or what was sending these files.

At 3pm the next day David parked almost opposite Klaus' office. He had come in Emily's car hoping to remain incognito, but then got out and took a selfie making sure the car, its number plate and the office were clearly visible in the background. He saved the picture to his shared drive, then drove a little further up the road towards the pharmacy.

Having chosen to come in a car that ought to be unfamiliar to his quarry he now felt quite vulnerable, having sent the picture. He might as well paint a target on his forehead. Surely it was only a matter of time before Klaus came along and shot him or stabbed him. Ok, he didn't have a history of doing it himself and maybe not on the main road, but David knew what the man was capable of. Maybe if he left his window open one of the bees would make it fast and painless.

His phone pinged, making him jump. It was just after 4pm and a short video was added to his shared drive. It showed Carl and Klaus leaving the office.

A couple of minutes later he saw Klaus drive past in his BMW. He also noticed the bee following it, which carried on up to the sign on the pharmacy then turned around, heading for home but the flight line deviated towards David. It stopped hovered over the bonnet of the car for a few seconds and then flew off over the roof.

A few minutes later he got to watch the same scene, this time from the perspective of the bee that had filmed it.

He sat staring at the screen dumbstruck and in awe of the video he had just watched. Whether it was a person or a computer system that was sending him these videos he still didn't know but he suspected, maybe hoped, that it wasn't Klaus.

What he did know was that this system was way more than just a method of killing people. As an active surveillance system, it would be unbeatable. It seemed to have been filming Klaus leaving and getting a date stamp to send to him and in the process of doing this it had noticed his car. It then appeared to change its mission parameters, mid-flight and add a fly-by of David in his car. He found it amazing that computer technology had come so far as to be able to think for itself and change its mission based on what it saw. Either that or a person was actually flying the drone.

David looked up at the flat he'd been shown in an earlier video. There was no sign of movement, but then there was no sign of movement in any of the flats. Sunset wasn't for another four and a half hours so there would be no lights on inside and any computer or TV screens wouldn't be bright enough for him to notice. He could hang around until it started to go dark, but this was Friday night. He'd already pushed his luck too far by going behind Sarah's back with this latest round of bee obsession.

39.

"Hi babe, how are you?" Asked David.

"All good, thank you. Two questions for you. How was your day and are we still meeting the thingy's tonight?"

"Today was good. And yes, Nat and Jeremy, and you were supposed to decide where."

"Oh,"

Over the weekend more pictures were added to his shared drive. He had set up the original cloud account and then given Sarah access for storing pictures. He thought that explained why he got notifications of her additions to the drive but she didn't seem to have seen any of the videos. He still couldn't explain how this other entity was able to add pictures, but he'd obviously been hacked somehow.

He kept getting notifications about the same series of pictures. His phone was pinging every hour or so. Eventually he put his phone on silent so that Sarah wouldn't think it was some new girlfriend that was texting him.

The pictures were always the same:

Klaus' car.
The centre console of the BMW.
Exterior door to the apartment complex.
Door into Klaus' flat or office.
A rack of servers that look to be the size of a small refrigerator.
A laptop.
A suitcase.

Some kind of docking station with eight bees on the top. A bunch of keys.

David had to stop himself looking at the pictures whenever Sarah was anywhere near. There was no way he could explain the pictures or how they'd come to be on his phone. He could imagine the conversation and he sounded like an idiot every time he re-ran it in his head.

Since he was making no progress understanding the pictures or whether their order was important, he moved on to thinking about how he might respond. Obviously he'd be sending a picture or a video as it was the same method of communication, but what did he want to say? Message received? Nice pictures? I have no idea what you're talking about? Yes, that sounded right... I have no idea what you're talking about.

He propped his phone up on the kitchen work surface. He selected the selfie camera and started recording. Making sure he was centred on the screen, he then shrugged his shoulders, pushed out his bottom lip and turned his palms towards the ceiling.

There was no point in editing the video to make it shorter or neater. And anyway, it would be shared automatically to the cloud before he could even start.

He checked the shared drive. Sure enough there it was, his attempt at communication. He kept an eye on the screen for a couple of minutes, but quickly decided that watching the phone wouldn't speed up a response. He double checked that the phone was on silent and stuffed it in his pocket.

They were meeting friends that evening. This particular couple were always great fun. The non-stop conversation usually resulted in whole evenings disappearing in what seemed like minutes. Despite the welcome distraction,

David couldn't help but fixate on his phone, or rather the message he was waiting for. He kept patting his pocket to make sure it was still there and kept finding excuses to leave the table.

He would disappear to the kitchen to bring more wine for everyone, though he himself wasn't drinking as he had volunteered to drive. He would go to the bathroom, anywhere he could be private and check his phone. But at the same time, he tried to make sure that when he was at the table he was engaged in the conversation. He really didn't need anyone to notice that he was distracted, and certainly didn't want to have to explain.

As they got into bed around midnight there still hadn't been any messages. Despite his efforts to sleep, David's brain had other ideas. He kept going over the pictures and what they meant. He thought he understood each individual picture, not much to it really, a computer, a door. He didn't understand the centre console of the BMW. It obviously made sense to whoever or whatever had sent the pictures, but David didn't quite get it. Maybe he was missing something or maybe it was just some pictures with no hidden meaning. Maybe it was him that was making them into a conversation when, in reality, they were just a series of pictures.

"How did you sleep babe?" asked Sarah the next morning as she placed a cup of coffee down on his bedside cabinet.

"Oh, on and off. Brain was too busy."

"It's probably everything we talked about last night still buzzing around in your head. And you were good last night, didn't drink anything, did you?"

"Well, I had one glass. But I usually sleep better with less alcohol."

"I brought you a coffee. You can have a lie-in today; we haven't got much on."

"Thanks babe."

Sarah gently closed the bedroom door. David reached for his phone. Somehow it was 9:30 already. And he had a notification, another series of pictures.

The BMW centre console.

Someone (probably Klaus) picking up a bunch of keys on a lanyard from the centre console.

Klaus using one of the keys to unlock the external door.

Klaus using one of the keys to unlock the internal door.

That had done it. The mystery picture of the centre console was actually a picture of a bunch of keys *in* the centre console. That picture on its own would have been enough. He felt like the pictures of them in use were more of a comment on his intelligence than an indication of how the keys were to be used.

Ok, so now he understood what each of the pictures was but was there an overall message? He slurped some coffee and began to get dressed. He understood that he was being shown how to get into the office and what equipment was there, but what was he supposed to do with that information. Destroy the bees and the system that ran them? Maybe he was being encouraged to steal them, but why and by whom?

He pondered the question for the rest of the day, trying to come up with other explanations that didn't involve breaking and entering and theft.

Having tossed all sorts of ideas around in his head, he decided he needed more information, he needed to send some pictures that conveyed the idea of being 'rehomed', as he was now starting to call it. He took a picture of his van with the rear doors open and a picture of the bench in his workshop - a method of transport and a new home.

Again, there was no reply forthcoming. This time he was more relaxed about being made to wait. Yesterday he had a message that he didn't understand and was hoping for more information to make the message gel. This time he thought he knew what the message was and was waiting for a response to confirm that he had understood what was being asked of him. But somehow he felt more relaxed about the patience required before a response would come.

The next morning he was up early and headed to Veronique's flat in Port de Pollença. He had checked his phone first thing and had received an answer to yesterday's photographic question. The reply was simply a picture of him smiling and giving a thumbs up. Apparently they or it, or whatever had found a suitable picture of David and used it. He took that to mean 'Yes, put us in the van and take us to your workshop.'

He parked the van near the coffee shop and left his phone in the glove box. Now, more than ever, he wanted this flat to stay hidden from Klaus. The fresh air on the five-minute walk to the flat helped to wake him up, a fresh bounce in his stride.

The house clearance people were the customary one hour or so late, but David used the time wisely and went down into the garage to get the car's battery on charge and check the oil and other fluid levels.

Once they did turn up the three young men got straight to work as David supervised from the kitchen. They worked quickly and in no time the flat had noticeably more space. As he watched them work, he suddenly had an idea. He smiled to himself and nodded. The workshop wouldn't be where he would rehome the bees, this flat would be.

Nobody else knew about it, apart from Sarah, and she had no need to come here either. This would be their little secret.

He was organizing the clearance, he was doing all the decorating and he'd be polishing the marble floor. They could be housed here quite safely until the point where they had to put the flat on the market. Almost certainly it would be Sarah organizing the pictures of the flat before advertising it for sale on the internet. The bees would need to be somewhere else before then.

Ninety minutes later he was walking back to the van. They had been able to pay him for some of the nicer pieces, but most of it was worthless. After they had driven off in the van, David had gone back to the VW in the garage and reconnected the freshly charged battery, the engine had then started on the first attempt. Today was turning into a success.

40.

He told Sarah that he was meeting some of the boys at the rehearsal studio, a lie which left him with a quandary. Did he take the van, as he normally would do? Parking that near Klaus' office was probably the opposite of camouflage, whatever that was. Or did he take Veronique's VW and park the van somewhere off the beaten track in Lloseta where there was a small risk that Sarah would see it?

He took the car. The van was parked in a side road they hardly ever used. Guilt flushed across him as he left the van and walked away. He had never lied to Sarah about anything before. Nothing real. They'd always been straight, equal partners in everything they did and every decision they made. Until now.

He got into Veronique's car and drove to Santa Maria. He tried to concentrate on the job at hand, with the idea that it would diminish his feelings of guilt. He hoped that further surveillance of his target might prove inspirationally more fruitful that simply thinking about it from afar.

Ideas spun in his head like leaves blown by the wind. Each thought having a moment in his mind's eye before being briskly moved on and replaced with the next. Was there an alarm? How would he get the keys? He paused on these thoughts for a moment before they were pushed aside by new worries. How would he get all that equipment out? Several journeys between the van and the office? Would that increase his chances of being seen? Could he disguise himself? Were there cameras?

The ideas continued circling, then he went back to the beginning. Was there an alarm? How would he get the keys?

Before he knew it he was coming into Santa Maria and would be at the apartment complex within a few minutes. He was seeing familiar landmarks and would soon be choosing a convenient parking spot with a good view. The traffic was a bit slow, but that was normal for this part of town, with traffic shuffling between junctions and traffic lights.

As he went to accelerate the engine hesitated, more of a stutter. He looked at the dashboard and confirmed the engine was running, the revs were up. This time there was more of a cough, a definite moment of zero power, but the engine jumped back into life. Briefly.

He looked at the fuel gauge. Zero. Not low or close to zero. Zero. He shook his head, disappointed with himself. Disappointed on another level. How could he run out of fuel? There had been no warning light, no buzzer or alarm warning him of his predicament. No range warning. Just zero. Nada.

The car trickled to a halt, choosing its own parking space as David guided it nearer to the curb. He slammed his hands against the steering wheel, then brought them up to his forehead. What an idiot.

He cranked the engine a couple of times but knew that it was pointless. Maybe he would be lucky and find a fuel can in the boot. Maybe the car did this a lot, had a history of running out of fuel.

He got out of the car and went around the back to check the boot. There were some shopping bags and an old pair of trainers, but no fuel can. Of course not.

He was just about to close the boot when a car crept up behind him and blasted its horn. It made him jump out of his skin, nearly banging his head on the boot lid. Why did people feel the need to sneak up behind you and scare the crap out of you?

He turned to face the car ready to punch whoever it was that had scared the life out of him. The reflection of the bright sky on the windscreen made it difficult to see who the driver was, but he recognised the car … Klaus.

He beckoned David over through the open driver's window. David slammed the boot shut, taking his aggression out on the car now that he wouldn't be taking it out on the driver.

"Hello David, what are you doing here?" asked Klaus.

"Well, driving along in my customer's car," he said indicating the VW, "and I've run out of fuel."

"Well, that's unfortunate. Look, it can't be far to the next petrol station, I can give you a lift."

Now David's adrenaline was surging. He could feel his chest tightening, his heart racing. He felt like it must be obvious that his face had flushed red. He couldn't think straight.

"Um. OK, I'll lock the car."

He walked slowly back to the car forcing his feet alternately to take one more step. Hopefully his shaking wasn't visible, and his dizziness wouldn't affect his balance. He lent on the VW for support as he opened the driver's door. He made sure all the windows were closed before locking the door. He patted his pockets to ensure his phone and wallet were present. He forced himself to take a long deep breath. He walked towards Klaus' passenger door like a lamb to the slaughter.

He got in the car, closed the door and fastened his seat belt. Klaus would now be going to tell him how much of an idiot he had been, how he managed to con David into believing the bees wanted to talk to him, needed his help in escaping. And how he was now going to be taken to somewhere quiet and killed.

"You don't normally run out of fuel do you, David? Maybe the fuel gauge isn't working properly?"

"Well, I guess that could be it. Like I said, it's not my car so I'm not very familiar with it."

"Oh well, not to worry. I'm sure the petrol station just up here will sell fuel cans."

David began to breathe a little more freely and his heart rate had come down a little, but he still felt dizzy. Instead of just aimlessly staring out of the windscreen like a rabbit caught in the headlights, David forced himself to move his eyes around more and tried to make himself relax.

He moved around in the chair to get himself into a more comfortable position. He suddenly remembered the picture and looked down at the centre console. The bunch of keys on the lanyard were in their usual place. Right next to them was a BMW car key - the type that was supposed to stay in your pocket not in the ignition.

That key was what he needed to get hold of. With that key, he could open this car at any time and take the keys to the office. If he was quick, he'd be able to take all of the equipment and then return the keys before anybody noticed they were missing. But if he took it now Klaus would know straight away who to blame. The engine would probably stop and he wouldn't be able to lock the car when he got home.

The car pulled onto the forecourt and parked carefully and precisely next to a pump.

"You sort your fuel out, David. I'm going to get myself a coffee and some cigarettes."

"Ok, sure. I'll go and buy a fuel can and fill it up."

David went into the shop and located the fuel cans. After a brief discussion he left a €20 note with the attendant, which would be more than enough to cover the cost of the fuel and the can. He headed back to the pump and filled it with five litres.

Having filled the can he left it near the boot of the BMW and went inside to settle the bill. Klaus had got his coffee and was about to pay. David noticed him patting his pockets the same way he did, looking for his wallet. He pulled it out to pay for his coffee, but it was the car key that came out with the wallet that drew David's attention. He had been keeping close eye on it and didn't think that he'd seen Klaus take the key from inside the car. Maybe this was another key. A spare.

Once Klaus had paid, David watched carefully as Klaus replaced the wallet and then the key in his pocket. David reminded the attendant which pump he had used and about the fuel can. He was keen to get back to the car to see if that key was still there, but the attendant was determined to go about their business in the usual lackadaisical manner.

He found himself drumming his fingers on the counter. He turned to see where Klaus had gotten to, expecting he'd be back at the car by now, but he was waiting by the door for David finish paying.

They walked back to the car together. Klaus opened the boot and David lifted the fuel can in. As Klaus closed the boot lid, David moved quickly around to the passenger door And as soon as he opened it, he could see the other key sitting there, waiting for him.

Why would he have two keys in the car? David wondered if he'd ever done this himself in his own car and realised that he probably had. Occasionally he might already have a car key in his pocket but then pick another one up on his way out of the back door.

Maybe the key sitting in front of him wasn't for this car. Maybe they had two BMWs. Anna drove a VW, so that wasn't it. He kept trying to think of other explanations, but time was running out. David's car wasn't very far away.

He started to think about how he could take the key without being noticed. He felt like it would be so obvious, him just taking the key right there in front of Klaus' eyes. There was no way it would go unnoticed.

Suddenly a cyclist flew across the pedestrian crossing in front of them, causing Klaus to brake hard. Klaus blasted the horn at the cyclist and hit the button to lower his electric window. He then began shouting at the cyclist, although David's German wasn't good enough to keep up.

He slid his hand over to the key and closed his fingers around it, keeping his movements slow and silent. He casually brought the key back to his lap keeping it covered and out of sight.

Certain he'd been spotted, David held his breath and felt his heart rate rise. Time passed slowly as Klaus finished his verbal assault on the cyclist. The car proceeded down the road. The driver's window was closed, and they carried on back to David's car with Klaus mumbling something about cyclists taking responsibility for their own safety.

They pulled up opposite his car and David got out. On his way to the boot he pocketed the key, keen to get it out of sight completely. He grabbed the fuel can and thanked Klaus. As the BMW pulled away, David couldn't believe he'd managed to steal Klaus' spare key from under his nose. Whether it would stay secret was another question.

41.

"So, the flat has been cleared and you've got the car running ok?" asked Sarah.

"Yep, all good. I'm hoping to start on the painting later this week, but there's still some fittings that need removing and some prep work."

"And how bad did the floor look under those rugs?""

"Actually, the floor is much better where it's been protected by the rugs. The worst bit is near the front door, where all the dirt gets dragged in and ground into the marble. But that's always the case."

"Do you think our machine will be able to handle it?"

"Oh yeah, no problem, but I'll do that last. Let's see how far I get with the prep this week."

The preparation work and decorating at the flat along with his other regular commitments were one thing. But, what really preoccupied David was the liberation of the bees, and he was well aware that he now thought of them as his bees. Whilst under the ownership and terror campaign waged by Klaus the bees had reached out to him and asked to be… what exactly had they asked of him? Did they want him to steal them? Rehome them? Did they want a new keeper, or were they just fed up with the last one? Did they just want to be switched off and left alone? Maybe they wanted freedom, to be let into out the wild?

Either he hadn't been told enough information or he wasn't seeing the message clearly. Normally he'd be able to discuss this with Sarah but, as he'd chosen to do this alone, he had no one to brainstorm with. He was sure he'd get more answers after he'd taken the equipment from the office. There had to be answers in there somewhere.

Whatever the bees wanted him to achieve, he knew that the next step in the process was to get hold of the office keys. According to the bees, or whoever it was that had been communicating with him, they usually resided in the centre console of Klaus' BMW.

His procurement of the car key had been a clumsy, opportunistic affair and he was still amazed that he had, somehow, gotten away with it.

He wasn't sure which approach to theft he preferred. The slow, considered, methodical approach, where every eventuality was foreseen and accounted for, or the grab and go technique. One thing he was sure of was that all the planning resulted in an ever-increasing pile of if's and but's, each of which made him feel less and less confident that he could do this without getting caught.

And that was just him getting caught by Klaus. The idea that he was also lying to Sarah was even worse. He seemed to be living with a constant stream of adrenaline pumping through his veins. He couldn't keep going like this. His ideas kept circling and repeating, as did his guilt. He had to stop this craziness in his head and get out. Get out and do something else.

He headed over to Veronique's flat and got stuck into some mindless menial labour. He hated decorating, but the scraping, filling and sanding was exactly the sort of physical distraction that he needed.

The flakes of old paint fell away from his scraper, defeated by its keen blade. Tumbling and spinning through the air until they landed clumsily amongst their fallen comrades. David's arm ached as the repetitive action wore on his muscles. He tried changing his angle of attack and even tried using his other hand, neither of which helped. He couldn't seem to get the power or control right, producing inefficient results. Inevitably he always returned to his favoured hand and angle, which still ached.

Some of the plaster beneath the paint had also become fatigued of its function and crumbled and fell like fresh powder snow on the marble floor. He swept the flakes and crumbs and powder into a neat pile, then pushed them into the dustpan. Some of the finer dislodged material had floated further, some had gotten on his clothes and some, he realised, in his nostrils. It had changed the aroma of the apartment for the better, but only for him.

The work, however, was having the desired effect – he wasn't getting himself into a spin over Sarah and Klaus. The work kept his mind occupied just enough to be able to plan without worrying.

The aim was simple. Klaus would walk Toto at about 10:30, just before his usual bedtime. As long as David turned up at the house somewhere between dusk and dog walking then he should be fine. Klaus would be eating, drinking and watching the TV. David could slip in, grab the keys and be gone in a heartbeat, very straightforward.

The driveway was empty when he arrived at the house – not part of the plan. He drove past with his mouth practically hanging open. He hadn't seen that coming. He drove a little further up the road and turned the engine off.

He closed his eyes and took a deep breath. It was a minor setback. Nothing major. He'd just wait here in the darkness until his opportunity came. He'd be ready. He was probably picking Anna up from the tennis club, or wherever. They wouldn't be long; everything was under control. Breathe.

The waiting was dangerous because it gave him time to think. The potential problems and ideas of him getting caught kept resurfacing and he kept pushing them away. He was in the middle of another imaginary explanation to Sarah when he was brought out of his recrudescence by the flash of headlights turning a corner behind him. There weren't many cars like that around here. David again made himself breathe.

There was no rush. It would take them a few minutes to sort themselves out and get into the house. Then there was the possibility of multiple trips back to the car, especially if they'd been to the supermarket. He looked at the clock on the dashboard and decided that they needed five minutes minimum. He gave them ten.

He had to force his brain to go off topic as he watched the clock. He imagined going fishing with his mates as a kid and before that with his father. Paying the day license to the bailiff from the few coins he kept in his tackle box. The floats and the weights. They all had a purpose, but as a kid he just liked how they looked and the promise they held. He never really knew if he was using the right ones for the fish he was targeting. He never knew that he was targeting any fish in particular. Anything that got caught on the hook was a bonus.

Ten. He couldn't say it flew by or that it dragged, but the time was up. He checked around the car and the road to see who might be around. Empty. He got out of the car and shut the door. He had decided not to lock the car to make his escape faster, but now he wasn't so sure. Did he need a fast escape? Do speedy exits make you look more guilty? On balance, he now thought that rushing wasn't the correct way forward, so he pushed the button on the car key, locking the doors. He then pocketed the key.

He tried to walk at a normal pace towards the Faber's house. Not too fast, not too slow. He decided that he would do an initial walk-by to recce the place. The lack of streetlights meant that the street itself was dark. Illumination was therefore limited to the areas where each house had installed their own lighting. In the case of the Faber's this meant the front door and the area between the front door and the driver's door of Klaus' BMW.

He had done a couple of passes. He knew that too many would look suspicious. It was time to either get on with it or give up.

On his next pass he turned and walked up their driveway, being sure to keep his gait and pace normal. He walked around to the passenger door, away from the driveway lighting and front door, and pushed the BMW key. The car obeyed as it flashed its lights and unlocked its doors. He checked around for witnesses then pulled on the door handle. It opened easily. He bent down and ducked into the car and put his hand on the seat to support himself and leant further in.

The keys were there, just as the videos had promised. He reached out his hand to grab the bunch, knowing that his would be the perfect time for Klaus or Anna to catch him in the act. He'd gone over this moment time and again in his head - this was one of the key points in tonight's theft that he was most worried about.

There was a noise from the road. Voices and footsteps. David froze. He could feel his breathing quicken even as he tried to make it quieter. He could hear his heartbeat in his ears. His silence only served to amplify the noises made by the people on the road. He'd definitely been spotted. Caught red-handed.

Then he heard laughter from the people. It wasn't mocking laughter, but happy laughter. He allowed himself a gentle peek around the headrest. He moved slowly, trying to see them out of the rear window of the car. It was a young couple enjoying their walk together. They were lost in their own world. Not knowing or caring who David was or what he was doing. They carried on past.

David found that he had been holding his breath. He grabbed the keys and got out of the car. Closing the door as gently and quietly as he could, he retreated out of the driveway and as he continued, he pushed the button in his pocket and again the car obeyed.

Back at Veronique's car he fumbled for his keys, his fingers searching in his pockets. They weren't in the left pocket, and they weren't in the right.

What? Oh crap, you've got to be kidding.

Left pocket again. Nope. Right pocket. Nope

But they were there, jumbled up with the BMW key and the house key and some loose change. There were the stolen office keys, filling his pocket. He made a note to be more organised next time. Why did he even have this junk with him? This job needed two keys: his car and the BMW. He also had two pockets in his jeans. Next time.

The car started first time. He double checked that he had the BMW and office keys. Everything was present and correct. Panic over. He wasn't ready to relax just yet, but a small smile did crack in the corner of his mouth. The car purred quietly as he crept away from the kerb. He accelerated to a sensible speed that wouldn't draw attention. Just right.

42.

David parked Veronique's car a short distance from the office. He chose a space where he wouldn't have to cross the road with the stolen goods. Having locked the car he made sure he knew which pocket the key went into.

David examined the office keys. There was no alarm fob and he hadn't been given a code. He hoped this didn't mean his break-in attempt would be short-lived and noisy. He rolled his balaclava up to look like a hat and put it on his head.

As he approached the front door to the apartment complex, he tried to control his breathing even though his body and hormones had other ideas. He inserted one of the two keys into the lock and turned. The door opened. He walked into the entrance hall, trying to look like he belonged there. Creeping around looking like you were going to rob the place would only make him look suspicious. The entrance hall didn't appear to have any cameras so he walked up to the lift and pressed the call button.

There was a brief pause before the lift arrived and the doors opened. He didn't pull the balaclava down just yet because if he met anyone, he really would look like he was robbing the place. Instead, He turned to face the door as soon as he was in the lift, trying to keep his back to any cameras that might be inside. The lift soon delivered him to the second floor, where he cautiously looked left and right down the corridor. There was no one around and he couldn't see any cameras near the door to the flat, but that didn't mean there weren't any. He rolled the balaclava down, leaving only his eyes and mouth visible. He felt like an idiot.

He crept towards the door with the key pinched between his thumb and forefinger. He inserted and turned. The lock clicked, releasing the door which he pushed open slightly and paused. Held his breath and listened. There was no sound from within. He pushed the door a little more, expecting there to be some kind of noise from the hinge that would give him away, or at least make him feel more self-conscious, but there was none. Having slipped through the door he kept a grip on the door handle and guided it back towards the jamb, making sure it closed silently. The air smelled of a typically unkempt office. A mixture of stale men and food leftovers. They obviously didn't have a regular cleaner or adequate ventilation.

Inside the office was dimly lit by assorted pieces of equipment. Green lights blinked on various computers. Part way down the hall an electrical extension cable with four sockets also seemed to act like a child's nightlight illuminating the corridor. David took the first door on the right, which he had been led to believe belonged to Carl.

The small office was also dimly illuminated by various pieces of electrical equipment. David knew this room would have the laptop and outside on the balcony would be the docking station. The rough woven wool of his balaclava made his face itch. He scratched. The movement of the material dislodged a bead of sweat which trickled down his cheek. Perhaps that was what itched rather than the material itself.

The key was already in the door to the balcony and it unlocked easily. David eased the door open. Once again it operated quietly and efficiently. Before him on the ground, was the docking station. He had to admit it was an impressive sight. It was about the size of a microwave with eight bees stationed on top. Presumably they were ready to be sent off on some clandestine mission. He bent over and hefted it with both hands, but it wasn't as heavy as he'd expected. As he brought it inside its electrical cable followed and he kept moving further from the door until the cable was completely inside. He carefully lowered the docking station to the floor, then went back to close the door.

The bees remained in place. He wondered if they were watching. If they didn't want to be taken they would have flown away, wouldn't they? He took a moment to look around the office to see if any of the other items were there. It made sense to gather all the items from this office together before moving on to the office next door, but he didn't see anything else on his shopping list.

He moved carefully down the corridor into what would be Klaus' office. Once again, the abundance of electrical equipment present provided dim but sufficient light. Most of it seemed to be coming from the racks of servers near the door. There were several computers contained within one cabinet - the one that had been shown to him in the pictures. It was about the size of a small dishwasher. Of all the equipment, this was the most likely to give him away when he unplugged it. He decided to disconnect this last.

Scanning the office, he saw the suitcase he'd been shown in the pictures. Now he could see it in real life, it was more of a transport case for equipment rather than a suitcase. It was made of hard plastic with two industrial latches keeping the lid closed. He picked it up and placed it on the desk.

With gentle encouragement the latches sprung open allowing him to lift the lid. The case had a foam inner lining where smaller, transparent plastic boxes were each inserted into their own recess.

The case, or at least the foam inner, had been specifically designed to accommodate the plastic boxes. Even though he didn't really have time to spare, he removed one of the boxes from the foam. It was a snug fit, but a small indent allowed him to insert his index finger which gave him the access and leverage needed to get the box free. He brought the box up in front of his face and angled it to catch the dim light cast by the server's ever blinking lights.

It took his eyes a moment to focus on the detail of the contents rather than the transparent plastic of the box. The container was subdivided into eight individual cells, each of which contained a thorax. A broad pair of wings attached to a central unit. He gently turned the box over allowing him to see the underside and the 6 legs extended straight out, under the wings at an unnatural angle. Now he could see why the legs gathered the way they did when he had disassembled the units in his workshop. It hadn't made sense then. But now, and he looked at them in storage, he could see why. Each individual thorax took up less space, making their packaging and transport more efficient. It also meant that the legs were less likely to get damaged in transit.

He kept hold of the box while his index finger probed further into the foam of the transport case. There were two more boxes each with eight abdomens and a fourth box that was empty. He assumed these were the same eight bees that now resided on the base station.

Perhaps the bees were supposed to be disassembled before transport. It probably depended how long and how rough the journey was going to be. His focus then came back to the room and the task at hand. He was supposed to be robbing the place, not wondering about engineering niceties. He put the boxes back into their slot in the suitcase and closed the lid. Having made sure the latches were firmly closed, he tried to remember what else was on his shopping list. He replayed the pictures in his head a couple of times. He needed to remember by himself. He was trying to avoid getting his phone out and wasting more time. After a few seconds of trying to remember, he gave in and looked at the phone. He figured it would be more efficient to get everything on the list tonight, after all his chances of being able to return for any missed items tomorrow were zero.

He hurriedly ripped the phone from his pocket and fumbled to unlock it quickly and get to the appropriate pictures. He looked through the photographic list of demands. Having mentally ticked off each item on his list he nodded to himself, pleasantly surprised that he'd managed to remember all items except one. The bunch of keys. In the picture they were on the desk that stood in front of him, but he couldn't see them. He picked up the case to make sure he hadn't put it down on them earlier, then started shuffling the papers and notebooks that obscured the desktop. He couldn't see anything there, so he opened the uppermost of the three or four drawers under the right side of the desk. The rollers in the drawers slide mechanism complained as he pulled harder than he'd expected on the handle. He could imagine years of accumulated dirt preventing the mechanism from operating smoothly. The drawer opened revealing a clutter of everyday objects inside. This is what Sarah and he would call the junk drawer. Had no idea what Klaus called it.

Laying on top of the various boxes of batteries, staples, discarded instructions and office accoutrements was the bunch of keys. He picked them up and slid the drawer shut. He cast his eyes over the items he'd collected in this room and wondered how he'd be getting them all down to his car. There was no way he could do this in one trip, in fact the server on its own was probably too large for him to move without help.

He was about to go back to the first office when he noticed a four-wheeled trolley half buried under boxes and discarded items of no-longer needed winter clothing. He removed the layer of detritus that camouflaged it, revealing an almost new trolley that was the perfect size for the job at hand. In fact, this was probably how they'd transported everything into the office in the first place.

The largest item was the computer cabinet, which he thought should be loaded first. He wheeled the trolley alongside. He would leave it switched on with all the cables connected until the last moment before he went out of the door. He made sure there was plenty of extra loose cabling so that nothing would unplug itself when he lifted the cabinet. It had a handle on each side which he grabbed and tested the weight, before trying to lift it onto the trolley. It was heavy but he was able to keep it under control as he shuffled and then placed it on the trolley.

He placed the transport case on the trolley in front of the computer cabinet, then calmly walked around to the first office. This was no time to be tripping over or dropping anything. The end was in sight.

The eight bees still sat obediently on top of the docking station. The top of the unit, where they were docked, was surrounded by a raised lip. It almost looked as if there should be some kind of lid but he couldn't see it, and frankly didn't have time to look. It was probably hiding under some notebook or discarded paperwork. He picked up the laptop and placed it on top of the docking station. It covered 90% of the area that he would have liked it to. It would have to be good enough for the moment. If the bees really wanted to escape they would. Probably could have already.

He took a breath. The time had come to start unplugging equipment. First was the docking station. He carried it, with the laptop still in place, into the back office and put them on top of the computer cabinet. When he unplugged that he would need to get moving.

Before that he wanted to make sure that he had everything he'd come to steal. He ran through the list again, but this time adding his car key, the door key on the lanyard and the bunch he'd taken from the drawer. Everything was present and correct.

He pushed the on/off button on each of the computer units, then lent down to where the cabinet had been against the wall. He unplugged the network cable first, followed by the power cable. The lights blinked out one by one. There were no sirens or flashing lights warning of the equipment being disconnected. At least, not here in the office. He could imagine various alerts going off on peoples' mobile phones. Hopefully, he'd be long gone before they could get here.

He shoved the trolley down the corridor towards the door. He realised that he needed to get to the door first, before the trolley. He should be pulling, not pushing, but it was too late for that. As he neared the door, he squeezed himself between the trolley and the wall. He got through fine but had probably removed five years of dirt from the wall with his butt.

He pulled the door open and wheeled the trolley through. Once in the corridor he made sure the door closed quietly and wondered at what point he should be removing his balaclava. At this point he felt like he still needed it as a safety blanket.

He pressed the call button for the lift and the door opened almost instantly. Either the lift had stayed on this floor for the duration of his visit, or someone had recently come up to this level. Either way he needed to get out. He pushed the trolley into the lift and hit the ground floor button. Time seemed to go into slow motion as he waited for the doors to close, expecting someone else to turn up at the last second and get in the lift with him. They eventually slid shut and the lift made its descent at a relaxed, almost torturous pace.

Finally. A ping indicated the lift's arrival on the ground floor, followed by another seemingly deliberate delay before the doors began opening. David was clamouring to get out before the doors were open wide enough for the trolley. As soon as there was room, he heaved it clear of the lift, then had to grab the docking station as it almost slid off the cabinet. He shook his head. Dropping everything would only delay him. Better to get this done in one smooth journey. More haste, less speed.

He began pulling on the front door handle, then realised his balaclava was still covering his face. He pulled it off and wedged it between the cabinet and the trolley. Once outside there was a small step down to the pavement, only a centimetre or two, which he negotiated without spillage.

Moments later he arrived at the car and unlocked it. He carefully placed the key back in his pocket, so as to make sure it didn't get misplaced. He placed the docking station on the front passenger seat, the laptop still acting as a lid. Various cables were thrown into the footwell along with the bunch of keys. The large computer cabinet fitted neatly into the boot with plenty of room to spare for the transport case. He was pleased that he'd thought to put the rear seats down earlier, avoiding another unnecessary delay.

He was left looking at an empty trolley. Where was he supposed to put that? It certainly wouldn't fit into the car, and it would look strange to just leave it on the pavement as he drove away. He pushed it a little further up the road and decided to leave it between two parked cars. Dumped, but not obvious.

He grabbed the car key from his pocket and checked that he still had the key he would be putting back into Klaus' car. Everything was in order.

He'd gotten away with it.

43.

As luck would have it, Klaus was out walking Toto when David passed him on the main road. David knew that Klaus was about ten minutes from home, maybe five minutes if he had seen David and the portly man moved quickly. He began slowing down to turn into the side road that led to Klaus' house. A check of the mirror revealed an unenthusiastic dog and a none-the-wiser old man.

As David approached the house, the BMW was exactly where he left it and the moving, flickering glow of a TV suggested that Anna would be engrossed in her favourite soap. He calmly parked the car in the same place he had earlier. He forced himself to breathe slowly and calmly. The job was nearly over, now was not the time to be drawing attention. He tried to walk at a normal pace. Not too fast, he didn't want to appear rushed. Not too slow because he wasn't loitering. He decided to act as if he was delivering a letter, a perfectly innocent activity for any time of day. As he approached the BMW he tried to replicate the way the lanyard had been wrapped around the keys.

One push of the unlock button and the car unlocked itself without fuss or noise. Almost like it was an accomplice. He opened the passenger door and replaced the keys in the centre console. He took an extra second or two to check that they looked at least similar to when he had taken them.

Satisfied with his work, He checked that he hadn't dropped anything of his in the car, then exited and closed the door gently. He walked back towards Veronique's car, just as any regular person who had delivered an envelope. He pushed the lock button and the BMW acknowledged with silent cooperation.

He had been trying to decide what to do with the key for the BMW. He could drop it somewhere near the car, on the driveway or maybe the pavement, so it could be discovered. Maybe Klaus would think that he had dropped it. He could throw it in the bin and forget about it. But, of course, he chose to keep hold of it. After all, access to another car might be useful in the future.

He pulled up onto the driveway at home and switched the engine off. He had already transferred the stolen equipment into the van. He figured it was less risky to have it at home, and potentially discovered by Sarah, rather than leave it in the back of a car on the street. The irony of someone else stealing it wasn't lost on him.

Sarah was chatting away on the telephone when he stuck his head around the living room door. The tone and subject matter suggested either her mother or father. She waved. He waved back and pointed at her empty wine glass on the coffee table, receiving a thumbs up in response.

In the kitchen David got himself a wine glass from the cupboard. Wine wasn't anywhere near strong enough an antidote to the evening's testing activities. He pulled the whisky bottle from the cupboard and took a large mouthful straight from the bottle. It burned on the way down, punishment for being an idiot. He reprimanded himself further with a second mouthful. He replaced the whisky bottle in the cupboard and carried the wine, and his glass, through to the living room.

He topped up Sarah's glass before filling his own, perhaps a little more than usual. He plopped down on the sofa and took a couple of sips while Sarah continued her conversation. He found that he couldn't sit still. Her conversation with whichever parent wasn't exactly stimulating and he couldn't put the TV on to distract himself. Maybe he should have gone for a walk to give himself time to wind down. He took another gulp and pulled his phone out. Social media distracted him for a while as did some of the news feeds but really, he was still keyed up on adrenaline.

Eventually the alcohol started to work its way in, and he could feel the tension being released. Sarah's conversation finished and she filled him in on the latest developments. At some point his glass was empty and she topped it up. Gradually he came around to the realization that his exercise in *liberation* had gone unnoticed both by Klaus and Sarah.

The next morning David went to the flat to continue his preparation and painting, but really he was there to move his little friends into their new home. Unlike his hurried exit the night before, he now had the luxury of taking as much time and as many journeys as he liked. Having moved everything back into Veronique's car, he parked it in her garage where he could work safely away from prying eyes. It didn't take him long to borrow a sack barrow from a local shop, then he started by moving the bulky items first.

He was about to unload the docking station when he noticed that it did have a lid after all. What he had assumed was the rear of the unit actually hinged over, neatly clipping into place on the top. Now he could see it in daylight, it was obvious. He was pleasantly surprised to see that it still contained all eight bees. He hadn't accidentally misplaced any and they hadn't chosen to leave.

He placed the computer cabinet in a corner next to a socket but decided not to plug it in just yet. He placed the docking station nearby, also unplugged. Same with the laptop.

His phone pinged as a new message arrived. It was the bee that he had kept captive in his workshop. Unbeknown to him it had paired to his phone which meant that it was both here and active. It was asking for 12 volts.

Giving the thing 12 volts ought to be easy enough. He would just plug the docking station into the socket on the wall. What worried him was that by giving it power he might also activate some kind of communications system which would tell Klaus where his stolen goods were. He was happy to give them their power, but he wasn't going to be hanging around to get caught.

He thought back to the office and could imagine the look on Klaus's face when he realised he'd been robbed. He'd love to be a fly on the wall. Or a bee.

Having double checked that he had everything in order, he plugged the docking station into the socket. After a brief pause a green light blinked into life and after a few seconds became steady, which was his cue to leave.

44.

On his drive home, his mind found things to worry about. He worried that Sarah would see straight through his lies and know that he'd been playing with fire. He also worried about the fire. He thought he managed to get away with the theft itself, but would the identity of the thief really be such a big mystery. How many people knew about project 79a and that it was located in Santa Maria. Klaus and Carl, of course, but there must be others. He hoped that the list of suspects went far beyond just him.

Why had Klaus waited until now to start killing off his ex-colleagues? If he just wanted them gone, eliminated as witnesses to a clandestine project, he could have gently bumped them off one by one over a period of time. And they'd all been killed by 79a itself. It kind of felt like Klaus was showing the world how clever his bees were. How cold, how surgical, how efficient. Maybe he wasn't showing the world, maybe he was polishing his own ego.

He felt like he was missing something about Klaus, the bees and the timing. What he really needed was to talk to Sarah about it. They would chew it over with a glass of wine and come up with all sorts of crazy ideas before ending up with an idea that was feasible. He felt like he was nearly there, but he needed his drinking buddy to help him get the ball over the line.

Having swapped back into his van he pulled up on the driveway and went into the house. It was strangely quiet. He had expected Sarah to be there cooking or cleaning or engaged in some other high-volume activity. It seemed whenever she was around there was always some kind of noise or laughter. But not this evening. Not now.

He wondered if his secret project with the bees had been discovered. She'd found him out.

Usually the presence of the other vehicle, the one he wasn't driving, meant that Sarah was at home. But now he discovered that her bag and keys were missing, which he hoped meant she had gone out with a friend. Maybe for a walk or a coffee.

He checked his phone, but there was nothing indicating where she would be. He checked the work roster and realised that he had missed out a flat in Alcudia that afternoon. He figured he could make that up in the morning. Maybe a quick drive-bye to see if the bees were still there, plug the router cabinet in, then retire to a safe distance. If powering up the computer cabinet meant giving its location away, he wondered how long it would take for the owner to turn up and retrieve it. It couldn't possibly take him more than an hour.

The silence of the empty house nibbled at him. Doubt hovered in his mind. He knew he'd been stupid to keep any of this from Sarah. The silence, the stillness. Punishment. A reminder of what life would be like. How the house would feel without her. Cold, empty, alone.

The evening punished him for a further half an hour, or so. He had sat on the sofa and flicked from channel to channel finding nothing of interest. Looking for things to occupy his fingers. He picked up his phone and tried to look at his social media and news feeds. It took a couple of minutes of clicking and swiping to realize that none of the stories were being updated.

Somehow his Wi-Fi and mobile data had been switched off. Maybe he'd done it by accident, though he couldn't recall why he would have needed to put his phone into airplane mode or switch the data off. Then he remembered that one of the bees had contacted him by Bluetooth in the flat. Was it one bee, or was it many bees that had asked for 12 volts? He wondered for a moment how he should think about a group of bees, then quickly realised that there was already a collective noun.

He turned his data back on and within moments had a series of messages and emails, one of which was from Sarah. She had bumped into a girlfriend that she hadn't seen for a while and was going for a 'coffee'.

Relief washed over him but somehow only served to make him feel more guilty. She didn't know and she hadn't left, either because of him or because of the danger he posed. Nothing had changed. She was back and he was still an idiot.

45.

David was up early and judging by Sarah's slurred speech and incoherence last night, she wouldn't be. He parked his van near the coffee shop and walked the rest of the way to Veronique's flat. It took him a moment to build up the courage to go in, but he needn't have worried. The flat was exactly as he left it. Nothing had moved. Even the eight bees were still neatly aligned on their charger.

Leaving the bedroom window open had definitely done something with the stale air. The flat no longer smelled of old lady. It now smelled of whatever the neighbour had been smoking on the balcony last night.

He ran the water from the tap in the kitchen and rinsed the kettle. He had no idea how long the water had been standing. Having filled it with fresh, he flicked the kettle and unpacked a cup he'd borrowed from home and some instant coffee. As he waited for the kettle to boil, he ventured out onto the balcony looking for any members of his fan club.

He hadn't seen any of them for nearly a week. He wasn't missing them, but he was beginning to have fun with them, it was all about the game. He enjoyed the sport of being the prey that had outwitted the hunter.

He heard the kettle click in the kitchen. He took another look up and down the street. Unless they were very good at hiding, no one had followed him or the hive. He ducked back inside to make his coffee. He stirred, then cautiously took a sip of the hot black liquid.

He placed the cup on what would now be his desk. Opening the laptop roused it from its slumber. The cursor sat blinking at him in the middle of the screen. Blinking and impatiently waiting for its password. David shook his head. Of course it needed a password, everything did these days. He was a little disappointed in himself for not foreseeing that it would. His eyes went over to the bees. They sat silently looking at him. It felt to him like they were looking.

"Passwo -" he began asking himself out loud. He stopped himself; that wasn't how you ask the bees questions.

He grabbed his phone and took a picture of the password entry field on the screen. The picture backed up to his cloud. David and his bees silently regarded each other across the room. He sipped his coffee and surfed his social media. He had no idea how long the hive would take to respond, or even if it knew the answer to his question. Generally, if the computer already knew an answer it seemed to respond within half an hour, or so. It was only when the hive needed to record fresh information, or conduct physical research that he had to wait until the next day.

David shook his head. He was glad he hadn't waited too long for the computer to respond, after all, it was still switched off. He cursed himself and slurped more coffee. If he was going to turn the computer on, he'd be leaving the building again. Immediately. He patted his pocket confirming the presence of his car key.

He rinsed his cup and left it to drain, then did one last idiot check to make sure windows and shutters were secure. He powered up the computer cabinet. Lights blinked and cooling fans spooled. It sounded like any other desktop computer warming up for a day's work. Just like any other computer except that, in this case, it had been designed for sinister purposes. This was, after all, the brain of the killing machine that was article 79a.

He left the flat ensuring the door was locked behind him and marched back to his van. The quicker he was out of here the better. He felt like he'd just lit the fuse on a bomb and needed to get the hell out of there.

He breezed through his morning's work, catching up with the flat he'd missed yesterday and then got on with today's work. He was part way through fitting clean sheets when his phone pinged. He had made certain he would hear it by turning the notification volume all the way up to maximum.

His shared drive showed a new thumbnail. He clicked revealing a picture of the laptop with the password on the screen. It was an older picture from before he'd broken into the office. He shook his head and marvelled at the intelligence of the machine. Either that or he was still being strung along by a human somewhere hiding behind the screen. He hurried through the remainder of his tasks acknowledging to himself that his work wasn't of the usual standard. He hadn't cut corners exactly, but it wasn't the normal quality they set themselves.

After a short drive across town and a forced march, he stood outside the flat again. Although still cautious about who might have entered the flat while he was away, his curiosity about the hive system as a whole was getting the better of him. He entered the building and went up in the lift. It wasn't until he had the door half open that he realised he should have listened first before committing to entry. If Klaus had been here they would all have been taken by surprise. David, not expecting Klaus, and vice versa.

Luckily the flat didn't contain any uninvited guests. The eight bees remained vigilant. As David looked at them, he realised that now they were connected to their computer, they would be able to receive instructions. Having been on the receiving end of some of these instructions previously, he slowly folded their lid over and clicked it closed. If they were able to receive instructions at least now they wouldn't be able to act on them.

He sat in front of the laptop and entered the password. After what seemed like a deliberately long time, it beeped as it accepted him and he was allowed entry. The program opened revealing an overly complicated and cluttered screen. It seemed to be a mix of German and English, interspersed with what looked like computer code of some sort. The insides of computers had never been his forté. To him, computers always seemed to randomly do, or do not do, whatever they liked. In his world, if you turned something on, it was on. In the world of computers, if you turned something on, there seemed to be a whole string of communications and instructions which occasionally led to the item being switched on, or not, depending on how it felt.

Over to the right hand side of the screen there was a small picture of Klaus and below it a picture of Carl. Next to each picture was the number 1.

A little further down the screen were pictures of each of the article 79a workers that had already been killed, the pictures of their deceased wives. Each of these pictures seemed to have been designated number 5.

David could see what the pictures meant. These had obviously been fed into the computer as a means of identifying targets to be assassinated. Perhaps that's what the number 5 indicated: deceased. Or was it an instruction? Was it more like 5 was an instruction to kill. And did that then mean that the number 1 didn't indicate a friend, but was more of an instruction to leave alone, one maybe to just watch?

A little further down he saw thumbnails of him and Sarah. They had been designated 1. That seemed strange. Had Klaus really designated them as friends? He'd have been expected them to be on the kill list.

He thought about ways he might be able to test the system, try to figure out what each number meant. For a moment he thought about going out onto the street and photographing a local shopkeeper or random tourists and going back to the computer designating them as a 5. He quickly realised that this approach would have pitfalls. For a start, he didn't know how to upload pictures to the system. Additionally, he supposed, there might end up being more dead bodies.

Instead, he changed the status next to his own photograph. He designated himself a 2. He waited for the thrum of beating wings against their plastic enclosure. There didn't seem to be any action. He walked over to the docking station and tapped the lid. He wasn't really sure what he was trying to achieve, maybe tapping would wake them up or attract their attention. All he got in return was silence. He tried opening the lid again, but it made no difference.

He sat back in front of the laptop. Whatever instruction he had given them by designating himself number 2, hadn't really stirred them into action. He went back to the screen, wondering if he dared elevate his status further towards what he assumed was an order to kill.

Having failed to understand the significance of status 2, he pondered for a moment on 3 and 4. Without additional evidence it would all be speculation. It was quite clear in his mind that 5 was a death sentence. But with the lid down the bees did seem to be well contained. Perhaps he could risk it.

He deleted his status 2 and replaced it with a 5. His finger hovered over the enter button. It didn't even cross his mind that he'd already identified a method that would defend him against an attack. He was too caught up with the computer in front of him to be able to stand back and see the big picture.

He figured he could always change his status back to 1. If he heard them revving up and trying to get out, he would still have time to abort. They couldn't get out with the lid closed. Could they? His finger hovered and he took a deep breath. Without any further thinking, or opportunity to talk himself out of his stupidity, he pushed the button.

He sat silently listening for any sign of activity, but after a few seconds there was still nothing. He wondered if his instructions had got through. Computers were often like this. Commands lost in the ether, a hundred different actions somehow wedged between the click of a key and the resulting action. Or in this case, inaction.

The status next to his picture once again read 1. Strange, he was sure he'd typed it correctly. He entered 5 again and hit the enter key, this time not taking his attention from the screen. There was a brief pause of less than a second before the status changed itself back to 1. He'd have to think about this. Maybe he didn't have the right security clearance to change peoples' status.

For one brief moment he thought about changing the status next to Sarah's picture, but he knew a thing or two about making your own luck. Designating Sarah as status 5 would be a monumentally stupid thing to do. But designating Klaus status 5 seemed appropriate. He hit the enter key without really thinking, and almost immediately heard vibrating from the docking station. He leaned over for a closer look and saw that two bees were active. Back on the screen he changed Klaus back to 1, and the vibrating stopped.

He knew from previous experience that the bees spent a few seconds with their wings beating, before lifting off. Perhaps they were warming up, or conducting systems checks. In any case, they hadn't had time to lift off before he'd deactivated them.

The lid would probably have prevented take off too. It looked like it acted as a physical safety barrier, preventing accidental or unauthorised launch. He though it best to keep it closed, unless he really intended to authorise a launch.

For a moment he wondered why only two bees seemed to activate. There could be a hundred different reasons within the computer and its programming, but then realised that it might be more simple than that. There might only be two killer units on the docking station. The others might have video or sound heads. This altered their capabilities, and therefore must determine which missions they could be sent on. With him designating status 5, the system had activated whichever units were capable of a status 5 mission. The computer wouldn't send video surveillance units for a kill mission.

Back on the screen he looked for an area that might show the contents of the docking station. He soon found two rows of four letters over on the left side of the screen.

    KKVM
    KKVM

There was no indication of what the letters represented, or even if they were English or German words, but they were all green in colour, which he took to be a universal indicator that their batteries were charged. If he had designed the graphics he would have come up with a much better way of representing unit capabilities and charge status. If he was honest he thought a 5-year-old could do better, but what did he know?

A light bulb clicked on inside David's brain somewhere. In theory, all he needed to do was lift the lid, open a window then change Klaus and Carl's status back to 5. If he understood the system correctly, he would then be free to go and enjoy a glass of wine while the bees sorted out his problems for him. That would be the end of the remaining members of the team. He wondered for a minute if he'd be capable of such and abhorrent action. To coldly program the units then send them on their murderous way.

A few days ago, when he'd been planning to break in and take the hive, he felt himself capable of any action bordering on illegal. But Klaus was different, he deserved it. It's not even really killing someone, he had told himself. It was just programming a computer. If Klaus could send these murder bees out specifically to kill individuals, then surely anyone could.

But everything looked completely different when viewed from the convenient comfort of distance and theory. It was different now that he had the loaded weapon at his fingertips. Actually pressing the button that ended a life was more complicated. He felt guilty for the casual manner he'd tested the bees a moment ago.

Klaus might well be a cold-blooded killer of men and women and it would certainly be poetic justice if his own bees turned on him. But David wasn't going to be the one to send them. He neither the jury nor the executioner.

Having discounted the idea of finishing Klaus, and probably the whole cycle of murders, David turned his attention back to the individual units and their mission readiness. He double checked that he hadn't programmed anyone with status 5, then lifted the lid on the docking unit and examined the individual bees.

He had seen a murder unit previously and had spent a great deal of time examining the one that was used to kill Gunther, the unit that landed him in the middle of this mess in the first place. There were the two units at the end of their neat lines that looked the same as the one he'd had in his workshop, the murder bees. Back on the screen, he now thought that M units might stand for murder, or the German equivalent. Having examined the other units, he came thought that V was indeed video.

His eyes flicked across the screen to Klaus. Changing his status to 2 hadn't produced any discernible change in the behaviour of the bees, at least not with the lid on. He now removed the lid and went back to the computer to try status 2 again. For a few moments, the bees and David looked at each other across the room, but there was no movement or sound. He tried status 3.

A single unit revved up and then disengaged from the docking station. It then flew out of the window, dead centre. It was a very impressive sight and he continued watching until it flew out of sight.

Back on the screen one of the K units had gone and was now replaced by a blank space. He wondered for a moment how long it would take for the unit to get to Klaus. How did it even know where he was, he certainly hadn't told it? Had he just sent it on a mission to search the whole island for Klaus? David was fairly certain that the battery wouldn't last long enough for a mission of that scale. He changed Klaus' status back to 1.

A short time later, the unit returned and docked. David could feel that he wasn't thinking clearly. He felt the need to rush everything, thinking that Klaus could turn up at any time. I needed to get away from the flat, get away from the hive and find somewhere where he could think about the system rationally. He took a picture of the screen, shut the laptop down and closed the lid on the docking station. He secured the flat and walked back to his van.

He drove in silence. He found that driving helped him to think about particular problems. It kept his brain just busy enough to stop his attention from wandering, but left enough processing power in reserve to work on the problem at hand. He was finished with his jobs around the port today, and was heading to the middle of the island to a large property in Alaro. He probably wouldn't get it finished today, but at least he could put a large dent in it.

As he drove, he thought of himself as one of the bees with someone else giving him mission instructions. He smiled as he realised what he needed was all of the Ws. Who, where, what, why and when. Well, the bees probably didn't need to know why, but everything else seemed necessary. He couldn't wait to look at his phone, the picture he had taken of the screen. He pulled over at the side of the road and tried to extract his phone from his pocket. The angle of the seat and the added restriction imposed by the seat belt all conspired against him, and the phone wouldn't budge. He slackened off the seat belt and raised his butt off the seat, producing a much improved angle for phone extraction. He unlocked the phone and examined his picture.

As he predicted, there were spaces available for him to enter longitude and latitude, as well as a mission start time. He figured that if the start time was left blank, it meant the mission started immediately, which is what he'd seen with the status 3 mission earlier. He cursed himself for not being able to figure this out while he was sat in front of the computer. At that time he would have been able to put his new understanding into practice. To test the system further. He shook his head realising that he couldn't get back to the hive until at least tomorrow afternoon, and more likely the day after.

He drove on to his villa, deciding he'd spend a couple of hours there then head home. He was quite annoyed at the lack of efficiency. If only he had realised what the other information on the screen had meant. He could have had units recording video of Klaus, while he was sweeping and polishing. Oh well. Not much he could do about it now.

He decided to use his time away from the hive to plan a better mission. Rather than just sending units out of the window because he could, this enforced break from his bees meant he could design a proper mission. He momentarily thought back to changing Klaus and Carl's status to 5. The poetry of Klaus stepping out of his BMW then being killed by his own system, on his own doorstep. One bee, one victim. Problem solved.

He shook his head to clear the murderous thoughts from his mind. Maybe he could find a better way of bringing him to justice.

46.

Sarah's car thundered up the road with her music blaring at full volume. As she rounded the last corner at the helm of her mobile disco, she could see David's van parked on the driveway. The tyres complained as she braked late, turned hard and crossed the pavement at speed, before finally thumping to a stop next to his van. She killed the ignition and the music stopped. Sarah was home.

The day's work was over, and her darling was inside. She had been out with a friend last night then he had left early this morning, leaving her in bed. She had missed him. She visibly bounced as she strode towards the front door. As she entered the house she was greeted with an unfamiliar silence. Normally she would expect there to be some kind of music playing, either on the stereo or David on his guitar. The silence was strange but not unheard of; perhaps he was in the shower or his workshop. As she closed the front door she saw something that was strange. David's keys were hanging off of the door lock on the inside of the house. The key to Veronique's flat was sticking up, kind of wedged between the key ring and the door lock.

Hanging door keys from the lock wasn't unusual. They sometimes did it when they were on their way out. If one of them was ready first, they might head out to the car to warm it up in winter or cool it in summer. The key would be hung on the lock so it was easy for the other to find. Hanging keys on the lock when entering the house was unheard of, they hung up on their respective hooks under the shelf. Sarah picked up the bunch by Veronique's key and hung it on the correct hook under the shelf.

As she made her way towards the kitchen, she noticed David's phone and wallet were on the dining table, along with his other van key. Now she was beginning to worry. She went through all the rooms on the ground floor calling his name. She rushed upstairs.

"David. Are you there? What's going on? David? David?" She called into the silence, but there was nobody there. No reply.

She rushed out to the workshop but found nothing. She ran around the garden. Hoping to find something. Anything.

She walked into the kitchen to get herself a glass of water. That was when she noticed the note on the work surface, held down by David's favourite coffee cup. The cup was still warm. In fact, it was nearly hot. He couldn't have been gone for more than ten minutes.

You have my bees and I have David. Don't involve the police or you'll never see him again.

I am willing to swap my hive for David. Talaiotic Sanctuary near Sencelles, 8pm tomorrow.

Alone.

K

So, it was Klaus that had taken him, or one of his cronies. But what was all this nonsense about her having the bees. She realised immediately. It had always been David that was interested in these damned bees. Even though she thought they'd got rid of the damn things and the case was closed, apparently David had been furthering his hobby without her knowledge.

The keys on the front door lock still didn't make sense to her. She gulped some water from her glass, then perused the contents of the fridge. She closed the door, shaking her head. No wine just yet. She needed a clear head. She also needed to somehow find these damned bees to trade for her little pest of a husband.

She figured he'd been spending a lot of time over at Veronique's flat. His bunch of keys being hung on the front door by Veronique's key made her mind up. She finished her water. She picked up David's wallet and phone, then headed straight back out of the front door.

On the way over to Veronique's flat ideas kept floating around in her head about what David had been up to. What secrets had he been keeping from her and why? What exactly had he been doing with these bees? Why was Klaus so upset about it all? What had David done?

Sarah decided that she needed to talk to someone with a level head, someone that was already involved. She unlocked David's phone and looked for Simon's number. It stood out to her that she needed to look on David's phone for this and not her own. Perhaps the fact that she didn't have Simon's number was an oversight, but the way things had been going recently she wondered if she'd been excluded deliberately. Had Simon and David been working together on these bees? Had they conspired to take them from Klaus and if so, what were their intentions.

She saved Simon's number on her phone, then called him. The phone rang and rang, but there was no response. Maybe he didn't answer calls from numbers he didn't recognize. She messaged him instead.

It's Sarah here. David has been kidnapped by Klaus. Please help.

She put the phone down on the passenger seat and kept driving. If she got the chance she was going to punch Klaus right in the face. She was then going to smack David around the side of the head as well, before giving him a big hug. What did he think he was doing, going and working on things behind her back? He knew they did everything together, even if it would get them into trouble, at least they'd be in trouble together.

Her phone rang, making her jump. She cursed and thumped the steering wheel.

"Hello, is that Simon?"

"Yes, it is. Hi Sarah, what's going on?"

"Well, I think David's been a bit silly. He's been playing around with these bees that belong to Klaus. He's been studying them, and I think he might have stolen some from Klaus."

Simon paused for a moment, like he was trying to find a quieter place to talk. She could hear some voices in the background. Not clearly, but she knew there were other people there. For a moment she thought she recognised one of them. Her heart leapt as she wondered if it was David. No, wishful thinking. On reflection it didn't sound anything like him.

"Ok. You said in your message he'd been kidnapped? How do you know?"

"Klaus left a note telling me. He said not to call the police, or I'd never see David again."

"So, does it say anything about what Klaus wants in return for him?"

"It says he wants his hive, whatever that is. I'm assuming it's something to do with the bees that David has taken from him."

"And you don't know anything about that?"

"No. Whatever he's been up to, he's been going behind my back."

"Well, I suppose you need to figure out where David might have them hidden."

"I've got a few ideas. I'm going to go and have a look later. I just want this whole thing to go away. I thought we'd put it all behind us. Apparently not."

"So, you're just going to go ahead with the swap."

"It seems ridiculous, but I don't think I've got any other choice. I'm going to have to trust Klaus to do the swap and let us both go."

"And what would you like me to do? How can I help?"

"I'm not sure you can, unless…oh, I don't know. I think it helps just to be able to talk about it."

"Ok, well if you need me, I'm around. Just give me a call and I can drop everything."

"Ok, well, maybe I will. The note said to come alone, but that doesn't mean I can't ask for help."

She thanked him and said goodbye. She had found the call very useful. She hadn't figured out what she was going to do and hadn't got the problem under control. At least she now felt that she could see its edges. It didn't go on forever.

As she drove to Veronique's flat, she wondered about the voices she'd heard in the background. She thought it had sounded familiar and she had immediately hoped it was David. Maybe it said more about her optimism than it did about who Simon shared an office with.

As she pulled up outside the coffee shop in Port de Pollença, she wondered how many times David had parked there. As she walked to the flat she wondered what other little secrets she was about to discover, what else David had been keeping from her.

47.

As she opened the door to the flat the smell of fresh paint greeted her, in contrast to the seasoned scent of the crowded, dingy flat she had seen with Veronique. There was much more space with the furniture gone. The whole place had been transformed with a few basic improvements. David's efforts with the property had made a huge difference but of course she wasn't here for that.

"Oh my god," she exclaimed as she entered the living room.

Now she could see what David had taken from Klaus, and why the note had referred to it as the hive. David hadn't just taken some bees There were computers, cases, units that did something, but she didn't know what. As she examined the computer cabinet with its ever-blinking lights, and opened the laptop, she began to understand that David hadn't just taken the bees, had also taken the control system, the hive. Everything. No wonder Klaus was angry.

"Oh, David." She shook her head, but couldn't stop a small smile from forming. "Well, you've stopped him from killing anyone else with these bees. That's for sure. It's a shame you forgot that he probably has other methods of killing people too, including you."

She looked at the password screen on the laptop, momentarily wondering what the password might be.

David's phone pinged. It was a notification that a new picture had been added to the shared drive. She clicked and it opened. It was a picture of her, sitting exactly where she was now. Looking at the picture she figured it must have been taken from... over there in the corner. She looked for the source of the picture and found two neat rows of four bees sitting on top of... what looked like a laser printer.

She then noticed other pictures in the folder that she didn't recognize. Squinting at the screen, she scrolled back through pictures and videos. She went back to when they were at the party and all hell had broken loose. One by one she examined the pictures and videos. They appeared to tell a story.

48.

Her alarm woke her at the usual time. She had stayed at the flat until late, trying to figure out how the exchange would play out. After hours of playing out different scenarios in her head, she eventually found herself falling asleep at the desk. She had jogged back to the car to help to wake herself, then driven home.

She found herself at a loose end for most of the morning. There was really nothing to do until later, when she would load the car then drive over to meet Klaus. She hadn't decided which car to take, but the van with the company logo emblazoned on the side definitely seemed like the wrong choice.

She had thought about calling Simon to see if he had any other ideas or tactics, but there was something about yesterday's phone call that still seemed off. Maybe it was just his logical approach as a cold-blooded service agent when she would have preferred a bit more emotional support. Whatever the reason, she felt like she'd rather call Anna than Simon, and that definitely wasn't going to happen.

She managed to occupy herself for a little while by watching TV. She then found jobs to do in almost every room in the house. She resisted the temptation to drink alcohol but gave in to caffeine. Having had one too many coffees, what she wanted next was a punch bag, but Klaus would have to wait.

She drove over to Port de Pollença a little earlier than planned and took a scenic walk around the old town and then along the beach. She had decided to use Veronique's mum's VW to do the exchange and found the keys upstairs in the kitchen. The engine started on the first turn of the key, just as David had said it would. Having loaded the bulky equipment in the back of the car, she kept the laptop next to her on the passenger seat. The set of keys on the round key ring didn't seem to fit with any of the equipment present. There was the occasional lock on the computer cabinet and armoured travel case, but none of the keys fitted them. She threw them into the boot anyway, figuring that they must be part of the kit.

She arrived at the old Talaiotic sanctuary a little earlier than the instructed time. It wasn't really by design, or part of her plan. It was part of her normal methodology, making certain she wasn't late by being early.

She pulled into the parking area and was jostled about in the driver's seat by the rough uneven surface. Rutted and worn by rain, wind and tourists, the surface was strewn with what could only be called small boulders. Halfway up towards the ruins was a simple metal gate designed to prevent cars passing, but not much else.

She paused as she thought about where she would like to park. Did she want to give Klaus a clear view of the contents of the boot as he arrived, or was a speedy getaway more important? In the end she decided that being seen to be playing the game was the best policy and parked the car nose in, towards the gate. Hopefully Klaus, or any of his cronies, wouldn't block her in.

She got out of the car and walked past the gate towards the ruins, the rutted and broken ground making her choose her footing carefully. She passed a large sun-faded sign which, from prior experience, told the history of the place in several languages. She noted that its condition had deteriorated dramatically since she'd last visited. How time flew. The last time they had visited this place would have been in the first year or two after their marriage. It seemed like a very long time ago. It seemed like she hadn't seen him in forever, even though it had been a little more than twenty-four hours.

As she picked her way towards the remnants of the uprights she cast her eyes across the slight valley towards the hills. It would be sunset in less than an hour. The light was turning everything golden and the shadows were getting longer. Even though Klaus hadn't arrived yet, she felt like she was being watched, and she wondered if she was right.

A car meandered along the road through the shallow valley and began slowing down on its approach to the car park. The brakes squealed. From her vantage point she couldn't see anybody in the car, but she hoped David would be in there. She gasped slightly as a thought entered her head. What if this car wasn't Klaus, wasn't David? What if it was just some random member of the public? This could all go badly wrong. All this preparation could be ruined by the simple arrival of an uninvited guest.

Once the car began turning into the car park she had a much clearer view of the occupants. It wasn't Klaus's BMW, but it was Klaus driving with one of his men in the passenger seat. She also thought, or maybe hoped, that she could see David in the back. As soon as the car straightened its wheels and entered the car park a small swarm of bees left the back of Sarah's car. Sarah's girls.

At that range Klaus would have needed the eyes of a hawk to see them. They quickly flew upwards and began circling. Sarah didn't need to keep an eye on them, she knew what she programmed them to do.

As the car pulled closer, she could clearly see David in the back. She hoped he was all right, that they hadn't hurt him. As she watched the car approaching the low sun glinted off of the roof, dazzling her for a moment. Klaus pulled nose first into a parking space up against the rocks. She wasn't blocked in.

She started carefully making her way back towards her car as David and Klaus got out. This would all be over soon. There was no need for her to rush.

Simon watched through the telescopic sight on his rifle. Klaus approached Sarah's car and inspected the contents. He seemed pleased with what he saw, and appeared to nod and gesticulate at Sarah. He then turned and indicated to Carl to extract David. Simon knew that at some point in the next minute David and Sarah would be embracing happily, relieved to be back in each other's arms. This was his cue to finish them. With a bit of luck he'd be able to finish them both with one shot, but he usually allocated one bullet per person for jobs like this. The range was a little over 400m and well with in his ability.

His breathing was even and his heart rate steady as he locked and loaded the first bullet into the chamber. This would probably be the loudest thing this valley had ever heard. One, but more likely two kill shots blasting across the sleepy valley. He would remain perfectly still for at least half an hour after the event, before invisibly skulking off while everyone was busy at the crime scene.

Another even breath as the two lovebirds drew closer, maybe now just 10 metres apart. He could feel an anticipation. Yes, he'd worked with them for a little while, but he had never connected with them. A job was a job, and he just happen to enjoy this part of his. He was looking forward to it.

He recognised his own anticipation and suppressed it. He couldn't let his pleasure get in the way of the work. The kill had to come first, the enjoyment after.

He heard a low buzzing above him. He recognised the sound immediately and looked up. Precisely the wrong thing to do when a murder bee is identifying its target.

Sarah heard the pop from across the valley, but no one else noticed. At this range it was actually quite subtle. A small smile appeared for a moment. IF the bee hadn't achieved its mission, they'd both be dead very soon. She was disappointed that she had been right about not trusting Simon, but also pleased.

The timing was perfect, almost as if she'd issued the command then and there. The swarm of bees screamed back into hearing range and, unlike the attack on Simon, this time everybody heard them coming. Instinctively, she wanted to cover her head and eyes. She didn't know whether to trust the bees with their mission. To believe, or maybe to hope, that her understanding and programming of the bees had worked as she'd intended. For a brief moment she debated whether to stand proud and watch her girls in action, or to add an extra layer of personal security by ducking. She ducked, as did David. They both went to ground and grabbed each other, holding each other close while the bees did their thing.

There were two pops in relatively quick succession and then heard two bodies collapsing to the ground. She held David tight, hoping that their enemies lay dead and that their ordeal was over. The frenzied and chaotic swarming sound of the bees faded and eventually disappeared.

49.

David dared to uncover his face slightly so he could see what had happened. What he saw was beyond anything he could have hoped. Carl and Klaus lay dead on the ground in front of him.

They looked around to see if anyone had noticed as they helped each other to their feet.

"Hey, how are you?" Asked David.

"All good, you?"

"To be honest I don't really know. It's been a long couple of days. Do you think we should … "

"Get the hell out of here?"

Sarah closed the boot, and they got into the VW. She started the engine and drove calmly out of the car park and turned left, towards Costitx. As she drove up the other side of the gentle valley, she figured there'd be a dead sniper hiding in the bushes somewhere nearby.

David looked into the back of the car and saw all of the equipment that he'd taken from Klaus' office. He had a lot of question and knew that he owed a lot of answers.

They drove in relative silence. She didn't really know where she was heading. Just being away from Klaus was enough. When her right hand wasn't busy with the chores of driving, she rested it on his leg.

"Look, I think I owe you an apology. I'm sorry." Said David.

She still didn't know what she should be feeling. She was happy that she had David back and that he looked relatively unscathed. She was also relieved that this whole nightmare might be over. Or was it? Sure, Klaus was dead. She'd sent the bees out to look for Simon in a 1km radius of the meeting point and had heard them complete their mission, so he was dead too. But that wasn't the whole story, was it? It couldn't be that straightforward.

She looked at him, but didn't respond to his apology.

"Who was that man in the car with you?"

"Oh, that was Carl. He's part of the Klaus clan. I think those were the last two of 79a."

"So, we might be in the clear then?"

"Maybe." She'd decided to tell him about Simon later. They'd almost become friends, it was a shame.

"Oh. I was hoping for a more positive response."

"There's still the potential issue of whoever was buying them."

"The Russians?"

"Yes, but we have no idea who or where they are. And also, how much money have they paid to Klaus? That will determine their level of further interest."

"Yes, if they paid millions they're not going to be going away anytime soon."

"Right, but if they've paid nothing then it's just an arms deal that never happened."

There was a long silence while they both thought about things. How close they'd come to paying the ultimate price for being in the wrong place at the wrong time. How they felt the immediate pressure easing away with each passing moment. How angry Sarah was at David for getting them into all of this in the first place.

The silence continued as they approached the motorway. "Left or right?" she asked. This was really a question about their destination. Home or Port de Pollença.

"Right."

The silence continued as the countryside blurred past on their way to Veronique's flat.

"Nice job with the bees." Said David, eventually working up the courage to break the silence.

"Thanks." She let the silence hang for a moment longer. "Of course,"

Oh, here we go. Thought David.

"If you'd left the damned things alone, this would never have happened."

"I said I was sorry, and I meant it."

"I know, and I've already forgiven you."

"Oh?"

"But now you owe me."

50.

They walked into the bar closest to Veronique's flat and ordered two beers. It was reassuringly noisy, ideal for covering up conversations, not that there was anyone left to listen in.

"Look, I get that you needed to follow up on your bees after that one started talking to you."

David stopped for a moment.

"Right … " He responded cautiously, unsure of where this was leading. When he'd told her about the messages, she'd thought he was talking nonsense.

"But you should have told me that you were still involved with them. We're supposed to be a team."

Ok, now he was confused. She wasn't angry about the bees anymore. She'd had a change of direction and was now upset about being excluded from the bees.

"I …"

"But they are quite cool, aren't they?"

"Dos mas, por favor." David semi-shouted across the bar to make himself heard over the cacophony. "They are. I'm guessing that you figured out how to program them?"

"Yep." She looked quite pleased with herself.

"And you managed to tell them that we are the good guys, so they don't accidentally pop our brains?"

"No. We were already in the system under status 1, but you didn't do that?"

"Not me."

"Well, someone's told them that we are off limits."

"Or they decided for themselves."

She gave him a deliberately longer look. They hadn't really spent an awful lot of time with the hive, but surely they weren't intelligent enough to make decisions like that on their own.

"Look," he said "we have a lot to learn about them. Hopefully, now that the threat of Klaus is gone, we can spend time understanding them without any pressure or urgency. Or we can just pack them away and forget about them."

"Seems like a waste."

"I agree. But maybe we should lay low for a while until we know that the buyers aren't going to be poking around our lives like Klaus was."

"Do we know for sure that Veronique's place is safe?" she asked.

"Well, not for certain, but I'm happy that it's Ok. It's more likely to be off of the radar that our house."

"Definitely," she agreed.

"Maybe we can set them up to look after the flat – keep an eye on it while we let the dust settle?"

"That sounds like a plan. We can get them to watch our house too, maybe with some killers mixed in, just in case?"

"You've figured out how to get them to do that?"

"Yep." She had a more-than-slightly smug look on her face, especially since David obviously didn't know how to get them to do that. He nudged her with his elbow, aware that this was turning into a competition.

"If you're good," she said, "I'll show you how to program them."

"Oh, I see. Miss *queen bee* now, is it?" he retorted. He could see from her expression that she liked the idea.

"Queen bee," she said, nodding slightly, "works for me."

"Oh, god. What have I done? This is going to be insufferable."

She continued her silly grin and left his protest hanging in the air.

The next morning began with sore heads and strong coffee. They'd put the world to rights with several beers too many, followed by whisky for good measure. They had been aware that they were letting their guard down, and in hindsight it had been reckless, but so far there had been no consequences.

Back at Veronique's flat, David struggled with unloading the car while Sarah put the kettle on. Once the hive was upstairs and switched on, David went into the kitchen to find Sarah while the system finished booting up.

"So, what's the strategy then?" he asked.

"I reckon that we unpack and build all of the bees that we have here. How many is that, thirty-ish? Then we can decide how many to leave here watching the flat. The rest can be used to protect us and our house."

"Maybe we should have a couple at Klaus' office, see if the Russians turn up."

"And see if they go away, too."

"Hopefully." He sipped his coffee but doubted that more caffeine was what was really needed to clear his head. "You know, we don't have to hang around here, the island I mean, while the bees do their thing."

"We kind of do, we have customers that we've been putting on the back burner while we have been busy getting kidnapped."

"I suppose." Even in times of extreme personal danger, the customer came first.

"But you're right, we shouldn't stay in one place. We know which flats are empty. We know when we can move into them and need to leave."

"Do we even need a house then?" he jokingly asked, which prompted another one of her side-eye glances.

"You know. I understand the bees, well I don't, but ... you know. I don't understand all of the ins and outs, but I get the idea. I get the main computer, it's like a central thingy ... server or processor."

"Right," he said, seeing if he could prompt her, get her ideas to coalesce.

"And," she'd caught his nudge to get her to make sense, "I get what the laptop is for."

"Mmm?"

"What I don't really get is the AI bit, the intelligence that they seem to have. Lots of small brains acting like a big one."

"Me either, computers have never been my thing. We probably need to find a school kid and ask them."

The thought made her smile, but her mind quickly landed elsewhere. "Also,"

"Mmm?"

"I couldn't figure it out before, but what is that bunch of keys for?"

Thank you for taking the time to read this book.

It took far longer to write and produce that it ought to, but life has a habit of getting in the way. The next instalment will be quicker. Probably.

If you want to keep up to date with my progress and other projects, please visit:

www.calum-e-rogers.co.uk

Printed in Dunstable, United Kingdom